AN AFFAIRE IN ATHENS

THE GRAND TOURS OF THE ARISTOCRACY
BOOK 2

LINDA RAE SANDE

Twisted Teacup
PUBLISHING

ALSO BY LINDA RAE SANDE

The Daughters of the Aristocracy

The Kiss of a Viscount

The Grace of a Duke

The Seduction of an Earl

The Sons of the Aristocracy

Tuesday Nights

The Widowed Countess

My Fair Groom

The Sisters of the Aristocracy

The Story of a Baron

The Passion of a Marquess

The Desire of a Lady

The Brothers of the Aristocracy

The Love of a Rake

The Caress of a Commander

The Epiphany of an Explorer

The Widows of the Aristocracy

The Gossip of an Earl

The Enigma of a Widow

The Secrets of a Viscount

The Widowers of the Aristocracy

The Dream of a Duchess

The Vision of a Viscountess

The Conundrum of a Clerk

The Charity of a Viscount

The Cousins of the Aristocracy

The Promise of a Gentleman

The Pride of a Gentleman

The Holidays of the Aristocracy

The Christmas of a Countess

The Knot of a Knight

The Holiday of a Marquess

The Snow Angel of a Duke

The Ivy of an Earl

The Heirs of the Aristocracy

The Angel of an Astronomer

The Puzzle of a Bastard

The Choice of a Cavalier

The Bargain of a Baroness

The Jewel of an Earl's Heir

The Vixen of a Viscount

The Honor of an Heir

The Rose of a Sultan's Son

The Ladies of the Aristocracy

The Lady of a Grump

The Lady of a Sultan

The Pursuit of a Duchess

The Lords of the Aristocracy

The Abduction of an Earl

Beyond the Aristocracy

The Pleasure of a Pirate

The Making of a Mistress

The Bride of a Baronet

The Caton of a Captain

Puss and Pots

The Betrothal of a Baron

Masquerade Meow

The Grand Tours of the Aristocracy

A Courtship in Catania

An Affaire in Athens

Revenge of the Wallflowers

The Wager of a Wallflower

Stella of Akrotiri

Origins

Deminon

Diana

The Lyon's Den (Dragonblade Publishing)

The Courage of a Lyon

The Lady of a Lyon

The Loyalty of a Lyon

Note: Translations of select titles are available in German, Italian, Spanish and Portuguese.

CHARACTER LIST AND FAMILY TREES

Will Slater, Earl of Bellingham (1792), heir to the Devonville marquessate

Barbara Higgins Slater, Countess of Bellingham

Donald Slater (1811), illegitimate son of Will and Barbara, father of Antony, Marchese Montblanc

Nicoletta D'Avalos (1815), Marchesa Montblanc and wife to Donald

David Slater, Viscount Penton (1819), heir to the Devonville marquessate

Randolph Forster (1817), heir to the Gisborn earldom, nephew to Will

Thomas Forster (1819), nephew to Will

Jasper Henley, Viscount Henley (1786)

Marianne Slater Henley (1798), Viscountess Henley, first cousin to Will Slater

Marcus Henley (1817), heir to the Henley viscountcy, second cousin to Randy, Tom, and David

Diana Henley (1820), second cousin to Randy, Tom, and David

Michael Henley (1819), second cousin to Randy, Tom, and David

Antonio Fitzsimmons (1817), heir to the Reardon viscountcy

Jane Fitzsimmons (1820), sister to Antonio

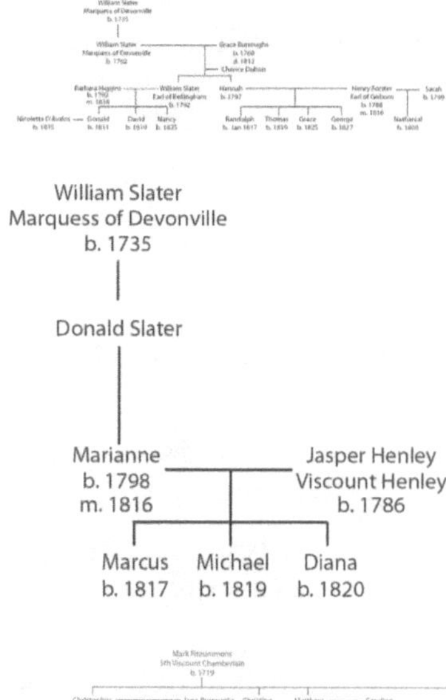

PROLOGUE

July 1840, near Girgenti, Sicily

From her vantage atop an ancient wall of stones not even two feet high, Diana regarded the design of a Roman mosaic with a grimace. "Another scene depicting a hunt," she groused. "The Romans were obviously obsessed with killing deer."

Below her, his knees pressed into a faded cushion, Viscount Jasper Henley glanced up and shrugged. "Deer and anything else from their daily life," he responded, wiping away another layer of dirt from atop what had at one time been the floor of a Roman villa.

His efforts revealed more details of an *opus vermiculatum* —a mosaic of tiny colored glass tiles—including a tanned, well-muscled young man garbed in a knee-length tunic, his short, golden blond, wavy hair, outlined in dark brown stark against the white tile background. His bare legs displayed well-developed calves, and his feet were adorned with sandals. One hand gripped a bow, revealing him to be the hunter of the deer.

"Oh!" Diana stepped down to join her father, careful where she placed her booted feet before stooping over to examine the newly uncovered scene. "This man is quite detailed."

Her father smirked at hearing her sudden interest in the mosaic. Given the size of the tiles used, the design had probably been created on a panel in a workshop by a Greek artisan and then installed when the villa was under construction. "Reminds me of the first time I uncovered one of these," he murmured. "A few years before you were born. Your mother blushed when she saw the hunter."

His daughter let out a rare giggle as she reached for the pad of paper she had left on the remains of a nearby wall. "Given her poor eyesight, Mother probably couldn't even see it," she said on a huff.

"She could see it rather clearly, actually," Jasper countered. "By then I had found an oculist in Palermo who could make spectacles specifically for her," he claimed. "She still blushes when she sees scantily clad males in artwork," Jasper said, grinning.

"Father," Diana scolded. "I'm not yet one-and-twenty," she added. "Talk of scantily clad young men is supposed to wait until after I've reached my majority." Pulling a pencil from the pocket of her breeches, she sat crossed-legged next to the hunter and quickly sketched the design.

"Don't remind me," he said with a grin. "And don't let your mother see you sitting like that. She'll scold you *and* me," he warned.

"Yes, Father," Diana said, not changing her position.

On any other day, she might have had to obey, but not on this day. Her younger brother, Michael, had completed another year of university at Oxford and had arrived by ship the night before with their older brother, Marcus, from London. Viscountess Marianne Henley hadn't seen her sons in nearly a year and insisted they spend the day in her company as she shopped in Girgenti.

Setting aside the small brush he had been using to clear away dirt from the tiles, Jasper struggled to stand, groaning as he straightened his knees. He surveyed his day's work.

The level of detail on this particular floor was far finer than the mosaic in the adjacent structure's floor. In that one, the *opus tessellatum* was created using larger tesserae laid directly in place. The red, white, and gold geometric border surrounded a scene featuring the Three Graces from Greek mythology. Their mode of dress left little to the imagination when it came to the shape of their bodies, but he wasn't about to mention it to his daughter.

"How can you be sure this mosaic is Roman and not Greek, like the one next door?" Diana asked, working to complete the sketch of the mosaic before the setting sun cast it in shadow. She would bring her paints in the morning to complete the illustration of the mosaic for use in her father's next book. He planned to publish a compendium of his finds in the Greco-Roman quarter of the Valley of the Temples, one which would include illustrations of as many of the mosaics as possible.

Jasper knelt to brush away some dirt from the edge of the scene. "Almost all of the mosaics I've found in this area have been Roman," he remarked. "I was lucky to stumble onto that one." He motioned over his shoulder to indicate the mosaic featuring the Three Graces. "I was about to give up digging when I didn't find anything at this level," he explained, smoothing his gloved hand over the newly uncovered mosaic. "As you can see, that floor is much deeper down."

"Another foot at least," Diana agreed.

"Which means that house was probably built and occupied well before most of these in the Greco-Roman quarter. Perhaps several hundred years earlier."

Concentrating on her drawing, Diana didn't notice how her father scanned the area around them. A line of Greek temples and other structures stretched for over a mile to make up the Valley of the Temples. Her father's work in the Greco-Roman quarter had been ongoing for the entire time he had been married to Marianne Slater, although the family had occasionally returned to London, usually in the spring, so he could see to his duties as a viscount.

When he didn't speak for several minutes, Diana glanced up and noticed him staring in the direction of the Temple of Concordia. "What is it?" she asked, setting aside the drawing.

"I'm trying to decide how I'm going to tell your mother we're moving on to another project," he replied, his attention still on the ruins surrounding them.

"Another project?" she repeated. "Where?"

He left out his breath in a *whoosh*. "Greece. Athens, to be precise," he said.

Diana blinked. "Athens?" From the way he had said the name of one of the oldest cities on the planet, she knew he was looking forward to the change.

"I've a patron who will pay for me to find evidence of a missing temple. The floor of it, at least," he explained. "So I wrote to who I think might be in charge of the restoration efforts there and have secured his permission to begin the work next month."

Her eyes rounded. "The Acropolis?"

When he nodded, she quickly stood and shouted with excitement. "Oh, Father. Congratulations!" she said as she embraced him.

Jasper chuckled softly. "Well, I'm glad to know at least one person in the family is happy to learn we'll be moving on," he said, mostly to himself.

She sobered. "The boys have been away at school more than they have been here," she reminded him. "We may only have to convince Mother of how wonderful this will be."

"She has so many friends here—not just Chiara," he said, referring to the wife of his partner in archaeology, Dr. Darius Jones. The brother of a duke and a decade older than Jasper, Darius had retired from active archaeological work to concentrate on publishing books about his finds on Sicily and along Hadrian's Wall in England. Although his original home had been in Cumbria, Darius had lived with Chiara in her villa near Girgenti for the past twenty years.

"Your mother could speak the language—mostly—from before I met her," Jasper continued after his moment of reverie. "I rather doubt she's going to like moving."

"Mother makes friends easily," Diana reasoned. "And she'll be happy that the boys are done with school and living with us."

Despite her excitement, Jasper merely nodded. "Still, I feel as if I need some really good news to help lessen the sting," he said on a sigh. "Or a very expensive bauble."

After a moment of thought, Diana's eyes rounded. "I think I know what would help," she said.

"Oh? Do share," he encouraged.

"Take her to Rome for a holiday. Before you go to Athens."

Jasper stared at his daughter for several seconds before he

grinned. "I think you might have a very good idea there," he whispered.

"The boys and I can go on ahead to Athens while you enjoy some time in the world's most romantic city," Diana went on, knowing full well her mother would object to leaving her grown children to fend for themselves. But if Jasper Henley had been invited—and his time there funded— that meant a house and staff would be arranged for their use. Given the situation in Athens, they would be paying witness to a city under post-war reconstruction. A city teaming with laborers and investors from all over the world.

A city where every dig of a shovel might reveal an ancient artifact. The remains of an agora. The foundations of an *oikos*.

"He was there," Diana stated suddenly.

Jasper blinked and regarded his daughter with furrowed brows before he chuckled. "Pausanias?"

"Yes," she responded, her manner guarded.

Sobering, he finally nodded. "I believe Athens is covered in his first volume," he said, referring to the series of books the traveler had written as he documented his tour of Greece. Pausanias's *Description of Greece* helped to tie ancient ruins mentioned in classical literature with the sort of archaeology Jasper was performing nearly sixteen-hundred years later.

The man's observations and subsequent descriptions of ancient temples, towns, artworks, and the people he met along the way were a travelogue of sorts. Pausanias never mentioned for whom his books were intended. They surely weren't meant as a guidebook for travelers—or those on their Grand Tours—since they didn't mention where a visitor should seek accommodations or where they should eat or drink. However, the books allowed someone sitting in the comfort of their *oikos* to feel as if they had been along on the trip.

"Would he have left some sort of evidence he was there, do you suppose?" Diana asked, hope in her voice.

Jasper straightened as he considered her query. "How could he have *not* been?" he asked rhetorically. "You've obviously read his works. You know how detailed he is about the paintings and statuary." When she didn't appear convinced, he furrowed his brows. "You mean, did he leave his name carved in marble?" he asked. He scoffed but considered the possibility. "I rather doubt it, but then, I haven't read all of his first book."

Diana's mouth dropped open. "You haven't?"

Chuckling at seeing his daughter's indignation, Jasper shook his head. "I learned about him, of course. I know there are ten or eleven volumes of his book. But I have not read more than the passages having to do with my own research," he explained.

"What if he did? Leave behind some sort of clue that he had been somewhere?"

Jasper's brows furrowed. "Well, I would think his books would be enough evidence of his having visited a place," he murmured. His eyes suddenly rounded. "Are you referring to graffito?" he asked. "You think he might have carved his name into marble to indicate he had been there? As some sort of… marker?" His face screwed into a grimace. "No." His expression softening somewhat, he added, "Well, it's unlikely."

"But not impossible?" she pressed.

He finally shrugged. "It's possible," he finally hedged. When his daughter displayed a grin of satisfaction, he shook his head. "But, please, if you don't find evidence of it, don't feel as if you failed," he warned.

Diana's shoulders dropped. "What are you saying?"

"I can see you are determined to prove your point... and it's a good one," he replied. "There are many a traveler who have left their marks in temples and on ancient artifacts all over the world. It doesn't mean Pausanias did so, or that someone else did it on his behalf, though."

Spreading her hands out to indicate the hundreds of Greco-Roman house foundations spread out before her, Diana said, "Have you ever felt as if you failed?"

He shook his head. "No, but then I always knew we would find evidence of Greek and Roman villas here," he said, pointing to the Temple of Concordia in the distance. "Had we not..." He shook his head. "We would have simply dug in another place, because we knew they had to have lived somewhere."

Considering her father's words, Diana angled her head to one side. "Since Pausanias wrote of Athens in Volume One— he described the temples on the Acropolis—"

"Did he?"

She blinked. "He did."

"Then we know he was there," he said with a shrug. "But it doesn't mean he left behind any markings to indicate he was there."

"True," Diana hedged.

"But you intend to look?"

She nodded.

Jasper sighed. "All right. I'll send word ahead. See if we can arrange permission for you to start work prior to my arrival," he murmured. "But be sure to document anyone else you might find leaving behind their mark," he instructed. "Someone else you might encounter along the way. You may find something—or someone—far more important in your search."

Diana considered her father's words and finally nodded. "I'll keep an open mind," she promised.

"That's my girl," he said, affording her a grin of satisfaction.

CHAPTER 1
AN UNEXPECTED FIND

August 1840, Acropolis at Athens, Greece

Wiping the sweat from his brow with a linen handkerchief, Randolph Forster, heir to the Gisborn earldom, paused on the last marble step leading up to the front of the Propylaea of the Acropolis and turned around.

His gaze took in the city of Athens below, many of the white houses built from the blocks of temples no longer atop the nearly flat acropolis.

"See anything of note?" his brother, Tom, asked from where he was still negotiating the worn marble slabs leading up to the escarpment.

"Anything not under construction?" their cousin, David Slater, Viscount Penton, asked from the bottom step. He was directing a pair of binoculars towards a nearby hilltop. "I think I found the Prison of Socrates," he added, struggling to focus the lenses of the set of small telescopes held together by a crude frame.

"Rubble and ruins and more ruins," Randy responded, his voice sounding his disappointment.

Holding an open book stuffed into the crook of this arm, Tom was studying a map. "According to this book, the Stoa of Attalos was there, in the agora," he said, pointing out toward the remains of a building where a number of columns were still lined up, their white marble made more so in the harsh morning glare of the sun. "Which means the Temple of Olympia Zeus would be around to the left," he guessed, his finger swinging through the air. When it came to rest, it pointed to the wall of marble blocks directly below the Temple of Athena Nike. "Out there somewhere."

"That was the group of columns we saw when we arrived in town," he said. You couldn't miss them they were so tall. We should be able to see them from the top," Randy said, grinning at Tom's antics.

"You would think Pausanias would have provided more detail about what's up here," Tom grumbled. "I read what I could last night, and it was damned difficult. He writes like he's an academic—"

"He doesn't even mention the Stoa of Attalos," Randy groused. "It was supposedly a dominant feature back then."

"I appreciate the detail with which he describes all the physical objects. The artwork," David stated. "I have no trouble with the language."

Tom and Randy exchanged quick glances as Tom rolled his eyes. Their cousin had always excelled at school, his ability to learn foreign languages a huge help when studying the Classics.

"Hey," David said by way of protest. "I admit his guide is not proving as useful as my brother's, but I still think it's worth reading," he explained. "There's a good deal of history, and his eye for art is unmatched. I finished Volume One last night and intend to start the next one after dinner tonight."

David had obtained several volumes of Pausanias' *Hellados Periegesis*, or *Description of Greece*, during their stay in Catania on Sicily, the second century text printed in its original Greek. Meanwhile, they had been following the guidebook his older brother, Donald, had written based on his Grand Tour from seven years prior.

Donald Slater's book was far more practical, providing information on where to stay, what to see, and how long it might take to explore certain cities and their monuments and temples, while the information in the Pausanias volumes didn't seem intended for an actual traveler but rather one who wished to learn about Greece whilst sitting in a comfortable chair in their study.

Tom looked up from the guidebook Donald had written and directed his attention down to his right. "The theatre appears to be mostly intact," he said in awe, referring to the Odeon of Herodotus. From his vantage, he could see the stage as well as the half-circle arcs of marble seats and the backside of the multi-arched facade.

"Pietro said it's still in use," David commented, remembering how easy it had been to understand the butler of their rented house in Athens. Although Pietro spoke some English, Randy and Tom had been forced to remember their Greek from university while David, who was fluent in the language, had stood nearby and pretended ignorance.

Randy watched Tom pass him and step around the columns making up the Propylaea—the entry to the Acropolis. "Where are you going?"

"The Erechtheion," he replied, excitement in his voice. In one hand, he held a loosely bound book, its pages opened to a drawing Donald Slater had done when he had visited the

Acropolis seven years prior. "It has the rest of those caryatids like the one that's in the British Museum."

"Why is it you're *always* after young women?"

Tom gave him a quelling glance. "I think you have me confused with Cousin David," he replied. "Where are you starting?"

From the moment Randy had begun the climb to the Propylaea, he had been curious about the stout white marble temple directly above and to the right of the worn steps. Now that he was nearly level with it, he wondered at its odd placement. "I'm going in this one," he replied, frowning at how out of place a tall, dark, square tower next to it appeared. "Such a shame the Franks had to build such an ugly fortress right here," he added.

"Made sense at the time," David remarked, his head dropping back on his neck to take in the worn blocks of the crenelated tower. "Made for a perfectly situated watch tower. From the top, you can probably see for miles. Are you going in?"

Randy's face screwed into a grimace. "Maybe later. I'm going into this temple first." Although it was only mid-morning, the day was growing warm. The tower's position cast a cooling shadow over the white marble temple. He glanced over at the book Tom held open, the pages displaying a sort of map of the location of the structures on the Acropolis. "The Temple of Athena Nike." He chuckled. "Ladies first."

"Suit yourself," Tom murmured, "but don't expect much. The original temple was dismantled by the Turks and had to be reassembled by Hansen and Schaubert a few years ago. The roof was never found."

Randy frowned. "Hansen and Schaubert?" he repeated. His eyes suddenly rounded. "Ah, the architects. Christian

Hansen and Eduard Schaubert," he remembered. The two had been responsible for some of the reconstruction efforts after the Greeks had won their war for independence.

Tom and David hurried off over a field of rubble toward a temple featuring a series of caryatids perched atop the walls of a porch protruding from the north side.

Randy continued his trek past the columns of the Propylaea and considered how best to navigate the partially buried marble blocks and broken rocks strewn about the ground. If he wasn't careful, he would end up spraining an ankle, or worse, falling and breaking an arm—or his head—on the unforgiving stone.

Once he made it to the entrance of the small temple dedicated to the goddess Nike, he paused in the entry in an attempt to allow his eyes to adjust to the sudden darkness beyond.

Darkness? This temple was supposed to be missing its roof. He glanced up, realizing a tarp had been strung across two of the cella walls while the Frankish tower behind the temple cast its sharp mid-morning shadow over the rest. There was a small light source, but he couldn't make out exactly what it was—at first.

"You're blocking my light." The feminine voice held complaint in its tone.

Quickly stepping to one side, Randy blinked when his vision returned and his gaze fell on the perfect globes of a derriere garbed in doeskin breeches. For a moment, he was reminded of the shape of an upside-down heart, until he realized said heart sat atop a pair of shapely legs leading down to a pair of black riding boots.

The very last thing he expected to find in the Temple of Athena Nike was a woman, although he supposed he should have expected to discover a statue of the goddess at the very least.

His cock reacted in a most undignified manner. Why it did, he didn't have a chance to consider. He had seen his younger sister, Grace, dressed in breeches a number of times. She was a tomboy, though, and she was still young. Even before he had left England on his Grand Tour, his mother, Hannah, Countess of Gisborn, had mentioned her hope that by the time he returned, Grace would have outgrown her affinity for doing everything their younger brother, George, did in favor of more feminine pursuits.

"Have you already finished your socializing?" the woman asked. She was still bent at the waist and holding a lantern near the marble wall, her attention clearly on the smooth stone.

By now, Randy realized the derriere belonged to a young woman. Tucked into the tightly-fitted breeches was a white shirt. Her reddish-blonde hair was pulled into a tight bun at the back of her head, and a red scarf was wrapped around her neck. "I haven't even begun," he replied, not sure what else to say.

She quickly straightened and glanced back. The lantern suddenly swung in front of her, momentarily blinding Randy. "Did my brother hire you?" she asked, the query making her suspicion evident.

Holding out a hand to shield his eyes from the glare of the light, he said, "He did not, Miss…?"

"Who *are* you?" she asked, stepping sideways so she was next to a large marble block that nearly reached her waist. From the alarm in her voice, Randy could tell she was either frightened or annoyed.

With her face cast in the golden glow from the lantern, he

realized he would prefer she be neither. "Forgive me, my lady. I am Randolph Forster, and—"

"You're English." It wasn't a question

"Yes. Oxfordshire, actually. I'm on my—"

"Grand Tour," she finished for him, the sound of disgust in her voice. "Well, there are plenty of other temples for you to see today. Be off, won't you?"

Randy bristled at her dismissive comment. "Yes, I noticed," he replied. "However, I am here."

Her free hand fisted and rested on her hip, a move he had seen his mother and his Aunt Barbara do on a number of occasions—times when they were annoyed and determined to make their displeasure known. The move emphasized the silhouette of her body, which had him swallowing any other response he might have made. She seemed familiar and yet he couldn't sort exactly why.

Had she been naked, she could have been Venus about to scold Eros.

CHAPTER 2
A BROTHER AND SISTER
TOUR A TEMPLE

Meanwhile, in the Parthenon

As her brother stood at the ancient wall near the Parthenon, his gaze taking in the city of Athens below, Jane Fitzsimmons glanced down the front of her gown to discover the hem displaying a band of dust. It was as if she had dipped the bottom of her skirt into a vat of dirt with the intent of adding a gray stripe along her hemline.

If she'd had any idea her brother Antonio, heir to the Reardon viscountcy, had intended for them to climb the hill and the steep marble steps leading up to the Acropolis on this day, she would have never chosen such a dark colored gown.

Made of navy British silk and wool with a V-neck fitted bodice and full sleeves cuffed at the bottom and gathered at the upper arm with lace-trimmed bows, the walking gown was far too warm for late August in Athens. At least the bell skirt, featuring a drape of furbelows over a crinoline of starched linen, seemed to keep her legs cool.

She had acquired the made-to-order costume from a ladies' tailoring department in Bath only a few days before their departure from England, having learned with little notice she would be joining her brother on his Grand Tour. She was sure the modiste charged her father more given the quick turnaround required to fill the order.

"But why?" she had asked when their mother told her of the plan.

Maria Paloma Silvestri y Arístegui de Benavides Fitzsimmons, Viscountess Reardon, had sighed one of those deep sighs only mothers were allowed to make when their youngest questioned their authority. "Because you need to travel, my dear. See the world as I did."

Her mother had seen the world—or at least some of the Continent and part of England—because she had been born in Spain, the daughter of the seventh Conde of Albacete.

"Besides, your father and I will be in London for the Season, and I know you despise the capital," Maria had added, arching a dark brow to emphasize her point.

Her mother had the right of it. Despite having spent nearly her entire life preparing for her come-out at the beginning of last year's Season—learning French, taking dancing lessons with a dance master, learning to paint and draw and embroider and play the piano-forté—she had discovered a Season was exhausting. Attending balls, *soirées*, and the theatre would have been more than enough, but then there were the *musicales* and garden parties. The afternoon teas in the parlors of matrons who could derail her come-out with a single word of censure.

Then there were the men.

Always attentive men. Young bucks, outfitted in the latest top coats and colorful embroidered waistcoats, who wore pantaloons so tight, they threatened to burst their seams should they so much as bend a knee. The older gentlemen, some widowers and some who had waited entirely too long to start their nurseries, oozed desperation as they sought her for dances and then paid calls the following day, bringing with them bouquets of hot house flowers whose scents always seemed to clash with their overpowering colognes.

If she never again smelled the scent of lime, it would be too soon.

A Season spent touring Europe, especially the countries bordering the Mediterranean, was far preferable to another Season in London.

Antonio had insisted they make the ascent to the Parthenon that morning, though, only their second day in the capital of Greece. "Marcus will meet us there," he said with excitement as he held a note that had been delivered by a footman to their rooms at the Hotel Aiolos.

Designed by architect Stamatis Kleanthis, the two-story, three-year-old hotel was located at the corner of Aiolou and Adrianou in the Plaka neighborhood. Although she had expected their accommodations to be simple, they were surprisingly elegant and comfortable. There were even balconies with wrought iron railings from which she could see the very temple in which they now stood.

"Eleven o'clock at the Parthenon. We should take a basket of food," Antonio suggested.

"Marcus?" she remembered repeating.

"Marcus Henley, heir to the Henley viscountcy and son of the famous archaeologist," he replied, acting as if she should have known the young man. "Have you already forgotten meeting him and his sister? They were the ones who were assisting me when we arrived here in town yesterday." Then his frown had deepened. "You met him last year in London. At one of the balls we attended."

She had been tempted to remind him he hadn't introduced her to either of the Henleys, but Anthony had been so excited to see a friend from England, she supposed he could be forgiven the oversight.

Given her visceral reaction to seeing Mr. Henley, she was almost glad she hadn't been forced to put voice to a greeting. Never had the sight of a young man of her brother's age had her so discombobulated.

She didn't even know why her heart had begun to race or why her breathing had suddenly hitched. Marcus Henley surely wasn't the most handsome man she had ever seen, but there was something about his masculinity—the manner in which he carried himself and the fit of his clothes—that set him apart from those who had vied for her attentions in London.

For an Englishman, his face was entirely too wide and too tanned, his hair a shade of light brown devoid of waves or curls. His jaw seemed terribly square, and his nose appeared a bit wider than most, but then it probably wouldn't turn into one of those hooked noses she found rather revolting on the older gentlemen. He was also too broad across the chest, as if he had been performing physical labor.

He probably had been if he was following in his father's footsteps as an archaeologist.

Digging in the dirt.

Although the thought should have left her wrinkling her nose in disgust, it instead had her experiencing a series of tingles she found both frightening and exciting.

Whatever was wrong with her?

"I know him from Oxford, of course," Antonio had added, when she didn't immediately respond.

At that point, she had merely sighed. While Antonio had

been off making new friends at Oxford during his three years at university, she had been left behind at their family estate near Bath, forced to learn all the skills necessary to attract a husband and run an aristocrat's household.

She pulled the glove from her left hand and used her thumb to wiggle the ruby betrothal ring she had accepted from David, Viscount Penton and the future Marquess of Devonville.

Overwhelmed by the number of suitors she had attracted during her time in London, she had been impressed by the amiable young man who had saved her from ruination in the gardens during a ball. David was far too young to be considering marriage, but he had made her an offer she couldn't refuse—a betrothal meant to help fend off unwanted suitors. Should she meet another she really wanted to wed, she had his blessing to break off their betrothal. Otherwise, she would be available to marry him when he was of a mind to actually settle down to the life of a married aristocrat.

She had thought he wouldn't be of a mind to marry until he was seven-and-twenty, which suited her just fine.

At the time.

Now, a year later, she was having second thoughts. Could she really wait until she was five-and-twenty—or even older— to marry David?

"Ah, here's Henley's heir now," Antonio said, turning from his perusal of Athens when he spotted a young man carefully picking his way through the half-buried rubble that covered the surface of the Acropolis.

Jane surreptitiously shook out her bell skirt in an effort to rid her hem of its ring of dirt and turned to face Marcus Henley.

With his attention on the ground in front of him, Marcus didn't stop until he was near enough to slug Antonio's shoulder with one fist while using his other hand to grab Antonio's for a vigorous handshake. "You look rather well for someone who has only arrived in the last day," he said, his greeting sounding more like an accusation. "I take it the hotel is comfortable?"

"It is indeed," Antonio replied. "And the trip from Thessaloniki wasn't arduous," he added. "Well, not for me, at least. My poor sister suffered with the less than ideal accommodations, though."

Jane resisted the urge to scoff at hearing her brother's assessment of the ship on which he had arranged their passage to the Athens port at Piraeus. Yes, her cabin had been on the small side, but all of the cabins had been tiny on the Greek steamship that frequently made the passage from Thessaloniki to Athens as well as a few Aegean islands before heading back north. "My brother exaggerates," she said when Marcus faced her and dipped a low bow.

He took her gloved hand and brushed his lips over the silk fabric. "I'm sorry we were not reintroduced yesterday," he said.

She managed an equally deep curtsy and was forced to pull her hand from his slight grip when he didn't let go. For a moment, she regretted having done so.

"Oh, that's my fault," Antonio said with surprise. "I was sure you two would remember having met last year."

"Of course I remember," Marcus said. "But given the parade of young bucks seeking your attention that evening, I rather imagine you have quite forgotten me."

Jane widened her eyes. "Not you, of course, but I admit your name escaped my memory."

Antonio chuckled. "Allow me. Miss Jane Fitzsimmons, may I have the honor of introducing Mr. Marcus Henley?" her brother asked. "Marcus is the heir to the Henley viscountcy."

"Mr. Henley," she said, giving him a nod. She was certain her face was red with embarrassment and hoped the shade cast by the brim of her hat hid it. She was also fairly sure the young man swallowed as he openly stared at her. His white cravat, still stiff despite the day's heat, hid his throat from view, though.

"Miss Jane," he murmured. He turned to her brother, his eyes wide. "You might have warned me she was more gorgeous than when I last met her," he accused.

Had any other man said what he had in her presence— and they had on several occasions—Jane's usual response would have been to scoff, roll her eyes in an effort to hide her revulsion, and say something insipid like, "You're too kind, sir."

She did nothing of the sort on this day.

Instead she simply stared at him, unable to form any words.

How could he appear even more arresting than he had the day before?

"Watch yourself, my friend," Antonio warned. "She's under my protection whilst we're on this tour, and I shan't abide any antics that might ruin her."

Jane's mouth opened as if she planned to argue, but she couldn't yet form any words to counter her brother's.

Whatever was wrong with her?

At least a dozen young bucks in London had said similar

words directly to her face the year before, and she had been quite prepared with a suitable response, one that not only thanked them for their consideration but also made it clear their attentions were not welcome.

Today she feared she was appearing as a fish in an aquarium, her mouth opening and closing with not so much as a bubble emerging.

Marcus lifted a hand to his chest, the sound he emitted a clear indication he took offense at hearing Antonio's warning. "I would never do anything to besmirch your sister's honor," he insisted. When he returned his attention to her, he lifted a shoulder. "Please, understand I am speaking words of truth when I say you are a vision of loveliness, Miss Jane."

She nodded her head, sure her face was still bright red, and not only from the growing heat of the day. "It's very kind of you to say, Mr. Henley."

"Oh, do call me Marcus." He inhaled as if he intended to say something more, but he instead turned back to Antonio. "So, allow me to give you a tour of the place. My brother is around here somewhere..." He surveyed the area around them, leaning his head back as he directed his attention around the side of a column toward the Erechtheion. "He's been studying the caryatids on the north side of that temple over there," he said, lifting a hand in a dismissive wave. "Before the local man in charge of this place puts him to work."

"Work?" Antonio repeated, his gaze directed to the Erechtheion.

Marcus nodded. "As you know, my father has accepted the assignment of finding one of the Greek temples that used to be located here," he explained. "With the proviso Michael be put on a team with some of the other archaeologists working over there." He waved in the direction of the Propylaea where, despite the distance, they could see several men dressed in suits. They looked as if they were having a serious discussion, their arms waving about as if to emphasize their point. "I expect they'll have him doing most of the digging," he added, grinning.

Jane moved to stand next to the fluted columns that made up the south side of the Parthenon, her attention going from the archaeologists Marcus mentioned to the Propylaea, where three young men were making their way past the columns there. Although one split off to disappear behind the dark Frankish tower, the other two hurried toward the Erechtheion. She inhaled softly.

"David?" she said, unaware she had said the name out loud.

"What's this?" her brother asked, joining her at the edge of the temple floor to follow her line of sight.

"I... I think that's David," she said.

"David?" Marcus repeated. He noticeably stiffened.

"Viscount Penton," Antonio stated. "You know him. He was at Oxford, although he was a year or two behind us. A rather amiable sort. In fact, he and Jane are betrothed," he said, a dark brow arching as if in a tease.

Marcus turned to regard Jane with what appeared to be a look of hurt. "Betrothed?" he repeated.

Jane dipped her head. "We are. I have not seen him since last Season, though," she said softly. "Are you friends with him?"

His features hardening into a scowl, Marcus shook his head. "I hardly know the boy. He's an heir to a marquessate, though, so..." He shook his head, as if he had come to a disappointing conclusion.

Eager to keep his attention, she asked, "Might you know the young man who is with him?"

Antonio was quick to say, "That would be Thomas Forster." He chuckled. "He's the Earl of Gisborn's spare heir. They must be on their Grand Tours, too."

"And the other?" She waved to where she had last seen the tallest of the three.

Antonio and Marcus exchanged quick glances. "There was another?" Marcus asked in alarm. "With them?" When she nodded and indicated the small temple near the entrance, he added, "Um, if you'll excuse me a moment, I should go check on my sister." He bowed to Jane, who dipped a curtsy. "I'll return shortly."

"Your sister?" Antonio repeated in surprise.

"Diana. She's doing some research in the Temple of Athena Nike," Marcus explained.

"Would you like us to go with you?" Antonio started to follow Marcus, but at seeing his upraised hand, he paused.

"I would never forgive myself if you turned your ankle whilst traversing this field of rubble," Marcus shouted. "I'll only be a few minutes. Please, look around if you'd like—this is quite an impressive temple—and when I return, I'll fill you in on what my father will be doing once he arrives." He hurried off in the direction of the tower.

Jane glanced up at her brother. "He left his sister unescorted?" she asked, censure in her voice.

Antonio merely shrugged. "I'm quite sure Diana Henley can fend for herself," he murmured.

"Tony," she scolded softly.

"Marcus doesn't speak very highly of her," he said. "She's her father's daughter but from what he's told me, she would have been better off born a boy, I think."

"Why do you say that?" she asked, her attention finally going back to her brother when Marcus disappeared into the squarish temple next to the tower.

"Like Lord Henley, she's apparently an archaeologist."

"Oh, how interesting," Jane said in awe.

"Hardly a suitable avocation for a young lady," Antonio countered.

"Why?"

He turned and began studying the fluted columns making up the Parthenon. "Digging in the dirt all day?" he said absently. He stood next to a column and looked straight up before directing his gaze along the line of columns. "Huh," he murmured.

"What is it?" she asked, mimicking her brother's moves. Her eyes widened in awe. "It's not a straight line," she whispered. "The columns—they're placed along the base, but it's clearly curved."

"The columns aren't straight either," he commented. "The sections are carved so they bow out about a third of the way up and then taper to form a smaller diameter at the top," he said, a grin appearing. "The Greeks were all about proportion and tricking the eye to make their temples appear taller than they really were. Quite a feat, really, considering they didn't have the benefit of machines to help with their construction."

"They carved all this marble by hand," Jane said as she stepped around the base of a column, tracing a gloved finger along the seam where the bottom drum of a column met the next one up. "And matched the fluting perfectly when they stacked them up," she marveled.

"The alignment must have been a challenge," Antonio remarked. "Although if I remember right, there are square holes cut in the middle of each drum. Once they were stacked one atop the other, a wooden dowel was inserted down the center to help keep everything aligned."

By the time Antonio had finished his explanation, they had arrived at a corner column.

While Antonio's attention was on the pediment up above, Jane scanned the flat area from the tower to the Propylaea and then to the Erechtheion. She lifted a gloved hand and waved when she realized both David Slater and Thomas Forster were waving in their direction. She smiled and then giggled for the first time since her departure from England.

Perhaps her stay in Athens would be more pleasant than she expected.

CHAPTER 3
A COUSIN FROM THE PAST APPEARS

eanwhile, back in the Temple of Athena Nike

At a loss as to why the young woman he had discovered seemed so annoyed with him, Randy considered simply doing her bidding by leaving the temple. He could join his brother and cousin at the Erechtheion to continue exploring the Acropolis.

He didn't want to, however.

She was still staring at him, one of her fists resting on a hip that merely accentuated her slender waist. Given how fitted the breeches were, he realized they had to have been made specifically for her. Made to hug her waistline and encase the perfect globes of her bottom and her thighs and knees. Below that, the Nankeen fabric disappeared into a pair of worn leather boots.

The mere sight of those breeches on her had his cock reacting again, and the thought that it could become apparent at any moment despite the length of the top coat he wore had him desperate to think of something other than her, naked.

His rescue came in the form of another man, who stepped into the temple and stopped short with a *huff.*

"What's wrong?" the young man asked in a familiar voice, directing his query to the young lady.

"Mr. Forster—"

"*Lord* Forster, actually," Randy piped up, deciding he would play his aristocrat card. "I am heir to the Gisborn earldom."

"Forster?" the other man replied in disbelief.

Randy regarded the interloper with surprise when he turned, the outside light illuminating his face so he could make out his features. "Marcus Henley? Whatever are you doing here, cousin?"

Marcus clapped him on the shoulder and offered his right hand. "Same as you, I imagine, but with a slightly different purpose."

"Oh?" Randy prompted.

"If you remember, father's avocation is archaeology."

"Uncovering mosaics in the Valley of the Temples on Sicily, wasn't he?" Randy asked, remembering they had seen some of Viscount Jasper Henley's work when they had visited the site the year before.

"He *was*," Marcus acknowledged. "His next project is here on the Acropolis, but before he starts, he thought to take my mother on a holiday. My sister and I have come on ahead to set up the household and such," Marcus explained.

"Your sister?" Randy prompted, his gaze darting to the young woman.

"Oh, forgive me," Marcus said. "Miss Diana Henley, may I have the honor of introducing you to our... second cousin, I believe you would be? Randy Forster. We attended Oxford together." He turned his attention back to Randy. "Diana is my only sister."

"Miss Diana," Randy said, reaching out to take her gloved hand to his lips. Although he sensed she was about to pull her hand from his grip, she seemed to capitulate as he brushed his lips over the worn leather. Even without looking up, he was sure she was rolling her eyes.

"You'll have to excuse her mode of dress. She insists on wearing breeches whilst she's working," Marcus explained.

"As does my younger sister, Grace," Randy countered, his face displaying his dislike of the practice.

Diana's manner seemed about to soften a fraction, her hand dropping to her side. When she paid witness to his expression, she resumed her previous chilly demeanor. Dipping the very slightest of curtsies, she winced at the sound of her boot heel scraping the marble floor. "Lord Forster."

Randy realized his mistake right away. "Does Lord Henley always take you along on his archaeological expeditions?"

She seemed to bristle at hearing the query. "Of course. I've certainly had no choice in the matter," Diana replied.

"Mother always comes along with Father," Marcus said, lifting a shoulder. "So, except when we've been away at school, we go where they do."

"Didn't you practically grow up on Sicily?"

"Indeed," Marcus acknowledged. "Same with Michael," he added referring to his younger brother. "Except for some Seasons in London, Diana and our parents could usually be found living near Girgenti. Since so many archaeological projects have started in Athens, my father has agreed to work on a project up here on the Acropolis."

"We just left my cousin—*your* cousin—on Sicily a few weeks ago," Randy commented, remembering Marcus' mother was a first cousin to his mother, Hannah, and his uncle, Will Slater.

"Which one?"

"Donald Slater. He's married to the Marchesa Montblanc, and they live in Catania with their..." Here Randy paused, realizing he couldn't exactly tell his friend that Antony, Marchese Montblanc, was really Donald's son. The aristocracy in Catania believed the young boy was the true heir of Ricardo Malgerei, Marchese Montblanc, when Donald's wife was in fact Montblanc's daughter from a secret *affaire*. Their marriage had been a ruse to see to it the marchese's grandson would inherit the title.

A hearty guffaw sounded from Viscount Henley's heir. "Slater finally *married*?" he said in disbelief.

Randy nodded. "He met Lady Nicoletta D'Avalos when he was on his Grand Tour over seven years ago. Fell in love with her, but she was betrothed to the marchese, so he had to wait for the old man to die before he could take her to wife."

"How romantic." The words were said with a sort of disdain that had Randy turning to regard Diana with a look of shock. About to respond, he couldn't when Marcus beat him to the punch.

"Come now, Sister. Just because *you* don't believe in love at first sight doesn't mean others don't," he scolded. He turned his attention back on Randy. "It *was* love at first sight, was it not?"

Randy blinked. Not having discussed the details of how Donald had come to fall in love with Nicoletta, Randy wasn't sure how to respond. "Isn't that how it is for most of us?"

Marcus let out another guffaw. "Then it's a wonder his younger brother hasn't already married. Penton seems to fall in love with every young lady he sees," he teased, referring to

David. He suddenly sobered, his expression conveying jealousy. "And they do with him, damn the lad."

Knowing Marcus spoke the truth, Randy said, "He's gone off with Tom to another temple."

"I saw them. They're with my younger brother, Michael, over at the Erechtheion," Marcus said.

"So… what are *you* in search of?" Randy asked.

Marcus was about to answer but Diana said, "That's really none of your concern."

Despite the warmth in the temple, Randy felt the chill in the young lady's response.

"Really, Diana, you needn't treat Forster as the enemy. I'm sure he's not here to pilfer Greek treasure."

Randy did his best to keep an impassive expression. *Treasure?* His only reason for visiting the ruins atop the Acropolis was to see them first-hand. The description of the Parthenon as provided in Pausanias' book suggested the traveler wasn't impressed by the building itself but only the artwork within. "Your brother has the right of it," he said, directing his response to Diana. "My cousin and brother and I are just looking, hoping to see some of the art described in Pausanias' book."

Diana's eyes widened a fraction at the mention of Pausanias, and she seemed to relax a bit, her rigid posture no longer betraying her suspicion. "Just don't go carving your names in the marbles, like so many of the other idiots who have come before."

Randy visibly winced. Although he hadn't done it himself, he had witnessed his younger brother, Tom, leaving his name and the date on the slab of a column from the Temple of Zeus at Selinunte. "I would never," he said defensively.

"Come, let's get out of here and leave my sister to her

searching," Marcus said. "I'll never hear the end of it if we keep her from her work, and I've a surprise for you over at the Parthenon."

"A surprise?" Randy repeated, once again giving the young lady a bow. "Miss Diana."

"Forster," she responded, barely dipping a curtsy.

"Another from our university days has come to Athens on his Grand Tour," Marcus said as Randy followed him out of the temple, the bright sunshine forcing both to lift a hand to shield their eyes before they had their hats returned to their heads. Even then, the thin brims of their top hats did little to help shade their faces. "We'll see if you recognize him."

"Do I need to be concerned about my brother and Cousin David if they're over at the Erechtheion?" Randy asked. "I don't wish for them to encounter any issues with the local archaeologists or unstable columns."

"Doubtful. It's not as bad a ruin as some of these others," he said, waving to the other structures on the Acropolis. "A sprained ankle will be the worst of it."

"Sounds as if you have some first-hand experience?"

Marcus chuckled. "Not me, but certainly others."

"How is it you're here today?" Randy asked, noting for the first time they weren't the only ones visiting the Acropolis.

"Father has taken Mother to Rome," Marcus replied. "Said he owed her a romantic holiday," he added, still grinning. "I don't expect them to arrive here in Athens for another week or so."

"Speaking of relatives," Randy hedged. "My uncle and aunt are with us, although they elected to spend the day in our lodgings. We let a house here in town. I think the heat is a bit much for Aunt Barbara."

Carefully stepping around an uneven marble slab that had

at one time been part of the path leading to the Parthenon, Marcus stuffed his hands into the pockets of his pantaloons. "If that isn't a secret code for something else, I don't know what is."

Randy nearly tripped on the remains of a metope. "What are you saying?" he asked in alarm.

"They want to be alone," Marcus replied, making a rude gesture with his hands.

"Marcus," Randy scolded. "They're too old for that sort of…" He stopped and cleared his throat. "Anyway, what makes *you* say that?"

Marcus once again guffawed. "Mother and Father engage in amorous society all the time. It's a wonder I don't have more than one brother and sister," he remarked.

"Where *is* your brother?" Randy asked, wanting to change the subject. His gaze took in the field of rubble through which they picked their path.

"At the Erechtheion. Probably talking your brother's ears off about those caryatids, as if he hasn't already studied every inch of the one at the British Museum."

Randy tore his gaze from the sandstone statues holding up the roof of the Erechtheion's porch to step around another obstacle. He had seen the one taken by Lord Elgin during the family's visit to the museum the week before they departed on their Grand Tour. They had concentrated on the Greek exhibits as a means of preparing for the trip. "I heard the caryatids are all different. Is it true?"

"You heard right. Their hair, mostly. The manner in which the braiding is done. It's rather interesting, if you're into that sort of thing."

"You're not?"

Marcus shook his head before hopping over a corner of a

capital. Randy grimaced at seeing its poor condition before he, too, had to avoid another marble block. "I take after my father when it comes to mosaics," Marcus explained. "Although I can't say I wish to spend the rest of my life looking for them."

Randy paused to study a column top, the Corinthian design made more evident by the dirt embedded in the carved creases. "Are you planning a different avocation?" he asked.

Marcus shrugged. "Truth be told, I prefer politics over digging in the dirt," he claimed. "I rather like London. There is so much to do, so I've been thinking of asking Father if I might move there. We have a townhouse, you see—an entailed property of the viscountcy—so I'd have a place to stay."

Surprised at hearing his cousin's plans, Randy asked, "Well, in the meantime, have you been doing any digging up here?"

His second cousin shook his head. "Although I have permission, I've not started any serious search up here. I thought it best to wait for Father." He gestured in the direction of a group of men who were working near the Propylaea. "I shouldn't wish to anger the ones in charge, so I'm rather glad Michael will be the one working with them. He's to assist them beginning in the next day or so."

Randy glanced over to see at least one of the men staring in their direction. He quickly caught up to Marcus to walk alongside him. "What about in the city itself? Have you discovered anything?

"Oh, yes. Mosaics are everywhere. You hardly have to dig to find them," Marcus acknowledged. "But I told Father I would provide protection for Diana while he's in Rome with my mother, which is part of the reason I'm up here today."

Randy thought of what Diana had been doing in the Temple of Athena Nike when he had first stepped through the opening. She had been studying the wall of the cella, the inner chamber. "So what's your sister in search of? Obviously not mosaics," he remarked, remembering the floor of the temple had been made of marble.

Marcus stiffened and paused his steps. "I suppose she has a theory she's determined to prove," he said, rolling his eyes. "She's always up to something."

Intrigued, Randy carefully stepped onto a marble disc with a square hole in the middle, his new higher vantage giving him the opportunity to see his brother on the porch of the Erechtheion. "Oh?" he prompted, lifting an arm to wave.

"You'll have to get it out of her if you want to know more. She's not told me anything."

Disappointed, Randy stepped down from the marble disc and turned his attention back towards the Temple of Athena Nike.

He wondered what he would have to do to get the secret out of her.

CHAPTER 4
A TEMPLE HIDES A SECRET

eanwhile, back in the Temple of Athena Nike

Wiping a stream of perspiration from her brow with a hanky, Diana Henley stood in the temple's opening and watched her brother and the Earl of Gisborn's heir as they made their way in the direction of the Parthenon.

For the first time in her life, she had felt true fright. That moment when the light from the opening in the cella had been briefly blocked, she had simply assumed her brother was checking on her. To discover a stranger regarding her with curiosity had her heart in her throat and a thought to flee filling her head.

Her legs wouldn't move.

Besides, where would she go? The interloper was blocking the only opening in the cella. The only structure within the cella was the altar. She glanced at the flat-topped block and thought of what she had set atop it. Her journal lay open to a page where she recorded the names she found on the walls. Next to it was an ink pot and her quill—hardly useful as weapons.

Given the lack of protection, she did what she always did when she was in a situation not in her control.

She lashed out. Behaved like a spoiled brat. Made herself the one to be avoided.

It usually worked. People gave her the cut direct in social situations. Nodded politely but left her company as soon as they could after meeting her. Made their excuses.

So why hadn't Randolph Forster?

She had to remind herself that her brother had joined them. That's the real reason the heir to the Gisborn earldom had stood his ground. Why he hadn't fled in an attempt to escape her wrath.

Returning her attention to the cella wall, Diana lifted the lantern and continued her examination of the smooth marble —smooth except for the scratchings from centuries of etchings in the form of names and dates of the visitors who had toured the temple over the more than two thousand years since its construction.

Surely she could find the name she was in search of somewhere on this wall.

If not here, there were other temples on the Acropolis where she could continue her search.

CHAPTER 5
FELLOW TRAVELERS UNITE

eanwhile, on the way to the Parthenon
"Surely you have an idea of what your sister is looking for?" Randy asked when they were halfway to the Parthenon. He cursed softly when he nearly stumbled on a marble block, its surface uneven but slick.

"'*Who*' is the more appropriate word, but my guess is as good as yours," Marcus replied, stopping to raise a pair of opera glasses to his eyes. His gaze was directed toward the Parthenon, where a figure could be seen near one of the marble columns at the opposite end. In the harsh light of midday, the column appeared white, but in the afternoon light, it would reflect a more golden color. "She hasn't yet shared a name."

Randy scoffed as he picked his way through the rubble. "On the wall of a temple?" he questioned, his confusion apparent.

"Of course. Those walls contain names and sometimes dates of hundreds of visitors—some who were explorers—

who came here over the centuries," Marcus explained. "Greeks, Romans, Franks, Turks..." He paused and gave Randy a pointed glance. "Young men on their Grand Tours." He once again brought the opera glasses to his eyes. "When we were in Rome last year, I heard an old man call it *graffiti*."

"Graffiti?" Randy furrowed a brow. "From *graffio?*" he guessed, remembering the Latin word for scratches. "Or *graphein*," he said, his eyes rounding when he realized the Greek word for writings and paintings on a hard surface could also apply.

He glanced in the direction his friend was staring, curious if it was the temple that had his attention or the silhouette of a well-dressed woman who lifted a hand and waved in their direction. The shadow from a column hid her features.

"A scratch, yes," Marcus replied, finally lowering the glasses. His gaze still directed on the Parthenon, he added, "Rather appropriate, and a far better word than 'carving', although I do have to say, I have seen some that look as if they really are a part of the artifact. Father used to warn me that sometimes the Greeks took days to make their mark on a temple wall."

Wincing, Randy shook his head before making his way around a capital. The elaborate carving was still in good shape, indicative of the Corinthian style of Greek temples introduced around 430 BC. "I'll never understand why someone would damage an ancient temple by taking a chisel to it," he complained. "Whatever happened to showing respect for history?"

Marcus chuckled. "I suppose for some, etching your name into old marble is a means of showing that you are a part of history as well." He held out a hand, his finger forming a line in the air as he added, "I was here."

"You condone it?" Randy asked in surprise.

"*I* don't," Marcus was quick to reply. "However, I have learned from my father it's been in practice for millennia. He's come across names and dates and symbols—some rather famous—during every dig he has been a part of over the years. Sometimes it even helps to identify a structure's name or the year when it was built." He paused as he negotiated his way around the half-buried disc of a column. "Surely you've seen them when you were in Sicily?"

Randy made a rude sound in his throat. "I actually didn't, but not many of the temples we saw still have their cellae," he replied.

Most of the ruins he and his brother, two cousins, and aunt and uncle had visited at the Valley of the Temples and in Selinunte were merely the remains of temples, with only a few standing columns. Given the raids of Carthaginians, Romans, and Normans and the shaking due to earthquakes, the structures stood little chance of remaining upright.

"Does your sister make note of the names? Catalogue them? Keep track of them somehow?" he asked, remembering he had spotted a journal or book resting on the remains of the altar at one end of the cella. An ink pot and pen had been perched on the altar as well, so he assumed she was making notes of her finds.

"If she does, she hasn't told me about it."

Pretending only a slight interest in his second cousin, Randy said, "Sounds as if you two aren't that close."

Marcus shrugged, his hands shoved into the pockets of his buff pantaloons as he led them to the far end of the Parthenon. The figure they had spotted upon exiting the temple was clearer now, the silhouette that of a lady wearing a navy gown featuring a fashionable bell skirt. "We tolerate one another," he admitted.

"Because we have to. I rather doubt I shall miss her when Father finally agrees to a marriage for her—if he ever does."

Randy's eyes rounded. "Why wouldn't he?"

It was Marcus' turn to scoff. "She told Mother she would prefer to remain a spinster."

Nearly tripping over a ragged step leading up to the temple, Randy cursed again. "A spinster?"

"That's what *she* said, and despite Mother's attempts to change her mind, she's quite insistent she doesn't want a husband."

Randy bent to study the remains of metope. "Prefers to be alone, does she?" he murmured.

His friend stopped in his tracks. "I hadn't thought that was the reason," he said. "In fact, she seems to genuinely dislike men."

Raising his face so quickly to regard Marcus with a look of shock, Randy was sure he heard his neck make a popping sound. "Why?"

Resuming his trek up the steep temple steps, Marcus lifted a shoulder. "She's really too clever for her own good. I would never say it to her face, but she's a bluestocking through and through. Learned everything she knows from Father and from books. Remembers *everything* she has read. Everything she's seen. Everything she's heard."

"Hm," Randy muttered. "Perhaps it's better for everyone if she doesn't marry."

Once again, Marcus paused, this time next to a column. "And do what?"

Randy shrugged. "My mother told me spinsters get their name from the women who used to weave and spin for their livings. Seems they made good blunt back then. They could live on their earnings and never have to marry if they didn't wish to."

Marcus let out a guffaw. "Not sure how my sister intends to earn her living, but I can't imagine Father extending her an allowance for the rest of her life."

"What of her dowry?" Randy countered. As an older brother and heir, Randy knew of his father's arrangements for his sister, Grace. She might only be nine years old now, but in a decade, he was sure she would be married off to an earl or a viscount. That is, if she wasn't still a hoyden.

Still standing in the shade of the column, Marcus regarded his friend with an inscrutable expression. "Oh, I'd quite forgotten about that," he murmured softly. "I suppose she could live on it. If she economized."

The way he made the comment had Randy thinking Marcus and Diana either might not be friendly siblings or that Marcus knew the dowry was a pittance. "And you?" he said, deciding to redirect the subject of their conversation. "What are your plans after you've finished visiting Athens?"

Marcus gave a snort. "If you're referring to the parson's trap..." He aimed a finger in the direction of the young woman leaning against the corner column of the Parthenon, her wide-brimmed bonnet shading her face from view. "*She* would be the cheese."

One of Randy's brows crinkled at hearing the odd comment. "You're not old enough to marry," he said, keeping his voice low as they approached the woman who was now standing with a parasol held aloft. Before they were close enough to exchange introductions, a young man appeared from behind another column, his face lighting up in delight when he spotted them.

"Forster? Is that you?" The young man hurried forward, his right hand held out.

Randy displayed a matching grin as he shook hands with another classmate. "Antonio Fitzsimmons, whatever are *you* doing here?" he asked of the man he recognized from their years at Eton and then Oxford. The viscount's heir sported wavy black hair and an olive complexion suggesting he wasn't English. Randy knew the features were due to Antonio's mother, a Spanish aristocrat's daughter.

"Probably the same as you," Antonio replied. "Grand Tour. Unlike you, though, we're nearly finished." He motioned for the young lady to join them. "This is my sister, Miss Jane Fitzsimmons," he said as she stepped forward and dipped a curtsy. "I'm looking after her since our parents have already set sail for England. We'll be departing for Valencia within a fortnight," he added before he turned to his sister. "This is Randolph Forster, heir to the Gisborn earldom."

Randy immediately reached for her hand. "You can call me Forster," he stated before kissing her knuckles. When he straightened, he understood exactly why she would be a temptation for Marcus Henley.

She was gorgeous. Compared to a traditional English miss, she was exotic, her black hair, hazel eyes, bow-shaped lips, and high cheekbones contributing to a regal appearance suggesting she could be the queen of some faraway land.

Apparently Marcus wanted her to be his viscountess one day.

"It's very good to meet you... Lord Forster, are you not?" she said, directing a curious expression to her brother.

Randy nodded. "Yes, but we needn't be formal here," he replied. His gaze darted between Marcus and Antonio. "You didn't tell me you had the Fitzsimmonses with you," he accused.

"Well, we're not exactly traveling together, if that's what you thought," Marcus replied, urging them to an area where a series of columns provided some shade.

"But we knew we'd be in the same place at the same time," Antonio added. His gaze darted to the west. "Did you leave your sister alone again?" he asked of Marcus in a chiding voice.

Marcus shrugged. "She'll be fine." He glanced around. "Didn't you have a picnic basket with you?"

"I left it in the shade," Jane said. "It is about time we ate, don't you think?" She turned her attention to Randy. "Would you like to join us? I'm sure we have enough food, although we may not have enough wine."

Surprised by the invitation, Randy considered the option for a moment. "Uh..." Remembering they had left Miss Diana alone in the Temple of Athena Nike, he moved until he could see the entrance to the temple from between two columns. Directing his attention to the Erechtheion, he noticed his brother was still examining the caryatids along with Marcus' brother, Michael. Although he couldn't see his cousin David, he decided the young man must have been inside the temple. "Thank you, but I'm not really hungry right now, and I'm still rather curious about that little temple," he said. "I can keep an eye on Miss Diana if you'd like," he offered, directing his comment to Marcus.

Marcus chuckled. "Be my guest. Oh, and do join us for dinner tonight. We're at Vouros Mansion in Vakchou Street."

"I will. Thank you for the invitation."

Giving one last cursory glance at the columns of the

Parthenon, Randy tipped his hat and made his way back through the field of rubble toward the Temple of Athena Nike.

Although he would have enjoyed a bit of food just then, his curiosity was greater than his hunger.

CHAPTER 6
A REUNION BOTH WELCOME AND NOT

eanwhile, at the Parthenon

As Marcus, Antonio, and Jane made their way to where she had left the picnic basket at the opposite end of the Parthenon, David, Tom, and Michael were traversing the field of rubble separating the Erechtheion from the Parthenon.

Marcus did his best to hide his displeasure at their impending arrival. Ever since Antonio had mentioned Jane was betrothed to Lord Penton, he had experienced a combination of disappointment and jealousy. Even the arrival of his good friend, Lord Randolph Forster, hadn't helped him overcome his melancholy.

When he paid witness to the manner of David's greeting, it was all he could do not to challenge the younger man to a duel.

"I wondered if I was imagining you, my sweet," David said as he approached, his gaze entirely on Jane.

She had blushed prettily and dipped a curtsy even as he took her hand to his lips.

Then he kissed her on the cheek.

Right in front of everyone and God.

The cur.

Worse, the young man was more handsome than he had been at school. He was another year older, yes, but the soft planes of his formerly youthful face had hardened somewhat. His resemblance to his father was unmistakeable, which also meant he would grow even more good looking as he aged.

Damn him.

"Lord Penton, this is such a surprise," Jane said, her smile glorious.

Marcus had to bite back an audible growl. Although she had met him with a pleasant expression and high color only three-quarters of an hour earlier, she hadn't beamed in delight as she was now doing for the benefit of Penton.

The cousins exchanged greetings and handshakes with Antonio and Jane before they continued their way to the basket.

"Oh, I do hope we have enough food for everyone," Jane said, lowering herself to remove the cloth cover from the basket. She shook out the blanket and spread it out over a shaded area of the temple floor. Antonio, Michael, and Marcus moved to sit at various corners as she placed hunks of cheese, bread, olives, and fruits in the center.

"Don't worry about Tom and me, my sweet," David said, assisting her at the basket. "Now that Cousin Michael has given us a thorough tour of the Erechtheion, we are going back to town for a bite to eat. I expect Randy will be joining us shortly."

"If you're sure, my lord," she said.

David seemed to hesitate for a moment before he said, "I am."

"More for me," Michael said, earning him a glare from his older brother.

"How long will you be in town?" David asked, his voice barely audible.

"A fortnight," she replied. "We're staying at the Hotel Aiolos."

"Is that all?" he asked, obviously disappointed.

"We're going to Spain next."

"To see your aunt?"

She grinned. "Yes. You remembered."

David dipped his head. "Of course I remember." He cleared his throat and spoke louder. "Will you and Antonio and..." He waved at the others. "Join me for dinner tomorrow evening? There's a taverna I'm told serves excellent local fare. We can make a party of it."

Marcus watched as she looked to her brother for guidance, and he winced when Antonio agreed and said, "I thought we might go to the caves—the Prison of Socrates, I think they're supposed to be—on the morrow. I hear it's a bit of a climb, but it shouldn't be too strenuous."

"I could see the caves from over there," David said, waving in the direction of where he had spotted the landmark with his pair of binoculars. "The path appears well worn."

"Perhaps you'd like to come with us?" Antonio asked, directing his query to the group in general.

"I'm certainly up for a hike," Tom said.

"I'll join you," Marcus chimed in.

"Sounds perfect," Michael said.

"Except you're due to begin your dig on the morrow, are you not?" Marcus reminded his brother, aiming a thumb over his shoulder to indicate the corner of the Acropolis where the archaeologists were still milling about.

"I hate it when you're right," Michael groused. "So, the rest of you have a pleasant day." He helped himself to a couple of figs and stood. "Come, you two. Let's let these three have their luncheon."

David and Tom joined Michael, but not before they bade their farewells and took turns bowing to Jane.

"I look forward to seeing you again before you take your leave of Greece," David said to Jane.

"And you, my lord," she said, giving him a deep curtsy.

The three younger men headed for the Propylaea as Antonio and Marcus returned their attentions to their luncheon and the wine Jane was pouring into small glass tumblers.

"Penton certainly took liberties with his greeting," Marcus remarked, directing his comment to Antonio.

Jerking his head up in surprise, Antonio glanced over at his sister before he said, "I hadn't noticed."

"Did he?" Jane asked. Her eyes widened. "But if you are referring to the kiss he gave me on my cheek—"

"I am," Marcus affirmed.

She angled her head to one side. "He is not one who shies away from showing his affection, it's true," she said, "but I find it rather flattering. He is my betrothed, after all," she added, before turning her attention to distributing food to the two young men.

"She will be greeted the very same way by our uncle and every other man we meet when we reach Spain," Antonio remarked, lifting a shoulder in a dismissive shrug.

"With a kiss?"

"On the cheek. Had it been anywhere else, Penton would have suffered a fist to his face," Antonio claimed.

"Tony," Jane said softly. She faced Marcus. "I do hope you'll join us for dinner at the taverna tomorrow evening."

Marcus straightened. "Of course, I will, Miss Jane." His heart raced when he saw how she beamed at him.

"You must tell me all about your archaeological finds," she added, pouring more wine into his tumbler.

Daring a glance in her brother's direction, Marcus realized this was his chance to impress the young woman.

They spent the next hour discussing his work on Sicily with his father before he escorted them to view the rest of the Acropolis.

The entire time, he made sure he directed his explanations to Jane. He knew if he had any hope at all of gaining her favor —of replacing David, Viscount Penton, as her betrothed—he had to show his affection any way he could.

CHAPTER 7
A DISCOVERY IN A TEMPLE

*M*eanwhile, in the Temple of Athena Nike

Having studied all the walls of the tiny temple from the ceiling to the floor, Diana stepped back and planted her fists on her hips. "Dammit," she muttered. Bending down, she lifted the lantern and was about to make one more pass around the interior when a shadow once again passed across the light from the entrance.

Stiffening, she quickly turned and held up the lantern between her face and the body that appeared in silhouette.

"Ack!" Randy said, his arms shielding his face from the glare of the lantern.

"You again?" she said, setting the lantern back on the floor.

"Your cousin, yes. Your brother and the Fitzsimmonses are about to enjoy a picnic in the Parthenon," Randy said, not bothering to enter the cella.

"And you're not?" she countered.

Randy paused, not expecting the curt response. "Did you wish to join them?"

Diana's attention had turned to the wall opposite the one she had been studying when he had first found her, her brows furrowed in concentration. "No. I'm not exactly dressed for it," she murmured, her head angling to one side as she continued to stare at the cella wall. "Certainly not if Miss Fitzsimmons is with them."

Randy sensed disgust in her voice.

Or perhaps it was jealousy.

"You are not friends with her?" he guessed.

She suddenly turned her gaze on him, her eyes round with shock. "Oh, that's not it all all," she quickly replied. "I only met her yesterday at the Aiolos Hotel. My brother introduced us when they were seeing to acquiring accommodations." She paused, her attention once again going to the wall. "You should join them."

Although he had the distinct impression she wanted to be rid of him, Randy's curiosity had him remaining in place. "I ate a rather large breakfast, so I begged off. I told your brother I would come look after you." His attention went to the same wall she was regarding with fascination.

"I don't need *looking after*," she whispered, as if she had said it a thousand times. Her manner softened as she regarded him, her gaze going from his head to his booted feet. "However, if you intend to stay, then I must put you to work."

The comment had Randy deciding it was as close to an invitation as he was going to get. He stepped into the cella. "What can I do to help?"

The enthusiasm in his voice had Diana crossing her arms. She had thought the warning would have him begging off. He certainly seemed unable to take a hint. "Follow directions. Do exactly as I tell you," she said before moving to the altar at the back of the small cella. She plucked a rolled up sheet of paper from the marble and, holding it by two corners, allowed it to unroll. "You're going to hold this up to this wall right here," she said, placing the blank sheet of vellum against the marble. "Hold it very still. Do *not* allow it to move."

Randy furrowed his brows. "All right," he said, stepping in to take her place as he gripped the corners between his fingers and pressed the sides of his fists against the thin paper.

"You'll have to move your feet back a bit so I can get in between you and the vellum," she said, returning from the altar with a black stick in one hand.

"What is that?" Randy asked, doing as he was told by straightening his arms and widening his stance. He was forced to move one foot back even farther from the marble when she stepped in front of him and faced the wall.

"Charcoal," she responded curtly. Before he could ask anything else, she began swiping the edge of the stick over the vellum, leaving behind a dark gray swath in her path. She continued working her way across and down the sheet of vellum before she was forced to reposition herself to continue the bottom half.

"You're doing a rubbing," Randy said in awe, his gaze going to where thin lines remained in white while the surrounding areas were filled in with the charcoal.

"Have you done one before?" she asked, bending even more so she could work on the bottom half of the sheet. In the process, her derriere touched his thigh. "Oh, pardon me," she said, shifting her stance slightly.

Randy did his best not to react, but his cock twitched, apparently aware of how neatly her derriere would fit if she simply bent over and supported herself against it. "It's all right," he said. "If you need to lean against me," he added, well aware of how she was having to contort her body in order to work in the confined space. "And, uh, no, I haven't done a rubbing like this before."

If she did use his body for support, he thought he would be doing a rubbing of his own sometime later that day and not on a temple wall. The mere thought of that upside-down heart-shaped bum pressed against his manhood nearly had him groaning with effort to keep it in check.

"Oh, my goddess," Diana whispered.

"What is it?" he asked in alarm, thinking she might have noticed his state of discomfort. At least her words had his cock settling down where it belonged.

"I think there *is* something here." She glanced up at him from where she was now kneeling. "I was sure this wall was smooth, but..."

"Graffiti?" he guessed. From his perspective, he could only make out the gray from the charcoal on the vellum and the few places where white lines seemed to have been left behind.

"I think it's Old Attic," she replied, referring to the language of the ancient Greeks. She slipped sideways, beneath his arm, and stood off to one side. "Let's take it out in the daylight and see what we've got."

Ensuring his feet were securely under him before he made to remove the vellum from the wall, Randy followed her out of the temple. He was careful to hold the large sheet well away from his body lest he smudge the charcoal on his clothing. The bright sun had him squinting, and a sudden gust forced him to turn his body so the vellum wouldn't become bent or wrinkled in the wind.

"There's a flat surface here," Diana said, hurrying to the block of marble he had stepped over earlier. She helped with spreading out the vellum as she took a seat on an adjacent column top and placed rocks over the four corners to keep the paper flat.

"It's terribly faint," Randy murmured, moving so he stood next to where she sat. "Can you read Old Attic?"

"Well, of course," she replied, obviously offended he would think she couldn't.

"I meant no offense," he quickly responded. "My mother can read Latin, but not Greek," he added.

Diana blinked and leaned away to regard him with surprise. "Cousin Hannah can read Latin?"

Relieved he had found a way to impress Diana, Randy nodded. "Despite looking like a fairy princess, she's always been a bit of a bluestocking. It's very disarming for people who have never met her before. They take one look at her and think she's a brainless twit when in fact she's really a rather clever woman."

Diana aimed a grimace in his direction. "Are you saying she still appears youthful enough to be a princess?"

Randy's gaze darted to the side. "Actually... yes. Maybe more of a fairy queen these days, but she's always had that willowy shape and pale blonde hair—"

"Gray, now, don't you mean?"

He scoffed. "No. She's not got a single gray hair. At least... she didn't when I last saw her. About a nine months ago. Father has some, though." He lifted a finger to indicate the side of his face. "At his temples. But otherwise..." He shrugged. "Except for your red hair—"

"It's not red. It's... reddish blonde," she said on a huff.

"—you look an awful lot like her, but I suppose that's to be expected given how closely you are related."

Diana blinked. "If you dare tell anyone I look like a fairy princess..." She let the sentence trail off as she turned her attention back to the lines on the rubbing, her features indicative of her concentration.

"What?" he prompted, suppressing the urge to laugh at her. "It's not as if you can help it," he added. "Besides, it's certainly nothing to be ashamed of. You must know there are probably a hundred young ladies in the *ton* who wish to look like fairy princesses."

She gave him a quelling glance.

"Apologies. I won't mention it again," Randy said.

Ignoring him to study the rubbing, Diana used the end of the charcoal to trace the characters that made themselves evident in the otherwise dark gray background. The darker edge along each whiter area reinforced their shapes until a word emerged.

Ἑκατόμπεδον.

"Is there a letter missing?" Randy asked.

"Why do you ask?"

He pointed to where the triangular symbol indicating a delta ended and a circle began a few inches away. "Unless," he angled his head sideways. "Oh. I see it now. *Heka*," he murmured.

She moved a finger to the next few letters. "*Tom*."

"*Pedon*," he finished for her. He frowned. "Hekatompedon."

Gasping, she stood and guffawed. "That's what this area was called back then," she said, waving to indicate the Acropolis. "There is mention of it in the old texts," she added, when he didn't immediately agree.

"Or it could be referring to the ancient city of that name. Somewhere near Epirus, wasn't it?" he countered. "Up north, in Chaonia? Eastern coast?"

She shook her head. "Without any other words to provide context, though? It doesn't make any sense."

He nodded. "All right. But wasn't there a temple of that name where the Parthenon is now? Or where that mosque is located?" he asked, pointing to the one remaining reminder of the Ottoman occupation of Greece and the Acropolis. He knew it wouldn't be long before the building was demolished. With the Greeks having gained their independence and the rebuilding of Athens well underway down below, it was only a matter of time before the last vestiges of foreign occupation were removed from the landscape.

"Father plans to look for it," she replied. "Or at least the floor of it. Back then, temples would have been made of wood, so it's unlikely anything other than a floor remains," she explained.

"So... do you suppose this area took its name from that temple? Hekatompedon?"

She grinned. "It's possible, of course," she replied.

"Do you think there are any other carvings in that wall?"

She shook her head. "I've been over and over it," she said with a sigh. "Hansen and Schaubert were obviously careful when they reconstructed it. The blocks fit together as they should, and what carvings I found in the marble match up at the seams," she explained. "The pieces for the roof were obviously missing, though," she said, pointing up to where the thick tarp acted as a temporary roof.

"You didn't find what you were looking for." He didn't make it a question.

She waved a hand over the rubbing. "This is a rather notable find," she said. "Besides, who said I was looking for anything in particular?"

Randy dipped his head. "Your brother mentioned you were in search of someone."

She chuckled softly. "It's a shame Marcus doesn't share our father's curiosity of antiquities," she said softly. "Ever since he returned from university, his interest in the past has waned."

"Replaced by his interest in the present?" Randy guessed. "Politics?"

She rolled her eyes. "His interest in the female sex," she stated, lifting her chin in the direction of the Parthenon.

Randy was glad for the harsh sunlight, sure his face suddenly reddened in embarrassment for his friend. "He said he wants to marry Miss Fitzsimmons."

For a moment, Diana seemed stunned by the comment, but she quickly recovered. "Ah, but will she marry *him*?" she asked, one brow arched. Her manner suddenly changed. "That's was terrible of me to say," she murmured. "Please don't tell him."

Randy regarded her with a furrowed brow for a moment. "You think she won't? Consider him for marriage, I mean?"

Diana shook her head. "I can't speak on behalf of Miss Jane. I hardly know her," she said. "But..." She paused.

"What?"

"Yesterday, when we were at the hotel, she removed her gloves, and I noticed she wore a ring. On her left hand," she said. "I'm quite sure it was a ruby, and the last time I was in England, I remember learning rubies were quite valuable."

"They are," he affirmed. "Are you saying you think she is already betrothed?"

For a moment, Diana seemed reluctant to respond. "I would assume so. But... I thought perhaps you knew."

"Although I know her brother from school, I hadn't met her before today," he replied.

"Mr. Fitzsimmons didn't say anything about her being betrothed?" she pressed.

Randy shook his head. "Not that I recall." He furrowed his brows. "What are you thinking?"

Diana lifted a shoulder and shook her head. "She is a very beautiful girl. Perhaps she accepted an offer of marriage as means to keep unwanted suitors at bay."

"Possibly," he agreed.

Diana arched a reddish brow. "Given my brother's interest in her, I believe I need to learn more about her," she murmured. "Perhaps as early as this evening. Marcus has invited her and Mr. Fitzsimmons for dinner tonight." She paused, her gaze directed towards the Parthenon. "If she's not betrothed, I expect she has a number of potential suitors back in England waiting for her return." She regarded Randy for a moment. "And she is probably in possession of a dowry of some value."

"Possibly," he agreed.

"If my brother intends to wed her, he'll have to court her while she's here on holiday and then see to gaining Lord Reardon's permission to marry her. Which means either a trip to England or a lengthy wait for correspondence to travel back and forth," she remarked.

"Marcus has a fortnight to win her over," Randy stated. "She and Antonio leave for Spain after that."

Diana heaved a sigh. "In the meantime, Marcus will be impossible to live with," she claimed.

Amused at how she managed to mention all the impediments to her brother's potential future with Miss Jane, Randy was curious how she might react to queries about the young lady's brother. "And Antonio? Has the heir to the Reardon viscountcy chosen his future viscountess?" he asked, half-expecting Diana might be under consideration for the role.

She shook her head. "I have absolutely no idea. I only met him yesterday." She waved her hands to indicate her attire. "I rather doubt I would make a very good impression on him, not that it really matters."

"It would be a shame if he didn't consider you."

Diana gave a start. "Apparently my brother didn't tell you of my plans," she said.

"Plans?" he prompted.

"I'm going to be a spinster."

Randy managed to hide a wince and merely nodded. "He might have mentioned it," he murmured. Noting how she suddenly began rolling up the vellum, apparently eager to return to her search, he glanced in the direction of the Erechtheion. "I should find my brother and cousin before they get your younger brother into any trouble," he said, straightening.

"Or the other way around," Diana replied with a grimace. "I expect we'll see one another about town," she said crisply.

Reaching down to take her hand to his lips, Randy ignored her attempt to pull it away, sure he felt a frisson beneath his lips as they made contact with her bare skin. "I'll make sure of it," he said, deciding not to mention he, too, had been invited to dinner by her brother.

He bowed and took off in the direction of the Erechtheion, sure she watched him as he negotiated the field of rubble. He was determined not to trip—or to look back.

CHAPTER 8
OUT AND ABOUT

eanwhile, in the city of Athens

Barbara Higgins Slater, Countess Bellingham and the future Marchioness of Devonville, gripped her husband's arm as they made their way along a street at the base of the Acropolis. In between centuries-old structures were new buildings, many still under construction, and laborers had suddenly ceased in their work and were heading in various directions.

"I was hoping to use this arm later today," Will Slater said, arching a teasing brow in her direction.

Gasping softly, Barbara released her stranglehold, straightening her gloved hand so it merely rested on his arm. "I'm so sorry. I don't know why I'm so nervous," she said.

"New city, strange customs, different language," he replied. "But you needn't be fearful," he added carefully.

"How can you be so sure?" she asked, obviously not convinced.

He lifted a shoulder as they strolled. "They love Brits here," he replied. "We helped them in their war for independence. If Lord Byron hadn't died from a fever, he might very well be their king right now," he added, although he was grinning as if he was teasing.

"I did wonder why I keep seeing his name," she said. "It's the one thing I can read."

"He used to live here. Or rather in the area they call Psyrri," Will explained. "When he was on his Grand Tour, he traveled with a friend and wrote several poems. Always claimed he was a poet because of his time here in Greece."

"But he was in London when I had my come-out," Barbara said, her gaze darting about as the streets seemed to empty of everyone but them.

"Did you meet him?" he asked, worry sounding in his voice.

Barbara inhaled slightly. "I was introduced to him at a ball, but we didn't dance or... or converse," she said.

"Well, that's a relief," Will said, although the dimple at the base of his cheek appeared to show he was more amused than concerned. "He had a reputation as a bit of a lady's man."

"I heard he was quite ardent with all his... *loves*," Barbara said, sure her face was red, and not just from the warm day. She reoriented her parasol to better shade her face when they turned onto a wider street.

"None more important than his love for Greece," Will replied. "Which is why he came back to help in the war. He died before Greece gained its independence, though."

He led them to stand before a cylindrical monument set atop a huge square marble base. "This is the Choragic Monument of Lysicrates," he stated, waving an arm in an exaggerated arc.

"What does 'choragic' mean?" Barbara asked as she studied the structure. Corinthian columns were embedded into a large cylinder at even intervals, and atop the structure was a torch with an ornately carved flame.

"*Choregos* means sponsor," Will replied. "Lysicrates was a rather wealthy man, and back then—"

"When?"

"Uh..." Will paused to think a moment. "Three-thirty-five BC, I think. They used to honor the god Dionysus by staging dramatic games—plays and such," he explained. "Which is why the frieze you see along the top depicts scenes from the life of Dionysus."

"What did a sponsor have to do to win such a prize?" Barbara asked, obviously intrigued as she studied the detailed reliefs.

"They were much like the producer of a play is today. They would pay for the costumes, the masks, rehearsals—generally any costs associated with putting on the performance," he explained. "This particular monument was to commemorate the first prize for one of the performances. The bronze tripod you see at the top was the prize." He glanced around. "There used to be several more which lined the road leading to the Theatre of Dionysus, but who knows where they've gone. This one survives only because a Capuchin monk bought it. Kept it from being taken by Lord Elgin when he was removing marbles from the Parthenon."

Barbara gave a start. "I saw those marble statues. Not long before I left London," she said quietly. "The lines of people waiting to see them at the British Museum were so long."

Will urged her to turn around as he extended an arm to point in the opposite direction of the monument.

Barbara inhaled sharply. "What is *that*?" she asked, her eyes round with fascination.

"*That* is Hadrian's Gate," Will stated.

"Hadrian? Wasn't he a Roman emperor?"

"He was. A builder, too. Left behind monuments all over the Roman world," he replied. "Finished some that had only been started, like what you see beyond the triumphal arch," he said, waiting for her gaze to go to a collection of huge columns in the distance.

"Was that a temple?" she asked, quickening her steps.

"The Temple of Olympian Zeus," Will said, grinning as he hurried to match her speed. "The road we're on now is actually a rather ancient one. It starts from the center of Athens and heads east to where an entire complex of temples were located. Most are merely ruins now, of course."

"Why do you say 'of course'?" she asked as they paused to allow a dray cart pulled by a donkey to pass. They crossed the street to the stand in front of the arch.

"Earthquakes and wars..." Will said before he shrugged. "Same as on Sicily," he added, his face aimed up to take in the huge arch.

They had traveled to Athens directly from the Mediterranean's largest island where they had spent nearly eight months touring ancient Greek towns and temples. They had also left behind their oldest son, Donald, his new wife, Nicoletta, Marchesa Montblanc, and their grandson, Antony, the current Marchese Montblanc. Another babe was due in the next month, which is why the newlyweds had remained at the Montblanc estate in Catania rather than join them for the next leg of their Grand Tour.

Barbara stared in awe at the ancient structure of the arch. "Is it made of marble?"

Will chuckled softly. "*Everything* is made of marble in this town," he replied.

"What do those words say?" she asked, pointing to two opposing inscriptions in the architrave. "Can you read them?"

Will gave her a quelling glance. "Testing me, aren't you?" he teased before he angled his head to one side. "This is Athens, the ancient city of Theseus," he stated before turning to regard the other, which faced the newer area of the city. "And this one reads 'This is the city of Hadrian and not of Theseus'." When he noticed her look of confusion, he added, "You have to remember, Athens used to be much larger than it is now. Thousands more people," he explained. "The war has left it in a sorry state, but it's coming along," he said. The evidence of rebuilding was everywhere, from homes and shops to a palace for the king, Otto.

"Where did all the workers go?" she asked. Even the traffic on the street had died down to almost nothing.

"Home. It's too hot to work in the middle of the day. They will return later, though," he explained, opening the canteen he had strung over his shoulder before they left their lodgings. He offered her a drink, and she took a few sips before he drank several swallows. The cook had assured him she had boiled the water before pouring it into the canteen, and although it had been hours since she had done so, the water was still warm.

"Are we going to the Zeus temple next?" she asked, her brows furrowing at seeing there were only a few columns still standing off in the distance.

"Why don't we go someplace a bit cooler?" he suggested, using his handkerchief to dab perspiration from his forehead. He wished he had worn a lighter colored top hat rather than the black beaver he sported.

"What did you have in mind?" she asked.

He pointed down the road to where a large green area was

located. "Queen Amalia's garden," he said. "Pietro said it's nearly finished."

"A garden?" she repeated, her gaze going to where he pointed.

"And it's open to the public," he said with a grin, offering her his arm.

"Aren't you afraid I'll get ideas about how to change our garden?" she asked, arching a brow.

He chuckled softly as they entered the green space where palm trees, evergreens, and shrubbery gave way to a riot of colorful flowers. "I rather doubt half of what we're about to see would even grow in England," he replied. "So do keep that in mind."

She grinned as she took a deep breath and sighed. "I think I shall enjoy our stay in Athens," she murmured.

Will nodded. "Let's hope the boys do, too."

CHAPTER 9
A YOUNG WOMAN CONSIDERS FAMILIAL RELATIONSHIPS

eanwhile, on the Acropolis

Safely tucked away near the entrance of the Temple of Athena Nike, Diana watched the departing backside of her second cousin as he carefully negotiated his way to where his brother, her brother, and their cousin David had earlier been attempting to imitate the poses of the caryatids mounted on the porch of the Erechtheion. The younger men were no longer there, though, apparently having spent some time with her brother and the Fitzsimmonses at the Parthenon.

Now the trio was making their way to the Propylaea, and it looked as if Randy would be joining them.

When she returned her attention to the porch of the Erechtheion, she winced, especially at seeing the space where one was clearly missing. Lord Elgin had arranged to have it removed and shipped to London after his visit to the Acropolis decades earlier, declaring it and the marbles from one of the pediments, as well as several metopes and triglyphs, needed to be protected.

She wasn't sure why it bothered her that he had done so. The statues, temples, and everything else on the flat rock had already suffered the ravages of wars and earthquakes, neglect and weather. Thieves had long ago removed anything of value from inside the remaining temples.

As for what she had been looking for, she would simply move her search to one of the other temples. Although there wasn't much of the cella left in the Parthenon—a cache of munitions stored there by the Ottomans had exploded during a bombardment by the Venetians in 1687, destroying the roof, most of the walls, and twenty-eight columns—there were still a few walls left standing at the Erechtheion.

Stuffing the rolled vellum into a tubular leather carrying case, Diana went about gathering her other belongings into a worn leather satchel. Slipping the strap over her head until it rested on the opposite shoulder, she adjusted the bag on her hip as she made her way out of the temple.

If her brother intended to have the Fitzsimmonses as guests for dinner that evening, she would need to inform the cook at Vouros Mansion as soon as possible.

She paused to wave in the direction of the Parthenon, not expecting her older brother to be on the lookout for her. She was pleasantly surprised when she saw him wave in reply, but when he made no move to leave the Fitzsimmonses to join her, she negotiated her way over the rubble-strewn ground and through the columns of the Propylaea. Once down the marble steps, she followed the ancient path that continued down the side of the Acropolis until she was finally on one of Athen's main roads.

Knowing there wouldn't be time for the cook to make additional bread for that night's meal, she stepped into a bakery. Pausing to inhale the familiar scents of yeast and baked breads—no matter the country, breads seemed to smell the same—she nodded to the proprietress and pointed to the two loaves left on the marble counter.

The old woman frowned, obviously not pleased at seeing Diana's mode of dress. The local girls wore layered gowns over what appeared to be trousers, though. Perhaps she would have to include a frock in her satchel and pull it on before leaving the Acropolis the next day.

Holding up two fingers, the baker spoke in Greek. Relieved she could understand the price, Diana pulled the lepta coins from a pocket in her breeches, thanked her, and helped herself to the bread. Holding the loaves in the crook of her arm, she left the small shop and resumed her trek home along the main road.

Lined with houses in various states of repair—some were old while others were under construction—the street teamed with laborers and donkeys, vendors and carts, and children chasing other children. She managed to avoid a dray cart pulled by a runaway donkey, but she wasn't able to sidestep a man who was walking backwards as he was shouting at someone.

She froze in place, determined not to give up ground despite the force with which the man hit her.

"Oh, pardon me," he said, whirling around and stepping back, his arms akimbo. "Miss Henley."

Diana's eyes rounded. "You again," she said with a huff.

Randy Forster stared down at her, his brows furrowing at hearing the rebuke in her voice. "Me again, yes," he replied. "I was…" He paused and pointed off in the direction in which two young men were headed.

"Admonishing your brother and…" Her gaze darted to

where he had been looking, but the boys were no longer visible.

"Cousin David," he finished for her. "They, uh, grew hungry and are in search of sustenance." He pointed to the bread she held. "As did you apparently."

Annoyed by the implication she would be eating two loaves of bread by herself, Diana gave him a quelling glance. "These are for tonight's dinner," she stated. "*I* had enough sense to bring a luncheon with me when I left the house this morning."

From how he dipped his head, it was apparent Randy knew he had made a fool of himself. "Apologies. I of course did not think you capable of eating *all* of that by yourself," he said lamely.

"Then you'd be surprised," she said, continuing her walk toward Vakchou Street.

Randy fell into step next to her, his hands shoved into the pockets of his pantaloons so that the front skirts of his top coat were pushed aside. Had they been in London, his manner would have been considered far too casual for the beau monde. Here in Athens, he appeared to be the best dressed man on the street.

"Are you saying you eat a lot?" he asked, a smirk betraying his tease.

Realizing he wasn't about to leave her side, Diana sighed. "When I am hungry, yes," she replied. "I expect you do as well." Her gaze darted to the side, and she quickly regarded his form from his broad shoulders to his dusty boots. For a moment, she wondered if the norm for an aristocrat had changed since she was last in London. Other than her own brothers, she had never seen a member of the *ton* sporting a physique that made him appear as if he did physical labor. There were those who participated in bare knuckle boxing and fencing, but when dressed in the typical uniform of a gentleman—shirt, cravat, waistcoat, pantaloons, and top coat—it wasn't evident.

Apparently he noticed her perusal, for he suddenly pulled his hands from his pockets and allowed his arms to drop to his sides. "Depends on what I'm hungry for," he said, arching a teasing brow.

Diana merely rolled her eyes. When she realized the other possible meaning of his comment a moment later, heat suffused her face. "Your words suggest you are a rake, Lord Forster," she said indignantly. "Are you a libertine as well?"

Not expecting the question, Randy stopped in his tracks. "No," he claimed, obviously offended. "I am not." He dipped his head, his face displaying what looked like regret. "All this talk of food is making me a bit peckish, however.'"

For a moment, Diana thought to mention he could simply buy a *koulouri* from one of the costermongers who usually manned carts parked along the side of the main road. The rings of bread covered in sesame seeds were a popular food for the morning. A quick glance around had her realizing the carts had disappeared. Either the increased heat of early afternoon had sent most vendors indoors, or they had sold out of their stock earlier in the day.

Tearing an end off one of the loaves of bread, Diana offered it to him. "Will this do?"

Randy hesitated before accepting the bread. "Are you sure?"

"Of course," she replied, lifting one shoulder in a shrug. The movement dislodged the leather strap of the tubular container holding the rolled up rubbing, and it threatened to slide down her arm.

Randy was quick to capture the strap before it would have ended up in the crook of her elbow, possibly upsetting her hold on the loaves of bread. "I would be happy to carry this for you. And your bag," he offered. Her look of uncertainty had him adding, "I shouldn't wish you to think any worse of me than you already do."

Diana gave a start, surprised he would say such a thing. "I don't think that," she claimed, although she knew her manner was at odds with her words. "I'm merely in a hurry is all."

"I suppose with your brother intending to host guests this evening, the responsibility of hostessing falls on you," Randy said. "I do hope your cook is accommodating."

"As do I," she replied, surprised he understood the situation.

Readjusting her hold on the bread, Diana allowed him to remove the strap from her arm. She watched as he easily hefted it onto his shoulder while he gripped the torn bread in the other hand.

"Give me the satchel, too," he said, moving to her other side to pull the bag's handle from her other shoulder to lift it over her head. Not expecting it to be so heavy, he nearly dropped it before hefting it onto his free shoulder. "Whatever do have in here?" he asked in awe. "Rocks?"

Left with only the two loaves of bread, Diana grinned at his surprise. "Tools," she said. When she noted his arched brow, she added, "Brushes, mostly. A small shovel, a ledger, a couple of pens. A sketchbook and an ink bottle."

"No rocks? No small piece of statuary pilfered from a temple?" he teased.

She gave him a quelling glance as they resumed walking. "I pilfered nothing, I assure you."

He ate some of the bread and swallowed before asking, "Do you do this every day? Go up to the Acropolis, I mean."

She shook her head. "Not every day. My brothers and I have only been in Athens a fortnight. It took a few days to do enough unpacking to set up the household," she explained. "I still have more to do before it's completely finished."

"So... the temple I found you in... that's your first... archaeological project here in Greece?"

She made an odd sound in her throat. "My second, actually. I spent a week in the Odeon of Herodes Atticus."

When he turned to look back in the direction of the ancient Roman theatre—they had both passed it on their way from the Acropolis—Diana once again studied her companion's body. Given their familial relationship, she expected Randy would bear more of a resemblance to her brothers in his facial features. At seeing him up close, she would never have guessed he was a cousin. All three young men were of similar heights and builds, although Michael was thinner. More lanky. He hadn't yet caught up to his older brother's athletic body but no doubt would given he would be working with the archaeologists on the Acropolis.

"Doing what?" he asked.

She blinked. "Apologies," she replied, not understanding his query.

"What were you doing in the theatre?"

"Oh. Uh. Searching for inscriptions in the marble," she stammered. She waved in the direction of an upcoming cross street. "This is where we must part, Lord Forster."

Randy furrowed his brows as he took in the neighborhood of multi-story mansions, several similar in appearance to the one his family was letting for their time in Athens. "I'll see you to your door," he said. "And please, do call me Randy. We are cousins, after all," he added.

"If you insist," Diana replied before turning at the next corner. She continued down the quiet street, the small trees and fledgling foliage indicative of newer construction. She wasn't surprised Randy stayed at her side, but she wasn't sure she wanted him to know exactly where she lived. If he didn't have his own agenda for what he intended to do whilst in Athens, she feared she might find him on her doorstep the next day, determined to join her again on the Acropolis. "How long will you and your family be in town?" she asked.

"A few months, I expect," he replied. When she made her way along the path of pavers to the front door of a mansion, he followed behind her.

Diana suddenly turned around, not at all surprised to discover his gaze had been directed downward. "Are you watching my...?" She clamped her mouth shut as her face reddened with embarrassment.

"Watching where I'm going?" he finished for her, innocence tingeing his voice. "Of course. These pavers are a bit uneven. Not as bad as the marble up on the Acropolis, though."

She was saved from having to say anything else when the butler opened the door.

Randy handed the straps of her satchel and the tube container to the servant before he tipped his top hat. "Thank you for an interesting day, Miss Diana," he said.

"You're welcome... Cousin Randy," she replied. "I expect we'll encounter one another again soon."

"Oh, we will," he replied. "Your brother invited me to dinner tonight."

Before Diana could react, he bowed, turned, and took off down the pavers to the street.

Huffing, she entered Vouros Mansion and hurried to find the cook. Apparently there would be six for dinner that night.

CHAPTER 10
QUESTIONING A BETROTHAL

*M*eanwhile, at Hotel Aiolos

"Thank you for the tour," Jane said as she curtsied to Marcus. She had already folded her parasol and retrieved the picnic basket from him, rather thankful he had offered to carry it down from the Acropolis.

Antonio had been oblivious to her struggle at managing her gown on the marble steps and the steep decline from the Acropolis. Marcus had been such a gentleman to offer his arm and the occasional warning should the ground be uneven or strewn with something over which she might trip.

"I look forward to hosting you for dinner this evening," Marcus said. "The hotel assured me they will have a carriage to take you to Vouros Mansion at six of the clock." He gave the picnic basket to the hotel clerk.

"So kind of you to have arranged it," she said, watching him as he took her gloved hand to his lips. She inhaled softly when he didn't merely brush his lips over the fabric but actually bestowed a kiss on the back of her knuckles. "Until then," she said.

"Until then," he replied, his gaze lingering on her perhaps a moment too long before he took his leave of the hotel lobby.

She and Antonio watched until Marcus was out of sight before making their way to their second-story rooms. After the day spent out in the sun, Jane was relieved to be in the cool confines of the hotel.

"I couldn't help but notice Marcus' regard for you," Antonio said before he opened her door. He glanced in to ensure no one was in the room before stepping aside to allow her entry.

Jane swept into the room and immediately fanned her face with a gloved hand. "I find that difficult to believe," she countered. "You practically ignored me all day long," she accused.

Antonio displayed a grimace. "When one has a sister as pretty as you, I hardly need to add my eyes to the gazing party," he murmured on a huff.

Gasping softly, Jane asked, "What does that mean?"

Antonio waved to a chair. She nodded and moved to sit on the edge of the bed while he took the chair, sprawling so his long legs were stretched out before him. "Your beauty attracts a great deal of attention—"

"I cannot help that," she said.

"—no matter where we go," he continued. "But Marcus..." He crossed his arms and audibly sighed.

"What about Marcus?" she asked softly. Usually she didn't care what men thought of her, but for some reason, she wished to learn what Antonio knew.

How he knew it. She had been with Antonio the entire day. He and Marcus hadn't spent a moment together in private. She was sure she had heard everything the two had said to one another.

Antonio rested his head on the back of the chair and allowed a sigh. "He is… smitten with you."

Jane inhaled softly. "Did he tell you that?"

"He wrote of it, yes."

Blinking at hearing his words, Jane fell back onto the bed, her legs left dangling over the edge. Despite having shaken out her skirts before entering the hotel, she had a thought the hem would leave dust on the counterpane. At that moment, she didn't care.

Marcus had written to her brother. About her.

"When?" she asked, suddenly sitting up again.

Her brother furrowed his dark brows. "Last year. Shortly after he met you at one of the balls we attended."

Why couldn't her brother be more forthcoming with his information? And why was she just now learning of the young man's regard for her? "What *exactly* did he write?"

Antonio leaned forward, his elbows resting on his knees. "He was smitten with you. Asked why I had never mentioned having such a gorgeous creature for a sister."

"Creature?" she repeated, obviously not impressed by the term as it applied to a young woman.

Once again, Antonio chuckled. "Well, you are," he accused. "When I mentioned you were betrothed to Penton, I couldn't help but notice the look on his face."

"Oh?" she prompted.

"The Green Monster appeared, I'm sure of it," he claimed.

"He was jealous?" she asked in awe.

"Angry, too, I think, especially when Penton joined us and then kissed you on the cheek." He rubbed a hand over his face and scoffed at seeing the evidence of his perspiration mixed with dirt. He took a handkerchief from his waistcoat pocket and wiped his face. "Did you know he was in Athens?"

Jane shook her head. "I only knew he had left England on his Grand Tour last year. He's not one to keep up with his correspondence," she replied, "but then, I haven't exactly written to him very often, either."

"But... you *are* betrothed to him." He didn't make it a question.

"Of course," she replied. "In... in a manner of speaking."

It was Antonio's turn to straighten, and he stared at his sister with a look of confusion. "What does that mean?"

Jane allowed a wince. "Only that, well, I accepted his offer of marriage as a sort of... well, a betrothal of convenience, I suppose one could say," she stammered.

Antonio blinked. "Penton gave you a *ruby*," he said, emphasizing the gemstone since it was the most valuable of all the stones found in jewelry these days.

Glancing down at her left hand, Jane wiggled her fingers and grinned. "He did," she agreed. She quickly sobered when she saw her brother's expression.

"You either are or you are not betrothed," he stated.

She lifted her chin in defiance. "I am. Although I have David's blessing to accept another offer should I decide I'm not willing to wait five or more years for him." She watched as Antonio's expression slowly changed, as if he was finally realizing what she had done.

"You accepted a ring from an heir to a marquessate *knowing* you would beg off?"

"Of course not!" she nearly shouted. "I had every intention of marrying David when I accepted his offer," she argued. "He was ever so wonderful to have even suggested a betrothal when he did."

"Go on," Antonio urged.

Jane swallowed. "He knew I was in distress. He could tell

how uncomfortable I was with all the attention. All those suitors. The bouquets of flowers that kept showing up every day—"

"I thought they made our townhouse smell rather nice," her brother remarked.

She gave him a quelling glance. "His solution—that I accept his offer as a means to ward off any other suitors—has worked rather well, don't you think?"

Antonio shook his head, although he finally said, "I guess it has. But you said only moments ago you *had* every intention of marrying him."

"Because I did," she assured him.

"*Did*. Not *will?*" he countered.

Allowing a long sigh, Jane finally nodded. "I... thought I could wait for him," she murmured. "Five-and-twenty wouldn't be too late to begin having children," she reasoned, although she couldn't help the wince that crossed her face.

"But?" he prompted.

"I want to have children now," she admitted. "I want to live in the capital—"

"Not Bath?" he asked, obviously surprised at hearing her mentioning London.

"Oh, Bath is a fine town, and although it offers much in the way of entertainments and comfortable living, I found I rather liked our time in London during my come-out. All the shops. The theatres. All those *soirées* and *musicales* we attended. I adored them."

"I thought you hated those," he claimed.

"I hated the attention from all the men," she countered. "They way they looked at me? It was as if I was a delicious morsel they wished to eat."

A strangled growl sounded from Anthony, and she noticed his face had suddenly reddened.

"What?"

He closed his eyes and swallowed. "I'm not about to explain it to you now, but you would be wise not to use that particular metaphor again."

Jane dipped her head, deciding it better she not ask why. "My betrothal with David has succeeded in ensuring I'm no longer pursued by unwanted suitors," she stated.

Antonio once again scoffed softly. "Indeed, but now that you know you want children—sooner rather than later—perhaps you and David need to reconsider your arrangement," he suggested.

"Perhaps," she agreed. "But whatever happens, please, don't tell anyone," she pleaded. "You're the only one besides David who knows about our agreement, and I shouldn't want word to spread that I am open to having my mind changed on the matter."

From his initial expression, Jane worried her brother might not agree, but he finally capitulated. "All right," he said. "But if a man decides to challenge Penton for your hand, I'm not going to interfere."

Jane widened her eyes as she nearly grinned. "You mean a duel?" she asked, managing to sound less excited than she felt at the prospect. "I rather doubt *that's* going to happen." She glanced toward the window. "What time is it?"

Antonio glanced at this pocket watch. "Nearly four o'clock," he replied.

"I best change for dinner. Will you order a bath for me?"

He nodded. "Yes, Sister," he replied. "I'll come for you in a couple of hours."

"Where are you going?" she asked in alarm.

"To take a nap," he said, displaying a grin.

For a moment, Jane wished she could do the same. But time soaking in a tub would be the next best thing.

CHAPTER 11
POST DINNER SHOWER

*L*ater *that evening, Vouros Mansion, Vakchou Street, Plaka*

The plates from the dessert course had been cleared away and small glasses of liquor delivered when Diana stood from her seat at the opposite end of the table from where her brother was holding court in the dining room of their rented house.

"My apologies, but I really must retire." She turned to Jane and displayed an apologetic expression. "I must leave you, Miss Jane, and you gentlemen to your drinks. Do have a good evening," she said, dipping a curtsy before she took her leave.

Marcus and Michael, Antonio Fitzsimmons, and Randolph Forster all stood and bowed as she did so, Antonio directing a questioning glance in Marcus' direction as the young man's sister departed.

"I'm surprised she even joined us for dinner this evening," Marcus said as he resumed his seat. "She was up rather late last night. On the roof. She was a sport to have arranged dinner and acted as hostess for me this evening. I'm afraid I didn't give her much notice."

"Did you say she was on the roof?" Randy repeated.

"Indeed. She was watching the shooting stars," Marcus explained. "I caught several arcing through the night sky last evening, and I wasn't even up there for five minutes."

"Are you referring to a meteor shower?" Antonio asked, his interest in the topic evident from how he leaned forward in his seat and glanced at their host.

"Indeed. Nothing like the one that happened seven years ago, though," Marcus said, referring to the Leonid meteor storm of 1833.

Attempting to suppress a yawn, Jane said, "Well, I wasn't up late last night, but I fear I have had too much sun on this day. I really must take my leave, or I may fall asleep here at the table," she claimed. "Brother, I'll send the coach back for you," she added as she stood from the table. A sound of protest came from Marcus, but she directed a grin in Antonio's direction. "I'm sure you and your friends have other matters you wish to discuss without a woman being present."

The men once again stood, Michael, Antonio, and Randy bowing as Marcus escorted Jane from the dining room to the front door.

"Other matters?" Randy said in a quiet voice, once the two were out of earshot.

Antonio shrugged. "If it's what I think it is, I'll make it clear he needs to discuss it with Father when he is next in England," he murmured, arching a brow.

"So... your father isn't coming to Athens?"

The heir to the Reardon viscountcy shook his head. "He and my mother boarded a ship out of Piraeus a few days ago. We've already been here in Greece for a few months, you see."

"Where?" Michael asked.

Antonio chuckled softly. "We started in the north. Epirus, Meteora, Thessaloniki..." He shrugged. "My parents have been to Athens before, and they weren't interested in returning. Father had to be back in England—something to do with the viscountcy—and so I agreed to escort Jane here before we leave for Spain."

Randy furrowed a brow, surprised the young man would be left to provide protection for his sister. "When are you and Miss Jane leaving?"

"We're here for another fortnight and then we'll board a ship to Valencia. We have an aunt who lives near there," he explained before retaking his seat at the table. "So we'll be her guest for a time before returning to England."

Marcus entered the dining room. "Well, it seems we are left to enjoy our drinks, gentlemen," he said with an expression that suggested he was disappointed.

About to return to his seat, Randy hesitated. "I, uh, I cannot help but think this is a discussion I shouldn't be a part of."

"I find I am in agreement with Forster. If you'll excuse me, I'm going to retire to my bedchamber," Michael said.

Antonio and Marcus exchanged quick glances. "It's... it's not private," their host assured them.

"Still... I'm rather curious about shooting stars," Randy said.

"Oh, well, if you'd like, you're welcome to go up on the roof," Marcus offered. "Just keep climbing the stairs and go out the last door. Although it's rather dark out there, there's no need to worry that you'll fall off the roof. It's flat, and there's a short wall all around it. Some chairs if you'd like to sit whilst you watch."

Randy nodded. "Sounds cozy. Gentlemen, I'm off to the roof."

Fairly sure his friends were discussing the future marital status of Miss Jane Fitzsimmons, Randy was glad to have an excuse to leave the dining room. Despite the open windows, the room had grown warm due to the number of lit candles in the chandelier and on the sideboard. Although they made the already elegant dining room appear more golden than the papered and mirrored walls did of their own accord, the odor of burning wax combined with the heat made the room oppressive.

Stepping out into the cooler evening air on the roof, Randy paused and inhaled deeply. He was glad for the short wall when he nearly collided with it, the night so dark he couldn't make out anything at first. Once his eyesight adjusted to the dark, he made his way to a set of small metal chairs and a table.

Before he even sat down, he realized he wasn't alone.

Diana was lying on her back on a thin pallet spread out on the roof, her hands resting on her midsection as she stared straight up at the night sky. Although the pallet seemed large enough for two, she was positioned in the middle of it.

"I wondered if I might find you up here," Randy said in a quiet voice.

"And yet you came anyway," she countered, not taking her eyes from the band of stars making up the Milky Way.

He resisted the urge to put voice to a sound of complaint. "This is an excellent location from which to view the night sky," he remarked instead, his head dropping back to admire the stars. "No clouds and so dark." The wall around the roof prevented the few lights from nearby houses from interfering with the view.

"No moon," she murmured, inhaling suddenly as a streak of light arced across the inky blackness.

"I saw that," Randy said with excitement, although the tail of the shooting star winked out almost as quickly as he caught sight of it. He moved closer to the pallet, finally glancing down on Diana.

"You're blocking my view," she complained, finally turning her attention to him.

Momentarily cowed—he had hoped the time they had spent together earlier that afternoon might have warmed her to him—Randy decided a bit of cheekiness might be necessary. "Might you move over a bit? Make some room for me?" he countered, undoing the two buttons of his top coat. He removed it and draped it over the edge of the nearby chair before lowering himself so he was sitting on the edge of the pallet.

She audibly scoffed and seemed about to put voice to a protest before she sighed and wriggled to her left, her hands pulling her bell skirt closer to her legs as she did so.

"Much appreciated," he whispered at the same moment she gasped. His gaze followed hers to discover a meteor disappearing in the east. "Damnation," he muttered, finally lying back onto the pallet. Stretching out with his hands clasped behind his head, he finally relaxed. He had left a small space between their bodies but made sure his bent elbow was above her head.

She glanced over at him before rolling her eyes. "Make yourself at home," she whispered, although her gaze was once again directed on the sky.

"I am, thank you. We could do with a thicker mattress, though," he commented. From the conversation during dinner, he had the impression the Henleys were used to rougher accommodations. He doubted he could sleep the night on such a thin pad.

"We?" she repeated at the same moment another meteor streaked overhead.

"Well, if you intended to sleep up here tonight," he reasoned. He turned his head to the left. From his vantage, he could make out her profile, see the edges of the tight curls that framed her face and a nose he thought matched the shape of his younger sister's.

"I suppose my brother told you I slept up here last night."

Randy gave a start. "He didn't mention it. Did you?"

"It was far too warm in my bedchamber to sleep there," she murmured.

An odd sensation occurred behind the fly of his pantaloons, and Randy realized that by removing his top coat, he no longer had the means to hide an erection should his cock decide to do more than twitch. "Was that safe?" he asked in alarm, at the same moment another light streaked across the sky.

"I rather doubt a shooting star was going to hit me," she replied, a hint of annoyance sounding in her voice.

"That's not what I meant," he replied. When he glanced down at her, he discovered she was staring at him. "And you know it," he added with a grin.

She tittered. "This house is well away from the others in this neighborhood, and it stands far taller. I can't imagine how someone could get up on the roof without coming up by way of the stairs." When he gave a start, she turned her head to follow the trail of another shooting star.

"Does this happen every night?" he asked in wonder.

"No. Only for a night or two a few times a year," she replied quietly, lifting a hand to her mouth when a yawn threatened. "There were far more last night. I take it you've not seen them where you're from?"

He shook his head. "A few over the years, I suppose, but I'm usually sound asleep when it's this dark. And then there are the clouds."

They lay in companionable silence for several minutes as the meteors streaked overhead. Turning onto his side and holding his head up with a bent arm, Randy waited until she turned her head to regard him with an arched brow before he asked, "How does spinsterhood work, exactly?"

She scoffed, her attention once again going to the sky. "You mean you've never met one?"

He considered the query. "No. Every woman I've ever known is either too young to marry, is married, or is widowed," he replied. "I know there used to be spinsters," he quickly added. "I've read about women who were, but that was... centuries ago."

Diana angled her head in his direction before she said, "A woman wishing to be a spinster merely remains unmarried. Lives her life wherever she pleases and does whatever she wants."

"Within reason, I should think," Randy murmured.

"I suppose. I wouldn't do anything illegal," she claimed. "My father says he'll give me my dowry when I'm one-and-twenty. Which is next year."

"Would you... live with someone?" Despite the dark, Randy could see when she furrowed her brows. "For protection?"

"I suppose it depends on if I'm living in England or still here. My preference would be to continue working on archaeological projects, but Father has warned me I may not be welcome unless he is the head of the team." She sighed. "I expect I may end up back in England for a time. If so, I'll have a lady's maid, of course," she said. "A staff for the house or whatever sort of abode I live in." She turned her head to face him again. "I shan't be alone if that's what you're asking."

"But... what about...?" He swallowed.

"What about *what*?" she asked, her attention now entirely on him.

"Companionship? Someone... someone to escort you to Society events and such," he clarified. "A companion?"

She grinned as she turned her head so she was once again staring at the sky. "Not that I expect many invitations, but should they be forthcoming, I think I can manage to attend events by myself. If I live in town, I will have a small coach, of course. A cabriolet or phaeton, perhaps. Two horses."

Randy sounded a grunt. "What about... at night?" he asked in a whisper.

She turned her head so quickly, he nearly gave a start. "What do you mean?"

Inhaling to answer, he hesitated when his cock seemed to understand what he meant before he did. He had managed to keep it in check for nearly the entire time he lay next to her, but the reminder it was night and dark and they were alone on a roof had it reacting as if it was expecting some attention. "A lover," he croaked. "Will you take a lover?"

"A lover?" she repeated in a hoarse whisper.

"Someone to...to warm your bed. To... to pleasure you," he stammered.

She suddenly lifted her torso from the pallet, her elbows supporting her as she stared down at him in shock. "That, sir, is none of your concern," she stated.

Randy swallowed. "What if...?" He broke off the query when he felt the vibrations of footsteps coming up the nearby stairs. He was up and off the pallet and seated in one of the metal chairs in a matter of seconds, casually resting an ankle on the opposite knee as he clasped his hands behind his head and leaned back.

Meanwhile, Diana cursed softly and lay flat on the pallet, her hands once again held at her midsection as if she was a corpse in a coffin.

"I didn't expect you'd be up here this long," Marcus said as he joined Randy at the table. He held a candle stick in one hand while shielding the bit of flame with the other. "Damn, but it's dark," he added, continuing to hold his hand next to the flickering fire to prevent the evening breeze from blowing it out.

"Makes for perfect viewing. These meteors have really put on a show this evening, although they seem to have stopped for a time," Randy remarked.

At that moment, a small streak had Marcus allowing a guffaw. "They're not falling like rain, though, are they?"

"Not like rain," Randy agreed. He straightened and plucked his top coat from the chair back. "I take it Mr. Fitzsimmons has gone home?"

"He has." Regret sounded in Marcus' voice.

"And did you have any luck convincing him you would make the perfect husband for his sister?"

Marcus shook his head, the gesture barely noticeable in the dark. "He said he would put in a good word with his father on my behalf, but any permission to court Miss Jane would have to come from the viscount, who it seems is currently on his way back to England."

"Well, that's to be expected," Randy said, shifting in his chair. He was sure Diana was listening to every word they said. "And recommended. As I'm sure you know, Lord Reardon was a military man."

"Captain in the British Army," Marcus stated, straightening so he was no longer staring at the sky. "Married a Spanish aristocrat's daughter before he went off and got wounded in the war."

"Which is why Antonio is so damned handsome," Randy groused. "All that wavy black hair."

"Indeed." Marcus chuckled. "And why his sister is so gorgeous. Accomplished, too, which is why I want her to be my viscountess when I inherit."

Wanting desperately to see Diana's reaction to her brother's comment, Randy had to resist the urge to turn his head in her direction. "How is it you've already decided you wish to marry Jane when you only just met her... what? Yesterday?"

"I met her when I was in London for part of the Season last year," Marcus explained. "After I finished university." He paused a moment, as if in thought. "I don't think she recognized me today, though. She had the oddest expression on her face at first."

"Oh?"

Marcus shook his head. "She was most gracious, though. Seemed happy for my company. I think she may be tired of spending so much time with her brother is all."

"I wasn't aware," Randy murmured. "Still, you needn't be concerned she'll accept an offer of marriage before you have a chance to return to England."

Marcus grunted his displeasure.

"You can make her an offer without her father's permission. Contingent on his agreement, of course," Randy suggested. He stilled when he saw an expression of guilt on his friend's face. "Or have you already?"

"I actually brought up the topic with her today. When Antonio went off to take a piss after our picnic." He paused. "She has accepted an offer of marriage." A hint of anger tinged his voice, which had Randy furrowing a brow.

"So... what's the problem?"

Marcus inhaled deeply and let the breath out in a *whoosh*. "The offer she accepted wasn't mine."

Blinking several times, Randy realized what Diana had said earlier was true. The ring on Miss Jane's finger was indeed a betrothal ring. He scoffed, though, at seeing Marcus' expression. "Well, it wasn't from *me*," he said, thinking he was being accused of stealing the young woman from his friend.

"True," Marcus replied, allowing the word to go on for a few beats. "But you know the culprit."

Randy swallowed. "I... I do?"

"Your cousin, Penton."

Fairly sure he knew exactly how a punch in the gut felt, Randy stared at his friend for several seconds before shaking his head. "That's... that's not possible," he whispered. "Well, I mean, it's *possible*, but even if he did indeed propose marriage, I'm quite sure David wasn't *serious*," he said. "Trust me when I tell you, he falls in love with every woman he meets. Besides, he... he was up on the Acropolis at the same time as I was today. Spent most of the time with Michael and Tom at the Erechtheion. Surely he would have remembered proposing to Miss Jane. Would have sought her out and reiterated his devotion to her if he was serious," he reasoned.

"He *did*," Marcus stated, one brow arching. "While you were helping my sister with whatever it was she was doing in that temple."

96

"A rubbing," Randy quickly stated. "On one of the walls." He cleared his throat, attempting to block the thought of her rubbing him. Imagining her hand wrapped around his manhood, her thumb stroking his tip, had him once again shifting in his chair in an attempt to stifle his body's reaction. "How *exactly* did David reiterate his devotion?"

Frowning, Marcus said, "He approached us, introductions were made—although it was obvious he had already met them both—then he bowed and greeted her by not only kissing the back of her hand, but also her cheek."

"Her cheek?"

"Her cheek," Marcus affirmed. "Said she looked especially lovely and called her 'my sweet'. It was most embarrassing. To make matters worse, he invited us to dinner tomorrow night at a *taverna*. Antonio and Jane accepted, of course, so I did as well."

Randy was glad for the dark, for he had trouble hiding the humor he felt at his cousin's expense. He stood, deciding it was past time he take his leave. "I'll speak with David's father. Discover... what he's about and see if we can't free up Miss Jane from her... obligation. If there truly is one."

Marcus stood and clapped a hand on his shoulder. "Much appreciated. He's far too young to marry—"

"As are you," Randy countered, heading for the stairs.

"—and I don't think it would be fair to make Jane wait so long to be wed when *I* would be willing to marry before the end of the year."

Randy stopped and turned to regard his cousin with surprise. "You're going back to England? That soon?"

Shrugging, Marcus said, "I don't plan to stay in Greece the entire year. We have a townhouse in London where I can live."

"You're sure you're ready for marriage, though? You can wait, you know. You needn't start your nursery so soon—"

"Jane Fitzsimmons isn't going to wait four or five years for me," Marcus countered.

Although he was tempted to say that if Miss Jane Fitzsimmons felt the least bit of affection for Marcus, she would wait, Randy asked, "What are the Fitzsimmonses doing tomorrow?" He skipped down the steps, relieved his host hadn't seemed to notice Diana lying prone only a few feet away from where they had been seated.

"They're planning to climb one of the hills—the one with the Prison of Socrates—and I've an invitation to join them."

"Well, that's something," Randy said. He pulled on his great coat before accepting his top hat from the butler near the front door. For a moment, he was sure he caught sight of an etching in its painted wood surface, but the light changed with his movements and the effect was gone.

"This time *I'm* bringing the basket of food and two bottles of wine for our luncheon," Marcus stated.

Randy winced but managed to show amusement as well. "I'll talk to Uncle Will as soon as I'm in residence," he promised, stepping out the front door when the butler had it opened for him. "Discover if David has spoken to him about a betrothal." He shook his host's hand and said, "Oh, and if you could thank your sister for me. For dinner," he added.

"I will," Marcus promised.

A moment later, Randy was down the short walk to the street and about to step into a waiting coach when he glanced back and up to the top of Vouros Mansion. Barely visible in silhouette against the star-studded sky stood Diana leaning on the short wall of the roof.

If she responded to his quick salute, he couldn't see it.

CHAPTER 12
CONTEMPLATING A FUTURE

eanwhile, on the roof of Vouros Mansion
Her hands firmly pressed to the top of the rooftop wall, Diana leaned forward and scanned the horizon and the grounds below. From her vantage, she could make out the silhouettes of the Parthenon's columns atop the Acropolis, and a few squares of golden light marked the windows of nearby houses.

Directly below, a lantern next to the mansion's front door illuminated part of the paved walkway leading to where an ancient town coach waited on the street. The snorts of an impatient horse reached her ears at the same moment light suddenly flooded the walkway.

Kyknos, the butler, had obviously opened the front door, and a moment later, the long shadow of a departing guest appeared on the pavers.

"Oh, and if you could thank your sister for me. For dinner," she heard Randolph Forster say before he hurried to the coach.

The driver had obviously stepped down from the seat and

opened the door, for the heir was about to enter before he paused and looked back.

Looked up.

Directly at her.

He gave her a quick wave before disappearing into the black equipage, and a moment later, the sounds of horse hooves on the stone street faded into the inky blackness.

Diana straightened, stunned at how her body reacted to seeing the heir to the Gisborn earldom again. To the memory of how he had simply settled next to her only the hour before, as if it was the most natural thing in the world to simply lie down next to her on a thin mattress and carry on a conversation in the dark.

So intimate and yet so chaste. He hadn't touched her. He hadn't made a move to take advantage. He had even left a modicum of space betwixt their bodies.

She couldn't decide if she should be glad or feel offended.

What would she have done if he had tried something? If he had tried to take advantage of her prone position?

If he had attempted a kiss, would she have allowed it? Welcomed it, even?

There had been that moment before her brother appeared, when he had asked if she would take a lover. She had been so shocked, she could only repeat the word. Until that moment, she had never given a thought to spending any of her time as a spinster in the company of a man.

To warm your bed. To provide you pleasure.

His quiet query had been said with such concern, as if he thought she might perish for the lack of it.

Of course her body had reacted before she could fully comprehend his meaning, her nipples hardening behind her corset as her breasts swelled, a fluttering of spasms in her abdomen providing the very pleasure she was sure he meant with his question.

On the one hand, she was rather relieved her brother appeared when he did, even though she had been surprised.

Randy hadn't been, though. He had obviously sensed something she hadn't, for he had moved away from her so quickly, she felt a moment of fear. To see how easily he pretended nonchalance as he sat in the chair had annoyed her as much as it had impressed her.

He had no doubt saved her from a scolding by her brother. Marcus hadn't even seemed to notice she was on the roof when he appeared.

If he hadn't come up the stairs when he did, she would have been forced to respond to Randy's question about a lover.

She would have denied needing a lover, of course. She almost wished she had claimed she didn't require one, just to see how he would react.

Would he be insistent? Would he simply accept her answer. Or... would he offer himself?

Diana scoffed, the sound loud in the quiet night. Randolph Forster wouldn't do such a thing. He was an heir to an earldom. He probably had a mistress back in England. He was probably already betrothed, perhaps to a young woman who was still in the schoolroom, the marriage arranged from the time he was at Eton.

She let out a sound of disgust. From what her mother had told her, arranged marriages were no longer the norm in the aristocracy, which was probably the reason her father seemed amenable to her idea of becoming a spinster.

If you really wish to remain unmarried, I shall not entertain offers for your hand, he had said when they were still in

Girgenti. *But I thank my lucky stars every night that I got caught kissing your mother when I did. She does, too, because she insisted she was going to be a spinster because of her poor eyesight.*

Even now, Diana wondered how much of her father's claim was true. She had seen the pair of black-rimmed glasses her mother used to wear, though, their thick lenses so heavy Marianne had been forced to strap the spectacles around her head to keep them on. Perhaps spinsterhood had seemed the only option for Marianne Slater.

It may not be my only option, but it's what I want, Diana thought as she made her way to the stairs.

If she was quiet enough, she could sneak into her bedchamber before Marcus made his way to his, and he would be none the wiser about her having spent time with Randy on the roof.

As for taking a lover, she would have to think about that particular option.

CHAPTER 13
PARENTS IN THE KNOW

An hour later, at the Engels Mansion in Adrianou Street, Plaka

William Slater watched his nephew depart the small salon of their rented house, a quizzical expression settling on his face as he crossed his arms. "What the hell just happened?" he murmured, not intending for his query to be overheard.

"Your nephew seems to have met his match when it comes to a woman," Barbara stated, stepping further into the salon. On her way to their bedchamber to prepare for bed, she had not intended to overhear the interchange between their second-oldest nephew and her husband. Curiosity had her pausing when she heard the name "Miss Diana", however, and a complaint about David's propensity to fall in love with every young lady he met had her listening to the rest of their conversation.

Turning on his heel, Will regarded her with an arched brow. "Met his match?" he repeated. He dropped his arms to his sides as she approached and then captured her shoulders with his hands before kissing her on the forehead. "I wasn't aware he was in need of a set down."

Barbara tittered. "Me, neither, but you were speaking of Miss Diana *Henley*, were you not?"

Will shrugged. "Yes," he hedged.

"In her most recent letter, your stepmother mentioned that we should seek out the Henleys since the viscount has taken on a new archaeological project here in Athens."

Will's eyes rounded before he allowed a guffaw. "Diana is Cousin Marianne's daughter," he said by way of recognition.

"Indeed. I wondered if you would make the connection."

Marianne Slater, the only daughter of Will's uncle Donald, was married to Viscount Jasper Henley, and Diana was their only daughter. The revelation had him chuckling as he smoothed a hand over his jaw.

"And she is the boys' second cousin, straight across," Barbara stated, her prim grin suggesting she was enjoying herself. "I take it you've never met Lady Henley or her daughter?"

Will shook his head. "Well, I met Marianne when she was born at Devonville House, but I haven't seen her since. She is younger than me—by six or seven years, I think—and she always lived with Uncle Don up in Canobie," he explained, referring to a small village in southwest Scotland.

Barbara winced. "She grew up in his distillery?"

Screwing his face into a grimace, Will once again shook his head. "Not *in* the distillery. Uncle Don has a rather nice country house, I'll have you know. At least, that's what Father has always said. I've not been there myself," he explained. "The land on which the house and distillery are located is part of the Devonville holdings, although I'm not sure if it's entailed."

"Next you're going to tell me your father helped fund the whiskey venture," she countered, not sounding very happy at the prospect.

Blinking, Will didn't confirm her guess but said, "Uncle Don has done rather well for himself with that scotch venture. He's become rather wealthy creating a liquor no one claimed to want or like," he added. "Since he doesn't have an heir, I could very well end up with the business," he warned, arching a teasing brow.

Barbara's eyes rounded. "No," she said in shock.

He cleared his throat. "Since Jasper Henley is married to Marianne, he is the more likely candidate to inherit it."

"Well, that's a relief," Barbara murmured, although the edges of her lips curled up to indicate she had been teasing him.

"I've not spoken to my uncle in years, so I've no idea what he plans. But... I can't imagine Henley running a distillery. Which means..." He chuckled softly. "It could end up with either Marcus or Michael," he said, referring to the two Henley heirs.

"Or Diana," Barbara said, arching a brow as she grinned. "Didn't I hear Randy say something about her wearing breeches when he met her today?" She stepped from his hold and placed a hand on his arm, intending they move to their bedchamber. Given the modest size of the house they had let for their stay in Athens, there weren't enough bedchambers for them each to have their own. Neither seemed to mind, though, since they often slept in the same bed back at Ellsworth House in Oxfordshire.

"He did," he affirmed. "She's, uh, apparently searching for something up on the Acropolis."

Barbara closed the door and stood in front of Will,

indicating he should undo the buttons down the back of her bodice. "Searching for what?"

"No idea. She wouldn't tell Randy, and Marcus doesn't seem to know, either."

"Randy spoke with Marcus?"

"He did. He ran into him up in one of those temples. He just came from dinner at their house. The Henleys have let a mansion here in town."

"So... the Henleys are *all* here? In Athens?" she asked, turning to regard him with surprise.

He nodded. "Apparently so, although I got the impression the viscount and Marianne haven't yet arrived. Apparently they are on a wedding trip or some such. We'll make arrangements to meet them when they get here."

Obviously bothered by his comment, Barbara said, "They left their children on their own?"

Will scoffed, undoing his top coat and waistcoat buttons. "They're hardly children, my sweet. Marcus is Randy's age. He's probably spent more time here in the Mediterranean than in England given Henley's avocation."

Barbara continued to frown, as if she were trying to remember something. "Wasn't Lord Henley working with Lord Darius in Sicily? At those temples we saw in that long valley overlooking the sea?"

"He was," Will acknowledged. "He spent a couple of decades working that dig near Girgenti—we saw some of his handiwork when we were in the Valley of the Temples," he reminded her. "Ancient Greek and Roman mosaics are his specialty, you see, but from what Randy said, Henley has a new patron who wants him to search for something here in Athens." He pulled off his ornate dinner waistcoat as he watched his wife step out of her dinner gown, his hands suddenly pausing.

"What is it?" she asked, hanging the gown from a peg on the wall.

"Are you intending to go to sleep?"

Barbara swallowed, immediately understanding the reason for his query. "Not for at least a half-hour. Forty-five minutes, mayhap." She arched a brow as she undid the ties of her petticoats, the white undergarments dropping to the marble floor in a *whoosh*, before she rushed to stand before him. "You have the horn *again*?" she whispered in surprise. She undid the knot of his cravat.

"I can't help it when you're half-dressed," he replied defensively. He was quick to loosen his cravat, attempting to unwind the silk from around his neck as Barbara reached out and pulled his shirt from his pantaloons. "Just... leave it on," she said, her hands moving to the sides of his pantaloons.

"You don't mind then? These unexpected tumbles?" he asked in a whisper.

"Well, obviously not," she replied as she attempted to push the pantaloons from his hips.

The top edge caught on his hardening manhood, and he chuckled as he stilled her hands and finished the task while attempting to step out of his shoes.

"I could just bend over the bed," she offered, about to do it.

"The hell you will," he said, his eyes darkening as he finished undressing. Not bothering to apologize for his curse, he lifted her into his arms.

"Oh!" she cried out, her body landing in the middle of the mattress. Will was over the top of her a moment later, his mouth covering hers for a long kiss before he moved his attentions to the soft mounds above the edge of her corset. After that, his head was between her quivering thighs, the stubble of his late evening beard scraping the tender skin as his tongue swept over her quim.

Barbara's chest rose from the bed when he pushed his tongue into her. The sudden orgasm had her barely able to breathe, her gasps for air accompanied by a series of "oh"s and mewls and an occasional "yes" as her hands gripped the bed linens.

When she seemed nearly spent, he rose over her and impaled her with his rigid cock, burying himself into her in one thrust. He barely paused before thrusting into her again and again before he, too, was swept away by his own release.

When his arms finally gave way and he rolled off of her, Barbara allowed a long sigh. She turned to see his eyes closed and watched as his breathing slowed until a soft snore sounded.

Knowing he would awake with a start in a few minutes, she rolled onto her side and allowed her thoughts to wander to their nephew.

To what she had overheard whilst she stood in the corridor outside of the salon.

She has me vexed, to be sure. Treated me as if I was a competitor for whatever secret she's trying to uncover when I know absolutely nothing about it. Nor do I care. But now... now I'm curious, dammit.

Barbara considered his comment. Had his mother, Hannah, overheard him, she was sure Hannah would think the very same thing as she was thinking.

Randy was smitten.

By a woman who wore breeches.

She couldn't help the titter that escaped as she stared at

her husband's profile, one that his nephew and their youngest son shared.

At three-and-twenty years of age, Randy was probably too young to be considering marriage, but perhaps he would require a reminder to be on his very best behavior around his second cousin.

A reminder that really should come from his Uncle Will.

"He's not going to ruin her."

Barbara gave a start at hearing Will's words. Despite his eyes still being closed, her husband was obviously conscious. "Well, I should hope not," she replied.

"So, you were *thinking* it?" he challenged, lifting himself onto an elbow as he regarded her with a smirk. Although he was awake, his eyes were barely open.

"Weren't *you* the one who told me Viscount Henley was forced to marry your cousin Marianne because he was caught kissing her in the gardens during a ball?" she countered. "During a ball at Weatherstone Manor, no less?"

A grunt sounded from her husband. "Jasper would have married her even if they hadn't been caught," he replied. "He was smitten by her the moment he laid eyes on her, or so he told my father."

The word "smitten" had Barbara sitting up in the bed. Apparently, Will had come to the same conclusion as she had. "You should warn Randy to be careful. Just because she wears breeches—"

"How do you know *that?*" he interrupted.

Barbara blinked. "I might have... overheard him mention it," she admitted sheepishly. "When I was walking by the parlor earlier this evening."

Will sat up and placed his stocking'd feet on the floor. His elbows on his knees, he ran a hand through his tousled hair and chuckled softly. "I'll, uh, mention it to him—and to Tom and to David—during breakfast in the morning. We might be in a different country, but I shouldn't want any incidents."

He stood and stretched before finally pulling the cravat from around his neck. The shirt followed, leaving him completely naked. In the dim light from a single candle lamp, it was apparent he had performed physical labor for most of his life. Although he had grown softer in the time since they had left Oxfordshire to join the boys on their Grand Tours, he still possessed a body like those featured in some of the statuary they had seen earlier that day.

"Apologies. I haven't yet found my banyan," he said when he noticed how Barbara watched him.

"Oh, you needn't apologize," she said, giving him a teasing grin. "If I had a marble pedestal, I could simply have you stand on it, and you could be my very own Greek statue."

"You minx," he accused. He strode to her side of the bed, leaning over to kiss her on the mouth. When he finally ended the kiss, he attempted to straighten and moaned in pain. "I don't think my back could handle such an assignment," he murmured, one hand moving to his hip as he leaned back.

"You wouldn't have to stand on it," she teased, rising from the bed. She made her way to one of the trunks shoved up against a wall and extracted his dressing gown. "You could recline."

He chuckled as she held the robe for him. "Or I could just be at your beck and call," he replied, turning to face her. "Much as I've been these past couple of decades." He pulled her into an embrace and leaned down to place a kiss on her forehead. His grin faded when he saw her expression change. "What is it? What's wrong?"

"David said something rather curious during dinner," Barbara replied.

His post-coital thoughts still on the two of them, Will furrowed his brows. "Remind me what he said."

She stared up at him. "He said he saw his betrothed in the Parthenon."

"Which one?" Will asked as he chuckled softly. He quickly sobered when he realized she was serious. "He tends to claim he's in love with every girl he meets," he added lamely. "I can't imagine he's actually proposed marriage to any of them."

For a moment, Barbara wondered if she should be concerned. Most mothers of heirs had to worry about their sons taking a wife in time to start their nurseries before duty kept them apart for months at a time. With David, her fear was he would marry but continue to fall in love with every woman he met.

Her reverie was cut short when Will chucked her on the chin. "You were telling me about his betrothed?" he prompted.

She sighed. "Well, Tom started talking about the caryatids and their hairstyles, and I never had a chance to ask David who he was talking about," she complained. "You do have a point, though. David does seem to fall in love rather easily. I had no idea he had actually *proposed* to anyone, though." Her eyes suddenly widened. "Do you suppose he was referring to Miss Diana?"

Furrowing a brow, Will shook his head. "I rather doubt he's ever met Diana, even if she is his second cousin—"

"And Randy and Tom's," Barbara reminded him.

He nodded. "The Henleys are rarely in London, so I think

only the boys have met the sons, Marcus and Michael, at university."

"Remind me why it was we didn't meet the Henleys when we were in Girgenti?" she asked, referring to the town closest to the Greek ruins at the Valley of the Temples.

Will held up a finger. "We missed them by mere weeks. I remember a letter from Cherise mentioning the Henleys were in London," he explained, referring to his father's second wife and the current Marchioness of Devonville. "Something about Henley giving a speech at the Royal Society and meeting with a new patron." He arched a brow. "Which is probably why he's here in Athens. Given the popularity of Greek artifacts back home, they probably can't dig them up fast enough to fill the demand."

Barbara winced but finally allowed a prim grin. "Then I suppose I should feel privileged to have my very own," she said, tapping him on the chest.

He chuckled, but is gaze was on his mind's eye. "I don't recall us ever being in town at the same time as the Henleys," he murmured.

"Well, I know I have not met them," Barbara said.

"Which means someone *else* from England was on the Acropolis today," Will mused quietly, moving back to the bed. "We'll ask at breakfast in the morning." He doffed his banyan and pulled on a nightshirt before he suddenly appeared to sway. He gripped the edge of the dresser. "Either I was in the sun too much today, or I drank more of that Greek port than I thought," he murmured.

"Tsipouro," she said before furrowing a brow in worry. "Or ouzo, if it tastes of anise," she added. When she saw his look of surprise, she added, "The cook explained it to me after I unwittingly drank some yesterday." She involuntarily shuddered before making her way to her petticoats, still heaped in a huge circle at the end of the bed. "Apparently it's a very popular drink here."

Will shrugged as he carefully made his way back to the bed. "When in Rome," he murmured.

"We're not there yet, darling," she replied, pulling up the petticoats to add them to the peg on the wall.

He grinned again, a dimple appearing at the base of one cheek. "Aw, but when we do get there..."

Her eyes rounded. "What's *that* supposed to mean?" she asked as she joined him back in the bed.

"Just you wait," he warned, leaving a kiss on her forehead as he pulled her against the front of his body. He grinned in tipsy delight. "Just you wait."

Although her grin matched his, it was soon replaced with a look of concern as she settled her head into the pillow next to his.

First her nephew and now her son—any other woman would be happy to learn the boys in their life had found women with whom to be smitten.

David was entirely too young to marry, though. Of that, she was sure. As for Randy, could she imagine him with a wife? At his age?

Perhaps.

CHAPTER 14
CONFESSIONS ON A HILLTOP

he following morning
"Did you sleep on the roof again last night?" Marcus asked when Diana joined him in the breakfast parlor of Vouros Mansion. He held a sheet of parchment in one hand and a fork filled with egg in the other. His garb was far more casual than usual—Nankeen breeches, blue waistcoat, simple shirt, blue cravat, and a pair of Hobys—and Diana was immediately reminded of what her father wore on the days he spent unearthing mosaics.

"I did not," she replied, giving the kitchen servant a nod when the young girl set a plate at the table for her.

"But you were up there?" he countered. "On the roof?"

Diana glanced up from the slice of toast she was buttering. "For a time. Saw some meteors streaking across the sky. Did you go up?" Although she desperately wished to ask him more about what she had overheard, she knew she couldn't without giving away that she had been on the roof while he was there speaking with Randy.

"I did. Had a chance to speak with our cousin in private."

"Oh?" she murmured, turning her attention to her eggs. "Did you know Lord Forster from school?"

Marcus nodded as he set aside the sheet of parchment. "Indeed. And you can call him Forster. Or Randy if you prefer. He is our cousin," he reminded her.

"Who's the letter from?" she asked, wanting to take her brother's thoughts—and hers—off Randy Forster.

"Father. He and Mother are leaving Rome—or left, rather —and are due back here in Athens the day after next."

"Did he mention if they enjoyed their visit?"

He plucked the paper from the table and handed it to her. "You can read it for yourself," he said. "What are you going to do today?"

Diana accepted the letter and set it next to her place setting. "I'm going back up to the Acropolis," she replied. "Continue my search in the Erechtheion. And you?"

"I'm going to climb a hill with the Fitzsimmonses. Antonio wishes to visit the Prison of Socrates, wherever that is."

"Philopappos Hill," Diana stated. "Eastern slope."

"Yes, that one," he acknowledged. "Anything I should know about it?"

Diana suppressed the urge to roll her eyes. Despite the two of them having grown up with an archaeologist for a father, beyond mosaics, Marcus had never gained an appreciation for the avocation as she had. "A complex series of caves carved out of the hill during the fifth century BC," she recited from memory. "Although it's rumored Socrates was imprisoned there, it's not known for certain he was ever actually there."

"So… what's the attraction?" Marcus asked.

"Well, there are a series of passageways connecting the

chambers, some murals on the walls, and a cistern at the back."

Marcus regarded her with suspicion. "From your description, one would think you have already been there."

"I have not," she responded. "However, I have read about it. At least three of Father's books include references to it," she explained. "It is my intention to see it, probably with Father."

"Does Pausanias mention this Socrates cave?" he asked. "In his first volume?"

Diana stiffened at hearing the Greek geographer's name. "No," she replied. "It was probably too obscure a location for him at the time he was in Athens."

Marcus nodded, but from his expression, he appeared suspicious, as if he didn't believer her answer. "You could come with us," he offered. "Today."

Although she was tempted—the series of caves would be interesting to explore—Diana shook her head. "Thank you, but no. I'll go with Father."

For a moment, he seemed uncertain of how to respond. "I'll be employing the town coach for the day, so it won't be available for you," he warned.

"I can walk to the Acropolis," she stated.

"Alone?" he said in alarm.

"I'll wear a hat. Everyone will think I'm a boy."

"Is that how you got home yesterday?"

"Of course," she replied, ignoring the rebuke in his voice. "Will you take a basket of food with you?" she asked, remembering what he had said the night before. "Seems only fair you supply a picnic today since the Fitzsimmonses did so yesterday," she added.

He nodded. "I told them I would."

"Have you told the cook?"

Cursing softly, he moved to stand from the table.

Diana quickly stood. "I'll see to it," she offered. "One bottle of wine? Or do you require two?"

Marcus regarded her with appreciation. "Two, and thank you for reminding me. You are so much better at all the niceties."

"Anything to help you secure Miss Jane's hand in marriage," she said, managing to sound sincere.

On the one hand, the thought of her brother married had her wincing on behalf of whoever agreed to be his future viscountess. On the other, the sooner he was married, the more likely he would be to go back to England. Perhaps he would live in the Henley townhouse in London, and Diana would no longer have to tolerate his censorious nature. He wasn't so judgmental when their parents were about, but ever since the two of them had moved to Greece while their parents spent time in Rome, Marcus behaved as if she were his charge rather than his capable sister.

"That is what you want, is it not?" she asked, pretending concern.

Marcus seemed reluctant to answer. "Do you like her?"

Surprised he was asking her opinion, Diana shrugged. "Miss Jane seems perfectly respectable. Obviously raised to be the consummate aristocrat's wife. And she is positively gorgeous."

"Isn't she, though?" Marcus agreed, apparently relieved to hear her assessment.

Diana inhaled and let the breath out. "If you do end up married to her, perhaps you wouldn't feel the need to also have a mistress." Prior to the night before, she wouldn't have even thought to say such a thing, but after what Randy had said when they were up on the roof—how he had responded to her comment about having a mistress—she secretly wondered if Marcus planned to employ one.

Perhaps he had when he was at university.

Her brother's eyes rounded with indignation. "Not that it's any of your business, Sister, but I would never want for a mistress if I knew Miss Jane was going to be greeting me at the door every night upon my return home."

Relieved to hear it, Diana acknowledged his comment with a teasing grin. "Good, because if she does agree to marry you, I'll finally have a sister."

Marcus blinked, as if he suddenly realized Diana could be an ally in securing Miss Jane's hand in marriage. "I suppose you would," he agreed.

She arched a reddish blonde brow and left the breakfast parlor in search of the cook. Although it took a few tries to make Elena understand her request—Ancient Greek and the current version of the language were somewhat different—the cook was soon assembling a collection of sliced meats, fruits, cheeses, bread, two bottles of wine, and a set of table linens into a basket.

Helping herself to a few items for her own luncheon, Diana stuffed them into her worn leather satchel, hung the strap of the tubular carrying case over her shoulder, and bade farewell to her brother with a reminder not to forget the basket of food.

When Kyknos opened the front door for her, she mentioned her brother's need for the town coach, knowing full well Marcus wouldn't have remembered to speak with the butler.

Although she still thought him too young to take a wife, the sooner Marcus married, the sooner she would be able to begin her life as a spinster.

CHAPTER 15
BREAKFAST COMES WITH A WARNING

eanwhile, at Engels Mansion

Barbara inhaled deeply as she descended the stairs and made her way to the dining room. Although she thought breakfast would be ready soon, she had not expected to smell the odor of cooked bacon or to hear the voice of one of her nephews so early in the morning.

The butler, Pietro, bowed deeply before he placed a platter of coddled eggs in the center of the table. Salvers of sliced bacon, a basket of breads, including rings topped with sesame seeds, and a plate of sliced cheese were already scattered about the cloth-covered surface. "*Kaliméra*," he said, turning to pull out a chair for her at the oval table.

"*Kaliméra*," she replied, happy to try out the morning greeting with the servant.

"*Kaliméra*, Aunt Barbara," Randy said from where he sat. Across from him, her youngest son, David, was studying what appeared to be a map.

Before Barbara could respond, Will and Tom joined them, moving to the chairs they had used during their first dinner in the house. Will paused to buss her on the cheek before he nodded to Pietro. "Coffee?"

Pietro nodded and lifted a conical cup from where it was perched on a grate over a flame. Gripping the long handle of the *briki*, he poured the thick, black brew into a small cup and placed it before Will.

Barbara swallowed before giving the butler a beseeching glance. "Might there be tea?" She was relieved when he said, "*Nai, kyria mou.*" *Yes, my lady.*

Lifting a teapot from the sideboard, Pietro placed it next to Barbara's serviette along with a cup and saucer.

Will chuckled. "The coffee does take some getting used to," he said before taking a sip, "but it's actually better than what we used to drink on the *HMS Greenwich.*" He had been the commander of the ship for several years before retiring from the British Navy.

David glanced up from the map. "Have you plans for the day, Father?" he asked.

Will helped himself to some eggs and bread while he shook his head. "I'll probably take your mother for a walk to the *agora,*" he said, referring to the area of Athens which included the Temple of Hephaestus. "We spent time in the Queen's Gardens yesterday." He passed the plate of cheese to Tom. "Did you have something in mind?"

David appeared momentarily disappointed. "I was thinking about going up the hill where the Prison of Socrates is located."

About to place an egg on his plate, Randy suddenly straightened and stared at his cousin. "Today?"

Noting her nephew's look of surprise, Barbara set aside her teacup. "By yourself?" she asked, directing her query to David.

For a moment, her son looked as if he couldn't decide how to answer. "I... I wouldn't be alone," he stammered.

Randy scoffed. "Neither will *she* be," he stated, his voice sounding a rebuke.

"I wouldn't expect her to be," David countered. "She'll be accompanied by her brother, of course. And others, mayhap."

Barbara was about to ask the name of the woman in question—and the identity of the brother—when she caught Will lifting his hand in a move to quiet the table.

"Before we start another day here in Athens, I wish to speak with you three," Will said, his manner rather serious.

Tom and Randy exchanged quick glances with David. "Is something wrong?" Tom asked, obviously confused by the conversation.

Will shook his head. "Not yet, but... I think it best you be reminded we are in a different country now. One with different customs."

"Has something happened?" Randy asked, straightening in his chair.

Although he seemed about to respond in the negative, Will furrowed his brows. "You tell me."

Randy blinked as everyone else at the table stared at him. "Well, as I mentioned last night, I... I attended dinner with our cousins, the Henleys," he said with a shrug. "We met them yesterday up on the Acropolis."

"Your brother told us all about it at dinner last night," his uncle said, nodding in Tom's direction.

"As far as I know, nothing untoward happened," Randy added defensively.

Will turned his attention to his son. "David?"

His eyes round, the viscount and future heir to the Devonville marquessate stared at his father in confusion.

"Does this have something to do with Miss Jane Fitzsimmons?"

Not expecting to hear that particular name, Barbara inhaled sharply. "Is *she* the girl to whom you're apparently betrothed?" she asked.

David squirmed a moment. "Sort of," he finally hedged.

It was Will's turn to scoff. "Betrothals aren't something that can be a 'sort of' arrangement. You either are or you are not," he stated. "Which is it?"

His shoulders dropping as if in resignation, David directed his next words to Randy. "You cannot tell Cousin Marcus."

"Tell him what?" Randy asked, obviously confused.

David winced. "Yes, I asked Miss Jane for her hand in marriage. During that ball we attended in London before we left for Sicily," he admitted. "But—"

"Miss Jane Fitzsimmons?" Barbara said, a tentative grin appearing. "Viscount Reardon's daughter?"

"Yes, Mother, but—"

"Well, this is quite unexpected." She had assumed David's comment about having met his betrothed referred to Miss Diana Henley.

"Yes, but—"

"You're getting married?" Tom asked, his face screwed into a grimace.

"I am," David stated, rising from his chair.

"What happened to waiting until you were at least seven-and-twenty?" Tom pressed.

The sudden silence in the dining room gave David the opportunity to provide his explanation. "My arrangement with Miss Jane is... *conditional.* Merely a convenience to assist her whilst she travels," he said, "and when she is in London. Nothing more." He visibly reddened before retaking his seat.

"Conditional?" Will repeated. "What... what sort of condition?"

David sighed. "Whilst at that ball, I discovered Miss Jane fending off an unwanted suitor in the gardens. I stepped in and... well, I might have bloodied Lord Brougham's nose."

Barbara inhaled softly. "He no doubt deserved it, that treacherous leech," she whispered hoarsely.

"I escorted her back to the house, and well, before we were back in the ballroom, I told her I would offer my services—to defend her honor—should she require them again."

"That's not exactly a betrothal," Will said.

"She, uh... might have... well, taken me at my word," David stammered.

"What do you mean?" Barbara asked.

David once again seemed to squirm in his chair. "She asked if I might be willing to be her betrothed should she have need of a means to prevent future unwanted suitors," he explained. "I agreed, of course, because... well." He shrugged. "I would gladly marry her—and I told her I would—once I reached seven-and-twenty."

Barbara settled back in her chair and emitted a sad sigh. "Miss Jane will be... what? Five-and-twenty?" she guessed, obviously not pleased by the details of the arrangement. "That's terribly late for a young lady to be marrying."

"Oh, I expect she'll decide on someone else before she's that old," David admitted. "But until then, she is free to mention me as her excuse to put off would-be suitors, and I am free to—"

"Kiss her," Tom said, the words coming out as an

accusation. "Like you did yesterday. Right out in the open, for everyone to see."

"You *kissed* her?" Will asked in alarm, before Barbara could.

"On the cheek, Father. I was merely... making it clear to Cousin Marcus she was... unavailable to him," David explained defensively.

Randy dipped his head as a chuckle threatened to erupt. "Cousin Marcus is none too happy with you," he murmured.

David straightened. "Was it awkward for you? At dinner last night? Is he angry with me?"

Lifting a shoulder in a shrug, Randy said, "You might have warned me of your arrangement." Turning his attention to his uncle, he said, "As for Marcus, even though he only met Miss Jane at a ball last year and then renewed their acquaintance a couple of days ago, he is quite smitten with her. Thinks he loves her."

Will's attention darted to Barbara, and he allowed a knowing grin.

Although she seemed to be staring at him, Barbara was remembering their first meeting. She was sure Will had been smitten with her, too, but she had been the one to encourage his attentions. The one to ask if he might kiss her. The one to coax an offer of marriage from him before he took his leave of England for a career in the British Navy.

Although she no longer regretted what had happened, there were years while Will was gone when she wished there had been time for them to marry prior to his departure. Their oldest son would then be the heir. Her life would not have been the hardscrabble struggle of a young woman banished from her father's London home. She wouldn't have been forced to live in a ramshackle cottage while raising an illegitimate son with dwindling funds.

She wouldn't have grown to despise Will Slater. To hate him with every fiber of her being. To wish she had never met him.

When she sensed movement to her right, Barbara glanced up to discover Will standing over her. He leaned down and kissed her on the forehead. "What is it?" she asked softly.

"You're crying," he whispered.

Blinking several times to clear the tears, she realized all three boys were staring at her, expressions of embarrassment leaving their cheeks stained red. "Whatever you all do, please do have a care in how you behave," she said quietly. "If you have any regard at all for the young women you are sure to meet whilst we are here, you will be on your very best behavior."

"Yes, Aunt," Tom replied, nodding emphatically.

"Of course," Randy chimed in.

"I... I won't kiss her again," David stated. "Unless... she demands it?" he added sheepishly.

Barbara gave him a quelling glance. "Only if you're placing a betrothal ring on her finger..." She stopped speaking when she saw him wince. "You already gave her a ring?" she asked in alarm.

He nodded. "Just a small one," he said, holding his thumb and forefinger so they nearly touched. "A ruby I bought in a London jewelry shop."

"Did you have her father's permission to do so?"

David shook his head. "He was at their home near Bath at the time, and we left England before he was due in London, so... no."

Barbara scoffed, her eyes still bright with tears, but before she could say anything, David asked, "Does... does that mean I shouldn't go to the Prison of Socrates today?"

Will returned to his chair, confusion showing on his face. "What does the Prison of Socrates have to do with Miss Jane?" he asked.

"She's going there today," Randy stated before David could reply. "With her brother, Antonio, and with Marcus."

Will inhaled softly, apparently understanding the issue. "You think you should be there so that Cousin Marcus isn't tempted to do something untoward with Miss Jane?" he asked, directing his query to his son.

David nodded.

"Even though her brother will be there?"

David shrugged.

Will straightened and crossed his arms. "I think I might have an idea of how *we* can spend our day," he said before returning his attention to his breakfast.

"What do you mean?" Barbara asked, sniffling. She blinked several times in an effort to keep more tears from falling.

"I think we should *all* go to the Prison of Socrates," he replied.

Randy shook his head. "I've already made plans to go back up to the Acropolis," he said. "But I can see the caves on my own another day."

"All right," Will agreed. He knew his oldest nephew could take care of himself. "Barbara? Will you join us? It might be a bit of a climb."

She gave him a watery grin. "Oh, I wouldn't miss it, darling," she said before tucking into her breakfast.

The opportunity to meet Miss Jane Fitzsimmons was entirely too tempting.

CHAPTER 16
ANOTHER DAY, ANOTHER TEMPLE

ater, on the Acropolis in the Erechtheion

Having adopted a slab of marble as a makeshift workbench to hold her tools, Diana moved to an area shaded by the east cella of the Erechtheion and dabbed her face with her scarf. Although the day wasn't particularly warm—yet—the quick climb up the steep slope had her struggling to catch her breath.

Unlike the day before, it seemed there were others at work on the Acropolis. A group of men were clustered near the mosque, its base and a spiral staircase the only remains of a structure that had at one time sported a minaret. The only portion of the religious building that could be seen from the city below, the minaret had been removed in 1832 after the Greeks had won their war for independence.

The animated discussion taking place was too far away for her to overhear, but she was sure the remains of the building would soon be removed.

Deciding she didn't wish to call attention to her own work, she had moved to the inside of the Erechtheion. She did a cursory review of the marble blocks, sighing when she didn't see any evidence of carvings.

"I thought I might find you here," Randy said as he sauntered in from the north entrance. The temple, mostly a ruin, could still boast most of three walls, several columns, and its porch featuring five caryatids.

Diana gave a start, surprised she hadn't heard his approach. "Found me you have," she said, pretending to continue her perusal of the marble wall.

Although she had experienced a moment of annoyance at seeing him, she decided she could be civil with him. He had kept her presence on the roof the night before a secret from her brother and no doubt saved her from a tongue lashing. "I suppose you would like to see the rest of what the Acropolis has to offer."

His gaze on the wall she had been examining, Randy shoved a hand into a pocket and allowed a grunt. "I would. However, I find I learn so much more when I am with someone who already knows all about them," he said.

She gave him a dubious glance. "I must warn you. I am not the most knowledgeable person when it comes to the Acropolis."

"Something tells me you know far more than I do," he countered. "Is it true you remember everything you read?"

Diana stiffened, unable to control how she turned to stare at him. "Who told you that?" she asked, immediately realizing it had to be her older brother. She didn't think Randy had even met Michael the day before.

"Don't be angry with Marcus," he said, moving to stand beside her. He stared at the top of the wall, his brows furrowing as he attempted to make out something he was sure was carved into the stone. "He's merely jealous of you."

Giving a start, Diana stared at him. She had never once thought Marcus envious of her ability to remember everything she had seen and read. Everything she had ever heard. "I rather doubt that," she murmured, moving her attention to the adjacent wall.

"*I'm* jealous," Randy said, unable to hide his smirk. "Do you know how much better I would have done at university if I'd been able to remember everything I had read?"

She glanced in his direction and realized he spoke the truth. "It can be a burden," she said, her hands moving to her hips as she bent to examine a lower portion of the wall she faced.

"I can't imagine how," Randy replied, his gaze following hers. "You must have done very well in…" He paused, wondering if she had been allowed to attend any sort of school. "Finishing school?" he guessed. If she had attended finishing school, her headmistress would probably faint at seeing how she was dressed in doeskin breeches, a man's shirt, and boots. Where a cravat should have been, she had a blue scarf wrapped around her neck. The color set off her reddish blonde hair and pale complexion, although most of it was shaded by a wide-brimmed hat.

This particular temple was missing all of its roof, and she was no longer in the shade of the back wall.

Diana scoffed as she rolled her eyes. "I was never a student, other than of my father's," she said, moving farther along the wall as a gloved hand skimmed over the marble.

"Having an archaeologist for a father surely made for an interesting education," he said, his attention once again going to the top of the wall where he was sure there was an inscription.

"I suppose," she murmured.

Randy turned and regarded her with a furrowed brow. "How did you even become interested in looking for graffiti?"

She straightened and stared at him a moment before she chuckled. "When I was learning about Egyptian temples, I suppose," she said.

Randy gave a start. "We've not yet been to Egypt, but we plan to go there from here," he said. "What... what exactly caught your attention?"

For the first time since he had met her, Diana displayed a huge grin. "I visited, and I did not like anything but the sarcophagus!"

Frowning, Randy shook his head. "What?"

"It's an inscription left in the Tomb of Ramesses the Fifth and Sixth in the Valley of the Kings," she explained.

Randy's eyes rounded. "Someone wrote that? Carved it in a tomb?" he asked in disbelief.

"It's just one of nearly a thousand random scribblings left in that particular tomb," she said with a shrug. "The tomb has been open since shortly after it was built, and the evidence of that is everywhere. The ancient tourists left their mark, sometimes in Latin, but most often in Greek," she explained. "They used black or red ink and sometimes they carved their thoughts in the walls."

Randy winced. "That's appalling," he murmured.

"Usually the inscriptions are down low on the walls, but some are up near the ceiling," she continued, appreciating how he had reacted. "Which suggests the desert sand had blown in and filled up part of the tomb. It had to be quite high when those graffiti were made."

"By the riff-raff of society, no doubt," Randy remarked, obviously not in agreement with the practice.

"You would be surprised to learn otherwise," she

countered. "Some of the visitors were doctors. Others were philosophers or high-ranking officials. For the most part, they weren't there as... as sightseers," she went on. "They were there on some sort of pilgrimage, believing the tomb to be that of Memnon."

"The hero from the Trojan War?" Randy asked in disbelief. "The king of Aethiopia? The one slain by Achilles?"

"That one, yes. But... that tomb is most assuredly not his. However," she settled a hip against the marble slab and crossed her arms. "There are two giant statues nearby, supposedly of Memnon," she said in a quieter voice, rather liking how she had Randy's attention rapt with her tale. "The Colossi of Memnon."

"Does one of those make some sort of singing sound when the wind blows?" he asked, his eyes widening with recognition.

"Indeed. You know of it?"

"One of my professors talked of it as if he had heard it for himself," Randy replied. "Turns out, the man has never left England. I cannot tell you how disappointed I was to learn that he only knew of it from a book."

She nodded. "If I had a crack in me like that statue does, I would sing in the wind as well," she groused. "But since it only happened in the mornings, it probably had something to do with water."

Randy chuckled. "I'll make sure the Colossi of Memnon are on our list. I can hardly wait to see them."

"Don't be too excited," she warned. "Some of the graffiti on those monuments is poetry, but most of it is the equivalent of 'I was here'," she explained. "Someone would write their name and their occupation, and the most common phrase used is 'I admired'."

Randy leaned against the cella wall and crossed his arms. "I suppose that's not so bad," he mused.

"In one case, some man had his secretary do the carving for him. All he wrote was 'I admired'." She held up a hand and waved it in the direction of the marble wall in illustration.

Randy smirked.

"How lazy does one have to be?" she asked rhetorically. "He's traveling all about Egypt with his own personal sculptor!"

Chuckling, Randy angled his head. "I'm almost frightened to ask if the Romans were so crass when they were there."

Diana seemed to suppress a chuckle. "I know it seems odd to think of them taking elaborate holidays, but that's exactly what they did. The wealthy ones would sail down to Alexandria, where they could see the lighthouse. After that, they would visit the pyramids at Giza, then board a boat, and cruise down the Nile."

"Two of the Seven Wonders of the World," Randy murmured in awe. "Do you suppose they had some sort of guide book? Like the ones Pausanias wrote about Greece?"

Diana blinked, staring at him for a moment before she said, "No doubt. They obviously saw the Colossi of Memnon, because those statues are absolutely covered in Latin graffiti. Even the Emperor Hadrian saw them," she claimed.

"Is that when his… *friend* drowned in the Nile?" he asked, curious as to how she would react to learning he knew something about Hadrian's sexual preferences. At least, according to one of his professors.

Diana visibly reddened. "Indeed. Not an unheard of situation given how they behaved on holiday."

"What do you mean?"

She shrugged. "Imagine you're a wealthy Roman citizen.

You sail across the Mediterranean for an exotic Egyptian adventure, seek out all the sights, attend some amazing Egyptian festivals, and drink copious amounts of beer. So of course you're going to see those two huge statues and all the tombs. Listen to them singing in the morning," she mused. "Believing them to be statues of Memnon."

Randy frowned. "Are they not?"

She shook her head. "They are of the pharaoh Amenhotep the Third," she stated. "The Romans thought they were of Memnon because he shared one of his names with a name found inside the Tomb of Ramesses the Fifth and Sixth, so they thought the tomb was his as well."

Scoffing, Randy uncrossed his arms and joined her next to the marble slab. "The timing... we're talking about a..." He paused a moment to think. "A *thousand-year* difference between their deaths and when the Romans would have visited," he murmured.

Diana's eyes widened as she displayed another huge grin. "Exactly!"

He winced, his face displaying a moment of confusion. "The Egyptians must have known the Romans had it all wrong."

"Yes!" she agreed enthusiastically, nodding her head for emphasis.

"So... why didn't the Egyptians correct them? Set the record straight, so to speak?"

Chuckling softly, Diana dipped her head. "Would you? You had all these rich Romans—including emperors—giving you their gold coins. Why correct their mistaken assumptions?"

"So history wouldn't get it wrong?" he replied, shoving a hand into one of his pockets as his momentary annoyance became evident. After a another moment, his face lightened. "The Egyptians were probably laughing behind their backs," he mused.

"Indeed," she agreed, secretly glad he seemed genuinely interested in history.

"You should be a professor," he stated.

Taken aback, Diana blinked. "A professor?" she repeated before she scoffed softly. "I rather doubt any of the colleges at Oxford would be amenable to hiring a woman," she complained. "They don't even allow women to attend."

He dipped his head and shook it. "Still, it's obvious you're passionate about this work." He waved in the direction of the Propylaea, where a small team of men were working. "Which has me wondering why it is the man who is overseeing the restoration efforts up here allows you to be here, too."

Diana glanced in the direction he indicated. "Only because I gave Mr. Pittakis a letter from my father asking that I be allowed to search for markings," she explained. "He was quite clear that I was to inform him of any inscriptions I might find that were anything other than graffiti," she added, rolling her eyes.

"So he can take credit for them?" Randy guessed.

Inhaling softly, Diana nodded. She hadn't expected him to grasp the situation so quickly. "Probably," she agreed. "Once I assured him I would share anything I found, he reluctantly agreed to allow me to bring my tools up here." When she heard him gasp, she asked, "What is it?"

"The rubbing you did—"

"I showed it to him this morning when I arrived."

Randy rounded his eyes. "And?"

Diana lifted a shoulder and sighed. "He thanked me but said he was already aware of the inscription."

"So…" He waved to the remaining walls around them. "What are you searching for here? Or rather, who?"

Diana stiffened, not sure she wanted to share a name. "I'll know when I find it," she finally replied.

He grimaced. "Well, seeing how everyone else in our parties have gone to see the Prison of Socrates, will you allow me to stay here and help?"

Angling her head to one side, Diana gazed at the wall where she had begun her search. Randy's height—he was at least a head taller than she—might prove useful. "Since you are obviously a student of history—"

"You have that right, professor," he acknowledged.

Diana felt the heat of a blush color her cheeks. "You'll have to do as I say," she warned. When she saw the eagerness in his eyes, she nearly changed her mind.

It was almost as intense as his happy countenance. Was he always in a good mood?

For a moment, she was sure she saw something else in his expression, but she didn't dare attempt to decipher it. She hadn't known him long enough to make any assumptions.

"I can follow directions," he claimed, holding up a finger as if to remind her of how he had helped with the rubbing the day before.

"Then you are welcome to stay." She struggled to maintain a passive expression as a frisson of pleasure fluttered through her abdomen at seeing his happy countenance.

What would he think if he ever learned she had never actually been to Egypt?

CHAPTER 17
AN INCIDENT ON THE HILL

*M*eanwhile...

Although they could have taken a carriage to the base of Philopappos Hill, Will and Barbara had asked their driver to drop them at Rovertou Galli Street, near where it met with Apostolou Pavlou Street. They planned to walk the rest of the way to where a path led up the hill to the Prison of Socrates.

"Why here?" David asked, noting they were very close to where he and his cousins had been the day before, prior to their climb up to the Acropolis.

"We're going to follow in the footsteps of St. Paul the Apostle," Will replied. "Or at least walk up to the street he used when he was here to institute Christianity into Athens," he clarified. He offered Barbara his arm and they set out down the well-traveled road.

While there wasn't much in the way of vegetation to their right, there were a number of holm oak and cypress trees marking the base of the hill they were to climb.

"According to Donald's guidebook, we can see more than

just the Prison of Socrates whilst we're on this hill," Will said. Tom and David had opted to walk abreast of Will so they could better hear him. "There is a monument to Prince Philopappos at the top."

"And he was...?" Barbara prompted.

"Gaius Julius Antiochus Epiphanes Philopappos," David recited, reading from Pausanias' book. "A prince from the Kingdom of Commagene—he was a Syrian, according to Pausanias. This hill used to be called Muses Hill back then." When he noticed his mother's arched brow, he added, "Oh, uh. Well, he died in 116 AD, and his sister, who was said to be grief-stricken, had the tomb built up on top."

"Can we go there first?" Barbara asked.

Will shrugged as they turned off onto the path leading up the hill. "If you're up for a climb, I am."

David glanced behind them, obviously in search of Marcus, Antonio, and Jane.

"They may already be at the caves," Tom said, elbowing David.

"Or they got a late start," David countered. Unlike most aristocrats, their family was used to rising early in the day.

The path up to the monument proved an easy, twenty-minute climb, the slight incline barely leaving Barbara breathless when they emerged from between some trees to where what was left of the two-story, semi-circular marble monument stood on a base. "Oh, this is quite grand," she said in awe. Her gaze went from the monument to the view of the Acropolis, and she audibly gasped. "Oh, Will," she whispered. She hurried to where some large stone blocks ran along the crest of the hill and looked out over the city.

He chuckled softly as he stood with her, admiring the Temple of Athena Nike, the Frankish Tower, and the

Parthenon. From this angle, they couldn't make out the other structures on the Acropolis, but the waters of the Saronic Gulf were visible. Tapping one of the ruined stone blocks, he said, "This was part of the Diateichisma."

Barbara glanced up at him. "A wall?" she guessed.

He nodded. "The Athenians built it in the fifth century BC when they feared the Macedonians were about to strike."

"What did Donald write about this monument?" David asked.

Having taken his cousin's guideline book from his uncle, Tom thumbed to the page featuring an elaborate drawing of the monument. "The lower level frieze depicts Philopappos as a consul. He's riding a chariot led by lictors."

"What's a lictor?" David asked.

"A Roman bodyguard," Will called out, grinning at his son.

Tom snorted before he continued reading. "The upper level includes statuary. Antiochus the Fourth—he was the grandfather—Philopappos is in the center, and..." He glanced up. "Apparently there was a statue of Seleucus I Nicator, the founder of the Seleucid Empire."

"Which was there when the Ancona humanist Cyriakos of Pizzicolli saw it in 1436," David said, reading from his brother's accounts. "He did several illustrations that showed it was intact at the time of his visit."

"Let me guess. It was partially destroyed during the war between the Venetians and the Turks," Will said as he joined the young men to admire what was left of the mausoleum.

"The Ottomans used part of it to build the minaret on their mosque atop the Acropolis," David confirmed. He shook his head. "I hate war."

Barbara wrapped an arm around the back of his shoulders

and leaned over to kiss him on the side of his head. "From your lips to Parliament's ears," she whispered.

He allowed a sigh and nodded his agreement. "It will be some time before I'm there," he replied. "Mayhap fifty years or more."

Will chuckled. "I rather doubt I'll live that long, although my father certainly might.

William Slater, Marquess of Devonville, was nearly eighty years old but still had his wits about him. Cherise, his much younger wife, was no doubt responsible for keeping him alive so long.

"Come, let's head to the caves," Will suggested. The four set off on the path to the north, and in only a few minutes, huge openings in the rock face appeared on their right.

Openings occupied by Marcus Henley and Antonio and Jane Fitzsimmons.

"So good to see you three again so soon," David said, rushing up to take Jane's hands to his lips.

Although he noted Marcus bristling at the sight of him, David enthusiastically shook hands with him and Antonio as the rest of the party stepped up to join them.

"Lord and Lady Bellingham, may I have the honor of introducing Miss Jane, her brother, Antonio Fitzsimmons, heir to the Reardon viscountcy, and our cousin, Marcus Henley?"

Will kissed the back of Jane's hand while her brother and Marcus did the same with Barbara.

"It's so good to meet you all," she gushed. "When my nephew mentioned having discovered you all atop the Acropolis, I had hoped we would meet."

"Thank you, my lady," Jane said. "Might I say it's a comfort to find so many others here from England?"

"Indeed. Are you...?" Barbara waved to the cave. "Already leaving?" From her expression, it was evident she would be disappointed at having missed her chance at spending time with the woman who might one day be her daughter-in-law.

"We've only just arrived," Marcus said. "We were admiring the view of the Acropolis from here and were about to go in. Would like to join us?" He glanced at Tom. "It appears you have the authoritative text on the matter."

"My cousin's guidebook," Tom affirmed, hefting the leather bound tome. "And we brought along Pausanias' book as well. For... well, the more historical aspects."

"What are we to find in here?" Antonio asked. He carried a lantern in one hand while a basket dangled from one of Marcus' hands.

Tom already had the pages of the guidebook opened to the description of the Prison of Socrates. "A complex of chambers and passageways, a cistern in the back, and murals on the walls," he read. "Carved into the rock in the fifth century BC."

They all moved to stand a few feet into the first cave, allowing their eyes to adjust as Antonio turned up the flame on the lantern and held it out to illuminate the murals.

"Was Socrates truly imprisoned here?" Jane asked.

"Possibly," Marcus replied.

"But why?" she asked. "I thought he was... respected by the Greeks."

"He was by most, but his teachings began to rankle those in charge," Antonio explained.

"What did they charge him with?" Barbara asked, her brows puckering as she studied the murals.

"Corrupting the youth of Athens and undermining the city's religion," Will replied. "He claimed he was only trying to help people understand the meaning of life and to encourage them to pursue the truth."

"He was found guilty, brought here, and ultimately sentenced to death by drinking hemlock," Tom explained, moving into the adjacent chamber. "So much for free speech and critical thinking."

"Was there nothing he could do in his own defense?" Jane asked, her gaze following David as he disappeared into the next chamber. When Marcus followed him, she glanced at the others in the party before she, too moved to follow.

"He was given the opportunity to take back his claims, but he refused," David replied, his voice echoing. "It's a reminder that even in the face of persecution and oppression, it is important to stand up for what you believe in and to fight for what is right." At the sound of a boot scuffing on the rock floor directly behind him, David turned to discover Marcus.

"What is it?" he asked in alarm. Despite the dim lighting, he could see Marcus was livid. He knew his cousin was about to do something untoward when the young man set the picnic basket he'd been carrying on the floor, the wine bottles inside clanking in protest.

"I'm standing up for what I believe in and for what is right," Marcus whispered hoarsely. "As I should have done yesterday when you dishonored Miss Jane with your inappropriate display of public affection." He balled up a hand into a fist and sent a punch in the direction of David's nose.

Well aware of what was about to happen, David nimbly ducked, which sent Marcus staggering to regain his balance. Moving backwards several steps, David's attention went to Jane. She had just come through the opening from the other cave and was standing behind Marcus, her eyes round and one gloved hand raised to her mouth.

"We should be practicing our pugilistic skills elsewhere, Cousin," David said, grinning in an attempt to indicate the two cousins were merely engaged in horseplay. When Antonio appeared and moved to stand on the other side of his sister, the lantern showed the confusion on his face. "Certainly not in the presence of young ladies," David added, lifting his chin to indicate they weren't alone in the cavern.

His eyes still blazing with fury, Marcus glanced over his shoulder and quickly straightened. "You're right, Penton. These caves tend to bring back memories of my youth on Sicily. A good location for horseplay." He turned and offered his arm to Jane. "Might I escort you, Miss Jane?"

Obviously uncertain of what had taken place, she gingerly placed her hand on his arm, her gaze lingering on David until Marcus had her moving in the direction of the cistern at the back of the cave.

At the appearance of his parents, David audibly sighed. "What is it?" Barbara asked, her gaze flitting from him to Marcus and Jane before she seemed to understand.

"Mr. Fitzsimmons, I understand you plan to take your sister to Cape Sounion soon," Will said, moving to stand next to Antonio.

The young man brightened, the tension from the moment before finally broken. "I am. Marcus said something about arranging a coach—"

"Actually, I wondered if we might all go together?" Will interrupted. "My wife would certainly welcome a female with whom to travel," he added. "We'd have to spend the night somewhere, of course—it's too far to make the trip back and forth in one day," he went on.

"I've been told it's fifty miles away, my lord," Antonio agreed.

"I can see to arranging a larger traveling coach," Will offered. "I realize we would still require two coaches as well as accommodations near the cape for a party of... nine or ten?" he guessed.

Antonio swung the lantern around to illuminate more of the back of the cave. "Marcus, I do believe Lord Bellingham has the solution for our upcoming trip to Sounion."

Marcus turned around, his manner far different from what it had been only a few minutes earlier. "Oh?"

"We can go as a group," Antonio said.

"There is safety in numbers, and the butler at our house has assured me there are accommodations with food very near to the cape," Will explained.

"Are you thinking of bringing everyone in your party?" Marcus asked, obviously struggling to keep his gaze from darting to David when he joined the group. David was pretending to read one of the pages of the guidebook by the light of Antonio's lantern.

"Uh, yes, which is why I thought it only fair I make the arrangements since there are only three of you."

"Four, actually. My sister will have my head if she's not included in the party," Marcus said.

"What of your brother? Isn't Michael with you?" Will asked, his gaze darting about.

"He is actually up on the Acropolis today and will be every day for the foreseeable future. Father was able to secure a position for him with the group working on some excavations near the Propylaea," Marcus explained. "He won't be joining us for the trip."

"So... there would be nine of us," Will stated. "I believe we can make that work if you're in agreement."

"*I* am," Antonio stated.

Marcus shrugged. "That would be capital," he agreed.

"Very good. I'll send word when the arrangements are complete," Will said.

"Oh, I do look forward to meeting your sister," Barbara said to Marcus.

The young man seemed surprised at hearing her enthusiasm. "I'm sure she's anxious to meet you as well," he replied. He glanced around. "Well, I think it's time we head up to the top and have our luncheon by the monument up there, don't you agree, Antonio?"

Appearing uncertain for a moment, Antonio glanced over at his sister, and she nodded. "If we're all finished here. David?"

"I think I've seen everything," he replied.

"Oh, it's positively beautiful up there," Barbara said. "We've already been. The view is spectacular," she added directing her comment to Jane. "Do enjoy your luncheon." She glanced around. "Oh, I believe you left your basket over there, Mr. Henley," she added, indicating the spot where Marcus had set it before he nearly punched David.

"Thank you, my lady. We'll see you again the day after tomorrow."

"Indeed. I look forward to it," Barbara said.

Will pulled David closer to him. "What happened?" he whispered. "Did he challenge you for Miss Jane?"

David shook his head. "Even if he had, I would not have accepted," he stated. "I know better."

They watched as the three were about to exit the caves until Jane turned and addressed David. "Penton, aren't you coming with us?" she asked. "We require your expertise on what we're about to see," she added.

Without so much as a glance in his parents' direction, David said, "Of course, Miss Jane." He closed the guidebook, tucked it under his arm, and hurried out of the cave. "Oh, and Mother, I'll be taking my dinner in town," he called out the moment before he disappeared.

Will and Barbara exchanged a nervous glance as Tom joined them to watch the party of four take their leave.

"I cannot help but think I've missed something," he murmured.

"You're in good company," Will replied. "Shall we head back? I don't know about you, but the mention of a luncheon has me feeling a bit peckish."

"I can always eat," Tom agreed.

Barbara tittered as she placed a hand on Will's proffered arm.

The three headed out of the caves and made their way down the tree-lined path, determined to find a costermonger before continuing their tour of Athens.

CHAPTER 18
A DISCUSSION DURING DINNER

*L*ater that night

Curious as to how Marcus had faired with Miss Jane that day, Randy ate the early dinner offered by the cook at Engels Mansion before heading out on foot to Vouros Mansion.

Although he had enjoyed the descriptions of that day's trek to Philopappos Hill offered by his father and by his brother—the two had been fascinated by the multiple interconnected caves they had toured—he had hoped David might provide him with an update as to his arrangement with Jane Fitzsimmons. The eventual heir to the Devonville marquessate had been absent from the table, however. When Randy asked as to his whereabouts, Will told him he was having dinner in town.

Had Marcus challenged his cousin to a duel? Or had David challenged Marcus?

"He hasn't been challenged to a duel, if that's what you are thinking," Barbara stated from where she sat at the end of the table.

Randy gave a start. "How—?"

"We discussed this very topic on our way down the hill," Will said, grinning. "But David assured me he has no intention of coming to blows with Marcus Henley."

"Which is a relief, seeing as how you are all cousins," Barbara added.

"But something happened," he guessed, not making it a question. Randy glanced from his aunt to his uncle and then to his brother.

"Nothing happened," Tom said firmly. "At least, no one has suffered a broken nose. Yet." He rolled his eyes as if in disgust.

"Thomas," Barbara scolded.

"My apologies, Aunt, but I did spend the day in their company, too. Marcus is quite vexed that David seems to have captured Miss Jane's heart when it's obvious he wishes to ask for her hand. The man is hopelessly in love with her. "

"He's done nothing of the sort," Will said, referring to David. "But I will admit, my son is playing his role as her intended well enough that even *I* believe they are betrothed, and I know the truth of the matter."

Randy groaned. "It's no wonder Marcus is vexed. I've half a mind to tell him the truth."

"You'll do no such thing," Barbara stated, which had all the men at the table turning to stare at her. "If the ruse is to be revealed, Miss Jane shall be the one to do it."

While the boys both grunted their objections, Will asked, "You don't think she likes Marcus enough to consider his suit?"

"Oh, I think she does," Barbara replied, which had the men displaying looks of confusion.

Tom angled his head to one side. "My father says I will

never understand women, and I believe this is a perfect example of why," he said, waving his hands. "Could you *please* explain what you just said, Aunt Barbara?"

Will and Randy both chuckled, but Barbara huffed before setting her knife and fork on her plate. "Having spent the day in her company, I find that Miss Jane is rather shy. Her beauty brings her much attention from those of your sex—most of it unwanted—which is why she is so glad to have arranged a faux betrothal with my son."

"But you think she likes Marcus?" Tom asked.

Barbara nodded. "Indeed, despite the fact that he is a bit young to be considering marriage."

At the other end of the table, Will cleared his throat.

Loudly.

"I was younger than him when I proposed to you," he reminded her.

A wash of red colored Barbara's face as she blinked several times. "Oh. Well, you were in the Navy and... well, you *seemed* older," she stammered. "Marcus..." She paused, as if struggling to describe the young man.

"Is not going to follow in his father's footsteps," Will firmly stated. "Although he's been trained as an archaeologist, he wants to return to London. Take up residence in their townhouse there and do his duty as a viscount once he inherits."

"And in the meantime?" she asked. "Jasper Henley is not that old."

"He's in his forties," Will argued.

Barbara's arched brow had him chuckling softly.

"Henley has rarely attended Parliament," he said by way of explanation. "But perhaps Marcus could be granted a writ of acceleration. Be given his father's seat in the House of Lords."

He turned to Randy. "You know him from school. What say you on the matter?"

About to take a bite, Randy hesitated before saying, "I believe you are right in everything you have said, Uncle. If he intends to live in the capital, he is going to need an avocation. Perhaps politics—and marriage—would suit him. Keep him out of the gaming hells and..." He clamped his mouth shut before the word 'brothels' could escape.

"If only the Henleys were here," Will murmured.

"Why do you say that?" Randy asked.

"Marcus would do well to discuss all this with his father," Will replied.

"And his mother," Barbara chimed in.

"They are due to arrive in a few days," Randy offered. "But in the meantime, I'm sure Marcus will continue his pursuit of Miss Jane. Do you know if he is having dinner with her and her brother this evening?"

"The Fitzsimmonses were to join Marcus for a supper at a *taverna* here in town," Barbara said. "Is that some sort of... public house?" she asked, her nose wrinkling as if she didn't think it appropriate for Jane to attend.

"Indeed," Will replied. "Miss Jane will be fine with three strapping lads to act as chaperones."

"Three?" Randy repeated. "So... David is with them?"

Will and Barbara exchanged quick glances. "He is, but he said he won't be staying out too late," his uncle assured him.

Even having been assured Marcus and David hadn't come to blows during their trip to the caves, Randy wondered if they would continue to be on their best behavior whilst in town. "What are your plans for the morrow?" he asked, finishing the last of his meal.

"I'm going to stay in all day and see to some correspondence," Barbara replied. "I owe everyone letters."

"While I arrange for a traveling coach to take us down to Cape Sounion the day after," Will said.

"To see the Temple of Poseidon?" Randy asked in awe. The ancient Greek temple had been completed in 450 BC, and unlike many of the temples built during that time, most of its columns were still standing. He knew Diana would want to go. The mention of markings and graffiti around the base of the temple could be found in a number of guidebooks.

"Of course. You will be joining us, I hope?" his uncle asked as the cook removed his plate and set a new one in front of him along with what appeared to be a plate of sweets. "Due to the distance, we'll need accommodations for the night."

Randy was about to reply, his thoughts still on Diana. Surely she would appreciate the opportunity to see the ruins of the temple overlooking the Aegean Sea. "Would there be room for six of us?"

Will shrugged. "I'll see what I can do."

At the other end of the table, Barbara dipped her head to hide a grin.

CHAPTER 19
A ROOFTOP RENDEZVOUS

half hour later

Determined to learn what had happened between David and Marcus earlier that day as well as to ask Diana if she might join his family on their trip to Cape Sounion, Randy quickened his steps as twilight descended over Athens. At the butler's suggestion, he carried a lantern, but he hadn't lit it, insisting he would reach the Henley residence well before dark.

When he turned onto Vakchou Street, he was relieved to see light in several windows of Vouros Mansion. The butler opened the door before he had a chance to lift the owl-shaped bronze door knocker.

"Lord Forster to see Mr. Marcus Henley," he said, not sure if the servant would recognize him.

"Mr. Henley is not in residence, my lord," Kyknos said in stilted English.

Giving a start, Randy glanced back toward the street. "Has he been home? Since this morning?" He dared a glance beyond the vestibule, half-expecting to see the young man either deep in his cups or in despair.

Instead he saw a number of crates stacked up in what he thought was the ground floor parlor, but there were far fewer than there had been the night before when he had come for dinner.

Someone had obviously been unpacking.

Diana, no doubt.

He couldn't imagine Marcus helping to set up the household in anticipation of their parents' arrival from Rome.

Kyknos shook his head. "I believe he has accepted a dinner invitation in town, my lord."

Randy remembered Marcus, David, and the Fitzsimmonses were to have dinner at a *taverna*, but he had expected they would have been done eating and home by now. Perhaps they had all gone to the Fitzsimmons' hotel. "Might I be allowed to wait for him?" he asked. He remembered the table and chairs on the roof and added, "Up on the roof? It appears to be a capital night for stargazing." With any luck, there would be more meteor showers.

Stepping aside, the butler waved to the curved staircase. "I will inform Mr. Henley you are there when he returns."

Randy nodded and set the lantern in the corner of the vestibule. "I'll find my way up," he said, heading for the stairs.

He was halfway up to the top when he realized he hadn't seen Diana upon his arrival. Was she with her brother? Or in her bedchamber?

A frisson of pleasure skittered under his skin at the thought he might see her again. Their day at the Erechtheion hadn't resulted in any finds of note, but his optimism had tempered her growing frustration—at least for a time. When she snapped at him for a comment he meant as a light-hearted tease, he had merely dipped his head and given her a moment to recover.

She had taken a deep breath and apologized, of course, but he knew not to attempt to mock her. The last thing he wanted to happen was to be evicted from her dig site and be told never to return.

He had been tempted to kiss her on the forehead, though. He had seen his father placate his mother with such a move more times than he could remember. Usually the kisses were enough. When it seemed they wouldn't be, Henry Forster took further steps, including once when he simply lifted his wife over his shoulder, stomped up the stairs while ignoring her pleas of "put me down" as her fists pummeled his back, and did who-knew-what to her after the door to their master bedchamber slammed shut.

Randy expected his parents wouldn't be speaking to one another for a week after that incident, but his mother had been especially happy during dinner that night, her color rather high.

Come to think of it, his father's mood had been rather jovial that night, too.

He wondered how Diana would have reacted if he *had* kissed her. Would she have slapped him? Been incensed he would do such a thing in an ancient Greek temple? Or would she act as if nothing had happened, returning to her search whilst essentially ignoring him?

There was a third alternative.

He dared not think of it, though, for he didn't wish to suffer with an arousal whilst he waited for Marcus' return.

As he reached the final flight of stairs, it dawned on him that Diana Henley was a bit of a grouch.

No wonder she didn't appreciate his incessantly good

moods, especially when he was determined to lighten hers. Was there anything he could do—short of tossing her over his shoulders and doing who-knew-what to her after he had her in her bedchamber—to make her happy?

He was thinking of asking his aunt for suggestions when he emerged onto the roof and quietly shut the door.

As he expected, the deepening night sky displayed the band of stars making up the Milky Way. Even before he started to make his way to one of the chairs, a shooting star streaked across the sky.

The inhalation of breath he heard was not his own.

Awareness of *her* had his body responding before he even realized Diana was there, lying prone on the pallet.

He didn't say a word as he lowered himself to lie next to her, settling so his arms were held atop his chest much like hers were. Although he itched to touch her, he was determined to keep his hands to himself. "How many have I missed?" he asked in a whisper.

"Only two," she replied. "But it's rather early." She turned her head in his direction. "What are you doing here?"

He turned his head to face her. "I wished to speak with Marcus. Discover what happened in the caves today," he said quietly. "Have you spoken with him?"

She sighed. "He sent a note saying he would be joining the Fitzsimmonses for dinner. At a *taverna*, I think is what he meant to write. His handwriting is shite."

Randy struggled to hold in a snort at hearing her curse. "He did not invite you to join them?"

When she didn't answer, he sobered. "Had I known, I would have invited you for dinner with us at Engels Mansion. Although it was more of a supper really. Nothing formal."

Diana had already turned her head so she could watch the black sky above. "I did not mind."

"David went with them," he murmured, lifting a finger when a streak of light speared the sky to the east. "He hadn't returned to the house before I left, though. He and my aunt and uncle and Tom spent the day with Marcus and the Fitzsimmonses at the caves."

She glanced in his direction before she asked, "Did they happen to mention if they paid witness to a duel?"

Randy gave a start and chuckled. "I asked the very same question," he claimed. "I was assured there was not, nor would there be a duel," he added. "I also came tonight to ask if you might like to join us the day after tomorrow. We're going to Cape Sounion to see the Temple of Poseidon."

Diana inhaled softly. "Your family?"

"The five of us. Uncle Will said he would see to finding a town coach to accommodate six. We'll have to spend the night, of course, but you and Barbara could share—"

"I should like to join you, of course," she answered, before he could say more. "I'll bring my sketch pad and paints."

"You paint?" he asked in surprise.

She tittered. "Of course."

Randy blinked, the musical giggle the first time he had heard her express humor out loud. He was also a bit taken aback by the idea of her painting. He wasn't sure why he thought her so different from any of the young ladies he had met in the capital. Well, none of them wore breeches or spent their days on archaeological digs, but she was a viscount's daughter. "I suppose you have other talents as well?"

Her scoff was loud in the dark. "I can draw, I can speak and read French, Latin, and Greek, and I can dance. I cannot play piano-forté, however."

"Oh! Such a failure," he teased, one of his fists striking his chest to emphasize his mock disappointment. He quickly sobered. "I am sorry I vexed you earlier today." He turned to regard her with a crinkled brow. "I should not have teased you. Nor pressed the issue of your reason for your search."

She turned to face him. "I am sorry for how I reacted."

"You were merely frustrated," he murmured.

"A situation that seems to occur far too frequently of late. I don't know why I'm so impatient. My father told me he knows of archaeologists who spend their entire lives searching for clues from the past and they find *nothing*."

Before she finished the comment, another streak of light briefly lit the sky. After her inhalation of breath had subsided, she added, "I think my father's successes have spoiled me. He has uncovered so many mosaics over the years. One after another, simply by digging and brushing away layers of dirt."

"Well, determining the location of the Greco-Roman quarter near Girgenti ensured he would find those floors," Randy reasoned. "Isn't that where all the residences were located?" When she didn't answer right away, he turned to discover she was no longer watching the sky. "What's wrong?"

She swallowed. "My father didn't find the Greco-Roman quarter," she murmured.

Randy lifted himself onto an elbow. "If not him, then—?"

"Lord Darius Jones did. The Duke of Westhaven's brother," she explained. "He and my father excavated the site, but it was Lord Darius who knew of its location."

Randy didn't know why she thought it important that he know there was another archaeologist involved. "Your father still made all those discoveries, though," he reasoned.

"True," she agreed. "Mother located a site where there was

a mosaic. She wasn't even looking for it, which had my father most vexed. Proud of her, though."

"Was she wearing her spectacles?" he teased, immediately regretting the query when she didn't share in his humor.

"I'm not sure," she finally said.

He furrowed his brows in concern, wondering why she seemed so sullen. The meteors continued to put on a show, the shooting stars arcing across the sky every minute or so.

"Do you fear you may never find what *you* are looking for?" he asked gently.

She gave a start. "Proof of Pausanias?" she countered, disgust sounding in her voice.

Randy stared at her in disbelief. "*That's* what you're looking for? That he was..." He waved a hand in the direction of the Acropolis. "That he was here?"

He watched as a grimace crossed her face. "Have you read his first volume of the *Description of Greece?*"

About to say he had, Randy reconsidered his response. "Parts of it. The volume having to do with Athens, of course, and the text about Sounion. I thought I would read the rest as we continue our tour," he explained.

"Have you read any of the *other* volumes?"

He allowed a shrug. "Parts of others. For the places we've already decided to go to," he added. "We still haven't settled on a final itinerary for the rest of the country, though."

"Did you notice anything... *different*... in his writings?"

Her careful wording had him furrowing a brow as he settled back down onto the pallet. "Well, Tom mentioned it seemed as if his later volumes are more... descriptive. Certainly better written, but then... that's to be expected," he stammered.

"Why?"

The query came at the same moment a brilliant white arc lit the sky. Although he didn't see it directly, the wash of light from it briefly illuminated Diana and lit her entire body. He was sure her nipples were tenting the fabric of her nightrail, their silhouettes evident in that fraction of a second. Then everything went back to black.

Randy struggled to keep his body's immediate response in check. His hand was mere inches from hers, one of his legs nearly touched hers. It would be so easy to simply lean over her. To cup one of her breasts in his hand while his lips sought hers.

He had held her entire body only a few hours earlier. Lifted her until she was level with an engraving that might have been exactly what she was seeking—except it wasn't.

"Uh..." He swallowed. "Pausanias probably hadn't written anything else. He started in Athens and worked his way around to the other sites. So he was learning to describe what he was seeing and simply improving upon it as he continued his tour of the country," he reasoned.

"Or he wasn't here at all."

The comment had him giving a start. "Why would you say that?"

He saw her shrug before she said, "He could have written it based on another person's recollections. Or of other travelers' descriptions."

"Why would you even think that?" Randy asked in dismay.

She audibly sighed. "If he *was* here, and if he was the one to write about it, then he obviously wasn't impressed by what he saw. There is no *passion* in his observations. No awe like there is in his later volumes."

Randy considered her comment before he dipped his

head. "You think that if he was here, he left markings in the marble somewhere?"

She nodded in the pillow under her head.

"And you think if you don't find any evidence he was here, then that... that means he wasn't?"

She once again sighed with frustration. "Not necessarily, but it has been something bothering me ever since I read his books," she admitted.

"And this is what has you frustrated?"

He saw how she rolled her eyes before she replied. "It's only one of many puzzles for which I would like to find answers, so you can understand why it is I am vexed."

When she didn't return her attention to the sky, Randy locked his gaze with hers. He waited another moment before saying, "A lover might help in that regard. Take your mind off your pursuit for a few hours."

She broke eye contact with him to scoff. "Did you hear what you just said?" she asked in disbelief. "What you're suggesting is... is scandalous," she scolded.

"Why? If you're a spinster—"

"Well, I am not yet."

"Can you be at the age of only one-and-twenty?" he asked, his face displaying one of concentration.

"I will still be unmarried and plan to remain so," she insisted.

He made an odd sound in his throat. "One man might not be enough for you," he murmured in a quiet voice.

Diana gave a start. Although the words had been said in almost a whisper, they sounded loud in the quiet night. "What do you mean?" She turned her head until she could see his profile. His gaze was still directed on the stars above.

"The reason you don't wish to wed," he clarified. "Is it

because you already know you would grow bored with the same man?"

She kept her attention on him and finally said, "Perhaps."

He suddenly turned to look at her. "Well, if not that, then why exactly don't you wish to wed? I would think you would appreciate the protection it would afford you," he argued. "For economical reasons as well as for your safety. Not to mention you would have someone with whom to attend entertainments. Someone to warm your bed."

Having heard all the usual arguments from her mother, Diana sighed. Loudly. "First of all, I have never wished to marry because I didn't want to..." Pausing, she swallowed.

"What?" he prompted.

"I don't wish to become someone's property," she hissed.

Randy frowned. "So... mayhap you *don't* marry, but instead you take a lover," he countered.

"You've already said I would grow bored with the same man," she accused.

"Which is why you would take more than one lover," he said, managing to sound excited by the prospect.

A sound of disbelief erupted from her, but it was tinged with humor. "Could I now?"

He turned onto his side and, supporting himself on an elbow, propped his head on a hand. "Surely you've read about sultans and their harems," he said. "The Ottoman Empire?"

Her brows furrowed. "I've read about them, of course. Up to four wives and hundreds of concubines for only one man." She made a sound of disgust in her throat.

"You could be a sultana," Randy said. "With lots of men at your beck and call."

She tittered. "Now you really are being silly. Besides not

having the funds to support a harem of men, I have no desire to manage them," she replied.

"So… mayhap start with seven. One for every night of the week?"

Obviously stunned he was still pressing the issue, Diana turned onto her side to face him, matching his pose with her elbow and hand. "For a moment, I thought you were seriously suggesting I take seven lovers—"

"Because I am," he interrupted, even though he was grinning.

She inhaled sharply. "Do you have any idea how scandalous *that* would be?"

Despite the position he was in, Randy managed to shrug. "Would you care? What others think, I mean?"

She winced. "Do you have any idea how… how ridiculous you sound?"

"Why?"

"Just because I wish to remain unwed does not mean that I wish to live a life of scandal," she explained.

"So… you start with one lover. Someone to warm your bed at night."

"My bed is quite warm enough, which is why I am up here on the roof," she said on a huff.

"So… separate bedchambers then," he whispered. "Hmm."

She directed a dubious expression at him. "One would think *you* are interested in the position."

"And what if I am?" he asked.

Staring at him for several seconds, she finally exhaled before saying, "How could you be? Knowing how easily annoyed I become? Especially with *you*?" She punctuated her words with a poke to his arm.

Although the comment stung, he pretended nonchalance.

His shrug went almost unseen in the dark. "I would think of it as a challenge. One that I would need to meet—and exceed—as often as I am given the opportunity."

She blinked and shook her head. "You say that as if you think—"

"Apologies!" he suddenly said, scrambling to get to his feet. "Forgive me," he added, reaching for her free hand to kiss the back of it.

The distant thumping of someone climbing the stairs had him rushing to one of the metal chairs. He managed to be seated before the door to the roof burst open.

CHAPTER 20
CONSOLING A MAN IN LOVE

moment later

Randy wasn't sure why he thought anyone but Marcus Henley was about to join them on the roof, but he still experienced a moment of relief at seeing his friend rather than a servant appear. The manner in which the young man had burst through the door and stalked in his direction had him on guard, though.

"Ah, Marcus," he said, hoping Marcus didn't notice his sister lying nearby wearing only a nightrail. He certainly hadn't when he first stepped onto the roof, his eyes needing time to adjust to the darkness. A quick glance in her direction showed she was lying down, her hands clasped atop her waist, her attention on the skies above.

"Oh, good. You're still here," Marcus said as he joined him at the table. He took a seat. "Our butler wasn't sure if you were up here. Damnation, but it's dark."

Randy chuckled, glad when Marcus leaned back to stare up at the sky. He had half-expected him to notice Diana, but she was to his back now. As long as he didn't turn around, he wouldn't know she was there.

Apparently Diana had come to the same conclusion, for she had quietly stood from the pallet and was making her way toward the door. Randy might not have noticed her but for the white fabric of her gown appearing almost ghostly, a slight breeze causing it to hug her body so that every curve was outlined against the darkness.

He had to suppress the urge to groan in frustration, his cock once again hardening. He was sure she noticed him watching, for she paused and seemed to stare at him before she slipped into the opening and disappeared.

Relieved her older brother hadn't noticed her departure—his eyes were probably still adjusting to the dark while the sound of the wind through some nearby trees was providing even more cover—Randy glanced up to discover Marcus still staring at the void. "Do I dare ask about your day with Miss Jane?" he ventured.

"You haven't spoken with your cousin?" The words sounded clipped but not angry.

"He wasn't at dinner this evening," Randy replied. "Which is why I came straight here." It wasn't the only reason, but Marcus didn't need to know he had developed a fondness for his sister and wished for her to join them on their trip to Cape Sounion.

More than a fondness, really. Beneath his obvious lust for her—did the woman realize how her choice of work clothing had him imagining all sorts of inappropriate scenarios they could be doing whilst she searched for evidence of Pausanias?—he had come to appreciate her determination to solve a puzzle. He found he wanted to be with her when she did. Surely she would display a happy countenance. Perhaps seriously consider his suggestion she take a lover.

"I may have ruined my chances with Miss Jane," Marcus murmured. He set a decanter and two glasses on the small table before he took a seat.

Not having noticed his host had brought the liquor and glasses with him, Randy straightened in alarm. "How?"

Marcus poured a generous amount of tsipouro into each glass. "I nearly punched Penton in the nose."

Randy swallowed. "But you didn't."

"I missed."

Randy's blink went unseen in the darkness. "Because…?"

"Because that damned coward ducked," Marcus complained on a sigh.

"Did he take a swing at *you*?" For a moment, Randy wondered why neither his aunt nor his uncle had mentioned the incident over dinner.

"Antonio caught us before he could. Miss Jane was directly behind him, though. I think she may have… paid witness to my failed attempt at pugilism. I'm not sure."

For a moment, Randy bristled at the thought of Marcus doing violence upon David. His cousin was an amiable young man, friendly with everyone. He couldn't imagine David doing—or saying—anything that would incense Marcus enough to have him punching him in the nose. "Did it happen in the caves?"

Marcus nodded before taking a huge sip from the glass. He reared back in his chair and coughed several times. "Damnation." The word came out sounding at least an octave higher than his usual voice.

Randy took an experimental sip. "It's not ouzo, if that's what you were expecting," he warned.

"I don't care what it is, as long as it's mostly alcohol," Marcus murmured, attempting to clear his throat before he took another sip, this one smaller.

"Did she say something? Scold you?" Randy pressed. He groaned when he realized what Miss Jane might have done if she thought Marcus a brute. If Marcus *had* punched David, Randy could just imagine her rushing to David's side to determine if he was hurt. David wouldn't say anything to dissuade her from showering her attentions on him, either. He would simply accept her concern and grin at her with his moon eyes.

For someone so young, he certainly knew how to make the young ladies swoon.

"She didn't, but…" Marcus winced. "I'm sure I saw censure in her eyes when she glanced in my direction. I tried to pretend like we were simply horsing around, but I'm not sure if my ploy worked or not."

"Did you all dine together this evening?"

Marcus drained his glass and refilled it. "We did, although I cannot say it was an appropriate place for a young lady to be."

Randy gave a start. "Where did you take her?" he asked, pretending ignorance. He remembered Barbara's query about a *taverna*. Her concern that it would be suitable for a young lady.

"*We* were all at the *taverna*," Marcus replied. "David invited us, but it was her brother's idea to go there. He has traveled a great deal and seems comfortable in such a place."

"Were there other women there?"

Marcus blinked. "Some locals, I think. An older woman waited on us."

"Then she was fine to be there with… what? Three of you?"

Marcus nodded.

"And?" Randy prompted.

"Well, she didn't say much. Listened mostly."

"Did you ask her any questions?"

For a moment, Marcus seemed flummoxed. "Oh, I asked if she found the climb to the caves to be too arduous."

"And?"

Marcus sighed. "She said, uh, 'Not at all. It was quite a pleasant excursion'," he recited from memory.

"Did you ask if she found the caves interesting? Or if she had a favorite from that day's events?"

"Uh, no. We mostly talked about London. About the next Season and Antonio's plans. And mine. I'm hoping I can convince my father I'm ready to take on the Henley viscountcy."

Resisting the urge to throttle his second cousin—did the man know nothing of speaking to members of the opposite sex?—Randy sighed. "Did you make plans to see her before she leaves for Spain?"

Here Marcus straightened. "Her brother wants to take her to the Temple of Poseidon the day after tomorrow."

Randy blinked at hearing the comment. Given his uncle's plan for them to do the same thing—on the same day—he had to think Will and Antonio had discussed it.

"You'll go with them, of course," Randy stated.

Marcus furrowed his brows, as if he hadn't considered the possibility. "What? Invite myself?"

For a moment Randy considered how the heir to the Henley viscountcy might arrange to join the Fitzsimmonses on their journey. Cape Sounion was nearly fifty miles to the south. An overnight stay would be required. "You could offer to make the arrangements for their accommodations. Find them suitable transportation," he suggested. "Offer to bring a basket of food and some wine for the trip there."

"I haven't been here long enough to know how to do all that," Marcus argued.

"You have servants," Randy argued. "You can speak their language, as can your sister."

Despite the dark, he could see Marcus' eyes widen with excitement. "Damnation. You're right." He drained his glass of tsipouro and slammed it onto the tabletop. "I'll send word to their hotel first thing in the morning. I'll tell them... tell them that my sister and I are making the trek and ask if they might wish to join us."

At the mention of Diana, Randy straightened in his chair. "That's a capital idea," he replied.

So capital in fact, he wondered how he might arrange for Barbara to invite Diana before Marcus informed her of his plans. Then she could ride in their carriage.

He briefly thought of Miss Jane. Would it be awkward for her to ride with Antonio and Marcus? The young lady seemed fine when she was with her brother, so perhaps she wouldn't miss the presence of another female.

Randy knew he would appreciate Diana's company, especially if they could discuss Pausanias' writings about the temple whilst on their way.

He really hoped he could convince Barbara to make the invitation. Although it might not matter in which coach they rode, it would matter with whom.

CHAPTER 21
A SISTER CONFIDES IN A BROTHER

*M*eanwhile, *in a coach on the way to the Hotel Aiolos*

When the hotel's coach arrived at the *taverna* to take Antonio and Jane back to the hotel, it was well past dark. Although neither had said much to one another at the noisy eatery where mostly locals were enjoying food and drinks, Jane had been wanting to discuss what she thought she had witnessed in the caves earlier that day.

She couldn't do it with the two protagonists sitting on either side of her at the *taverna*. What had happened to make Marcus Henley wish to hurt Lord Penton?

Could it be because Marcus had learned she was betrothed to Penton? Was he jealous? She remembered their time on the Acropolis the day before. Remembered the look on Marcus' face when David had stepped up to her and not only taken her hand to his lips but had kissed her on the cheek as well.

Had they been in Spain, it would have been a perfectly acceptable greeting. Atop the Acropolis in the company of the sons and daughter of a British aristocrat, it was wholly inappropriate.

"All right. Spit it out," Antonio said after he helped her step up into the coach. "Somethings's bothering you," he added when she scoffed softly at his edict. He took the bench opposite the direction of travel.

"Did Mr. Henley attempt to do violence upon David?" she asked. "I'm quite sure I saw David ducking in order to avoid being punched whilst we were in the caves today."

Antonio chuckled. "I saw that, too. Rather immature of them, but they are second cousins, Sister. Prone to horsing around like most young men do," he claimed.

"But... what if David hadn't ducked down in time?"

Sobering some, her brother considered the query. "Well, I suppose your betrothed would have taken a hit to the nose," he reasoned. "But I could tell it was all in good fun. Nothing to concern yourself with."

"Oh," she breathed in relief. Her brows remained puckered, though, and her brother noticed.

"Was there something else you wished to know?"

She dipped her head. "So... Mr. Henley's attempt at fisticuffs wasn't in some way a means to gain my attentions?"

Antonio stiffened on the bench. "Uh, well, he hasn't exactly hid his regard for you."

"Regard?" she repeated, tamping down the bit of excitement she felt at the thought of Marcus Henley fighting for her favor.

Once again chuckling, Antonio crossed his arms and leaned into the leather squabs. "Regard, yes," he said a bit too forcefully. "Like every other man who meets you, Marcus seems to have fallen in love with you," he accused, his voice betraying his annoyance.

"As women do with you," she argued. She could see Antonio's eyes widen when the exterior lantern bounced and cast its light across his face.

"They do?"

Jane scoffed. "You know they all do, Brother," she said. "Well, maybe not *all*. Miss Diana didn't seem to fall heels over head in love with you when she met you a couple of days ago."

"Which is just as well, since Marcus claims she plans to be a spinster," he countered. "Besides, I don't think I would want a wife who remembers everything she reads or sees or has heard in her entire life."

"What's this?" Jane asked in alarm.

Antonio waved a dismissive hand. "Miss Diana. She is apparently very clever. Very well read. Marcus claims she would have graduated at the top of any of our classes at Cambridge."

"Did you even attend any of your classes?" she asked in a tease.

He seemed about to put voice to a complaint, but the coach came to a stuttering halt in front of the hotel. Before the driver opened the door, Jane asked, "Do you think there is more to Mr. Henley's regard than his attraction to my beauty?"

Antonio inhaled and let the breath out in a *whoosh*. "I think if he was allowed, he would marry you tomorrow, move to London, and get lots of babes on you," he claimed, a moment before the door opened. He stepped out of the coach and turned to assist her.

But Jane remained on the bench, her mouth open in shock at hearing her brother's claim.

The thought of marriage to Marcus Henley might have

seemed far fetched to her the day before, but having spent the day in his company, she'd had the chance to admire the ease with which he conversed with others he had only just met. His confidence whilst navigating the terrain. His knowledge of their surroundings. His rugged handsomeness.

If only he hadn't tried to punch poor David.

He was obviously jealous of David, for despite her brother's assurances that Marcus and David were merely enjoying a bit of horseplay, she was quite sure Marcus intended to do harm to his second cousin.

To her betrothed.

She wasn't quite sure how she felt about it.

"Are you coming inside?"

Torn from her reverie, Jane gasped and immediately saw to exiting the coach. "Apologies," she murmured, stepping down to the pavement in front of the hotel.

She took his proffered arm and glanced up to discover he was watching her. "Marcus is one of the better ones," he said. "Should you decide you don't wish to wait for Penton to grow up."

Scoffing softly at hearing his opinion of David, she said, "I appreciate the information." She didn't try to hide her annoyance—how could anyone form a poor opinion of a young man who was so amiable?

"I'll have water brought up for your bath and come to your door when it's time for breakfast," Antonio said, opening the door to her room for her. "We can go to Hadrian's Arch and see what's left of the Temple of Olympia Zeus," he suggested. When she was beyond the threshold, he added, "Good night." He closed the door before she had a chance to respond, and she was left alone in the dim room.

Settling onto the edge of the bed, Jane sighed. At the

thought that they wouldn't be in the company of any others from England the following day—Antonio hadn't mentioned Marcus or the Bellinghams and their nephews—Jane wondered if it was for the best.

Time away from young men would be good. It was too bad she had to spend it in the company of her brother, though. He was as bad as all the rest.

CHAPTER 22
AN AUNT SUSPECTS SOMETHING IS AFOOT

*L*ater that night

The half-hour it took for Randy to make it back to Engels Mansion gave him an opportunity to rehearse what he planned to say to Barbara.

"Might you be so kind as to send word to Miss Diana that you would like to have her join us in our carriage for our trip to Cape Sounion?" he imagined asking. "I'm sure she would appreciate having a female with whom to speak", he added to himself as he made his way.

What a wonderful idea, Randy. I shall write her a note right now and send it with a servant, he thought Barbara would say in reply.

His lantern dangling from one hand, Randy entered the vestibule and opened the glass door on the lantern. He blew out the meager flame before giving it to the butler. "Has Lady Bellingham retired?"

"She has not. She is in the parlor with Lord Bellingham, Lord Penton, and Master Thomas."

Randy resisted the urge to curse. It didn't bode well that all three of them were still awake. He made his way up the stairs and ducked his head around the edge of the doorway to discover the family was seated around a gaming table. "Are you playing whist?" he asked, joining them to stand next to the table.

"We are, and your aunt is winning. Again," Will replied, the complaint in his voice belying the grin on his face.

She played a card and all three men moaned loudly. "And she has won," Tom said on a groan, tossing his cards onto the green felt. "Did you find Marcus?"

"I did. He is planning to go to Cape Sounion the day after tomorrow with the Fitzsimmonses," he said, his attention going to David. When his cousin didn't react, he turned to Barbara. "I wondered if you might be so kind as to send word to Miss Diana that you would like to have her join us in our carriage for the trip? I'm sure she would appreciate having a female with whom to speak."

Barbara blinked. "I should think Miss Jane would like her company in their coach," she reasoned, turning her attention to her son, David. "Besides, if we host both Miss Jane and Miss Diana in our carriage, you boys will have to beg for rides with Marcus Henley in his coach, or we'll have to find another."

Randy gave a start, realizing David had already put in a request for Diana to invite Jane.

Damnation!

"Perhaps we should put all the men in one coach and allow the ladies to ride in the other," Will offered as he collected the cards and began shuffling them. From the bit of humor he displayed, it was evident he was teasing.

Her face lighting in delight, Barbara said, "Well I shouldn't like to intrude, but that is a most excellent idea. Do you suppose it would be acceptable for me to propose such an arrangement? I could write a quick note and have it delivered in the morning."

It was Randy's turn to blink. This was not going at all as he had imagined. "I suppose," he hedged.

"Given the size of their skirts, it's best if they do ride together," Tom said. He motioned with his hands to indicate the shape of bell skirts in close confines. "I'm always afraid I shall be accused of wrinkling the fabric or stepping upon toes because I'm unable to see their feet due to all that… *gown volume*," he complained.

"But shouldn't there be a man with them? Someone to provide protection?" Randy asked, attempting to insert himself into the all-female coach. "If all the men are in one coach, that would be six… seven of us," he said, remembering to include Michael Henley. He realized too late that desperation sounded in his voice, for Barbara aimed a curious expression in his direction.

"If the carriages travel together, we should be fine," Will said. He lifted the back of his hand to his mouth to hide a yawn. "I'll see what I can arrange in the way of a traveling coach in the morning. In the meantime, I am off to bed." He leaned over and kissed Barbara on the forehead.

"Me, too," David said.

"Me, three," Tom added as the two stood and joined Will as he made his way out of the parlor.

"Aren't you going to retire?" Randy asked, surprised when Barbara remained in her chair.

Her attention on the parlor door, Barbara waited until everyone else had left before she turned to regard him with an arched brow. "Are you sweet on Miss Diana?" she asked, crossing her arms on the tabletop as she leaned forward.

Randy felt the heat of a blush and knew his ears were probably bright red. "Maybe," he murmured. "Probably."

From the way his aunt regarded him, her brows furrowed as if in worry, he thought she was about to scold him. He was instead surprised by her response.

"Oh, this such good news," she murmured.

Randy blinked. "It is?"

She chuckled softly. "Well, to have a son supposedly betrothed to Miss Jane and a nephew wishing to court a viscount's daughter is not what I would have expected for our first week in a new country," she said, grinning.

"Courting might be a bit... *unlikely*," he stammered. Before she could ask why, he took the chair his brother had abandoned and sat down. "She doesn't wish to wed, Aunt Barbara," he blurted. "She claims she wants to be a spinster."

Barbara angled her head to one side and sighed. "What is she? Twenty years old?"

He nodded. "Her father has said she can have her dowry when she turns one-and-twenty."

Boggling, his aunt rounded her eyes in disbelief. "So soon?"

Randy nodded. "She believes she can live comfortably on those funds for the rest of her life."

"Doing what? And living where?" she asked in alarm.

Randy inhaled to answer and realized he didn't know. Diana had never actually mentioned where she intended to live. Surely she wouldn't give up archaeology, though. She apparently loved what she did, even if it did seem to vex her.

She was too invested in solving the puzzles of the past.

"I don't know. She didn't say if she planned to go back to

England, but Marcus intends to, I think after his father and mother are settled here in Athens," he explained. "Perhaps you can learn her thoughts on the matter whilst on the way to the cape?" he suggested.

"Oh, I intend to," she said, although she displayed an expression of resignation. "It's too bad there's nothing for her to dig up in England."

Inhaling sharply, Randy stared at her for a moment. "That's not true," he countered. "The country is full of Roman sites, not to mention evidence of older inhabitants. Why Father says he's fairly sure there was a Roman villa near the river."

When Barbara merely grinned at him, he scoffed quietly. "You were being facetious," he accused.

"I merely wished to provide a suggestion that might have her more amenable to returning to England," she claimed. "As for marriage..."

"The promise of becoming a countess is not much of an incentive for her," he warned. "I don't think she likes London very much."

"I can certainly agree with her on that point," Barbara said sadly. She dipped her head. "You haven't done anything—?"

"No," he replied, shaking his head. "I admit I have been tempted to kiss her, but I haven't." He didn't mention what else he had wanted to do to Diana earlier that evening, when they were lying side by side watching the shooting stars. He was sure Barbara would blister his ears if she knew.

"Do you have reason to believe she would welcome such an act of intimacy?"

The query was so quiet, Randy almost asked her to repeat it. "Uh, no. In fact..." He crinkled his brows in frustration. "No."

Barbara sighed. "Well, I shall discover what I can from the young lady. Your uncle tells me it might take us five or six hours to reach Cape Sounion," she said. "I'm sure part of that time will be spent discussing men."

Randy visibly winced. "No doubt," he murmured.

CHAPTER 23
SIX MEN IN A COACH

Two days later, on the way to Cape Sounion

Although both Marcus and Randy would have preferred to ride in the coach carrying Miss Jane Fitzsimmons and Miss Diana Henley, the two were stuffed into an ancient coach with Antonio Fitzsimmons, Tom Forster, and David and Will Slater.

At least they would not have to censor their remarks for the opposite sex's delicate ears.

The coach was also not as full as it might have been. Michael had elected to stay behind in Athens to continue his work with the archaeologists atop the Acropolis. The older men no doubt saw him as a strapping young lad who could see to the more physical aspects of the dig.

Randy had a passing thought that Diana was probably feeling jealous she hadn't been included in the invitation. If she hadn't agreed to join his family on this jaunt to Cape Sounion, though, Randy wasn't sure he would have agreed to go. For some reason he couldn't quite fathom, he felt a need to provide protection for the young woman.

Marcus certainly didn't seem to show concern for his sister. His infatuation with Miss Jane was obviously clouding his judgement. For the young man to have almost come to blows with David Slater during their tour of the Prison of Socrates was certainly evidence enough, but his disregard for Diana was unconscionable.

Randy's gaze went to the ceiling of the ancient coach. Despite its age, the equipage was still in good shape, although the trap door appeared as if it might come crashing down at any moment. The driver had only opened it a couple of times since their departure from Athens to inform them when they would be stopping to change horses.

For a moment, he wondered about who else might have ridden in the coach—what sights they might have seen whilst touring the ancient country—but his thoughts drifted back to Miss Diana and her brother's lack of regard for her. He might have continued to mentally berate Marcus, but a conversation had begun amongst the others in the coach. He thought it best he pay attention.

"*H*ow is it that you served in the British Navy when you are the oldest and the heir?" Antonio asked, his query directed to Will.

"My grandfather was an admiral in the navy, and since I didn't have a younger brother…" He paused and reconsidered his answer. "At least, not one that I knew about, I asked if I might be allowed a naval career," Will explained.

He had finally met his illegitimate brother, Stephen, when he was commander of the *HMS Greenwich*. Stephen, identical in appearance to Will, was assigned to the same ship. The first time they had come across one another, they had stopped and stared in disbelief before Stephen explained he was Will's half brother by way of one of their father's mistresses.

"My father allowed me to pursue the career with the caveat I had to return to British shores unscathed."

"I take it you did so?" Marcus asked, emerging from a nap he had begun the moment they had taken their seats in the worn velvet squabs of a coach that had at one time belonged to an Ottoman nobleman. It was the largest traveling coach available, and a team of four horses was pulling the equipage.

Meanwhile, the ladies' carriage, a smaller but newer coach, was pulled by two draft horses and had settled into a comfortable trot up ahead of them.

"We were fortunate not to engage in any wars at the time," Will replied.

"Where was your ship assigned?" Antonio asked.

"The Mediterranean, mostly," Will replied.

"So… you've already been here," Marcus reasoned.

Will nodded, although he was quick to say, "Piraeus, of course, but the Ottomans controlled Athens at the time. All of Greece, really. We had to be careful not to cause any incidents."

"You mean like the one that British Navy cadet caused?" Marcus asked. "Back in thirty-three?"

Will gave a start. "I'm not familiar with it. What happened?"

"He broke the nose off a sculpture from the Parthenon. From one of the friezes," Marcus explained.

Will visibly winced. "Deliberately?"

Marcus shrugged. "He had to have climbed up there to reach it," he reasoned. "I'm not sure what he intended."

"Damn. What happened to him?"

"He was fined three pounds."

A low whistle sounded from Antonio. "Did he pay it?"

Marcus lifted a shoulder. "Someone did. The man who is in charge of the ancient monuments here—Mr. Pittakis—asked that the money be used to help fund the first excavations around the Parthenon," he explained. "Mr. Pittakis wrote to Admiral Malcolm—"

"He was the commander-in-chief of the Mediterranean Fleet," Will interrupted.

"—and those funds helped to keep the excavations going," Marcus continued. "Otherwise, the work would have had to stop due to lack of money. They had already spent all the funds provided by some Athenian antiquarian society."

"Three pounds for a nose," Tom said as his eyes rounded. "What did they accomplish with the money?"

Apparently enjoying his status as the one in the know, Marcus said, "Pittakis cleared all the medieval and early modern buildings from the site—"

"All except the Frankish tower," Randy remarked. "It's still there."

"—and he recovered a number of artifacts including three fragments from the north frieze, a metope, and various inscriptions."

At hearing the word 'inscriptions', Randy stared at Marcus. "Any graffiti?" he asked.

Marcus blinked. "I don't think so." He furrowed a brow and leaned toward Tom, his attention on the book his cousin held open on his lap. "What are you reading? And is that... is that Ancient Greek?" he asked in surprise.

"Pausanias' *Description of Greece*," Tom replied. "Thought I would read more about what we're to see today."

"What did he write about Sounion?" Will asked.

Tom held up the tome and recited, "On the Greek

Mainland, facing the Cyclades Islands and the Aegean Sea, the Sounion Promontory stands out from the Attic land. When you have rounded the headland you see a harbor and a temple to Athena of Sounion on the peak of the promontory." He paused. "Those are the opening lines to the book."

"Athena?" Marcus questioned.

"He got it wrong," Tom said. "It's a temple dedicated to Poseidon."

Randy scoffed softly. "If he got that wrong, what else did he mislabel, I wonder?"

"He tends to be more interested in art, I think," Tom murmured. "His descriptions of buildings are lacking, to say the least, but he's quite eloquent when it comes to describing statuary and paintings. He admits he's rather selective in what he includes."

"Admits it where?" Randy asked.

"Volume Three." Tom shuffled through the book before holding it open, his moves overly dramatic. "To avoid misunderstandings," he recited, "in my description of Attica I stated that I was not listing everything in order, but had chosen what is most noteworthy. I repeat the same before I write of Sparta."

Will chuckled softly, which had David briefly waking from the nap he had been taking since the moment the coach had jerked into motion. He hadn't even stirred when the horses were changed in Glyfada. His attention went to the window. "Water," he whispered.

"Saronic Gulf," Antonio said from the other side of the coach. "I think we're about halfway to Sounion."

David allowed a grunt before he nodded and drifted back to sleep.

His manner still guarded when it came to David, Marcus

lowered his voice to say to Tom, "Whatever you do, don't mention to the ladies what boys used to do in Sparta."

Tom furrowed a brow before he widened his eyes. "Oh, the bit about the youths sacrificing puppies?" he asked before adding a look of disgust. "Before they fought one another?"

"No need to elaborate," Will said.

"I don't understand why Pausanias would even mention it," Marcus complained. "Let alone describe it in such detail."

"He frequently digresses," Tom said, "but if he hadn't written about it, we wouldn't know. It's not as if there are any other references to such a practice since no other writings seemed to have survived from that time."

"He is good about mentioning his sources," Randy remarked. "He was obviously wealthy."

"What makes you say that?" Tom asked, apparently ready to argue.

"He was Greek. Well-educated, able to travel, and he had time to pursue cultural interests," Randy replied. "Not unlike some aristocrats we know," he added, waving a hand to include everyone in the coach.

"Except we're not Greek," Marcus reminded him.

"Wouldn't he have been a Roman?" Tom asked absently. "Given the time period? Uh... one-fifty AD?"

The others nodded their agreement.

The memory of Diana's talk about the Colossi of Memnon and Romans in Egypt had Randy suddenly straightening. "He wrote this book for Romans," he said in awe.

"What? What makes you say that?" Tom asked, his attention on the opening pages of the book.

"Wealthy Romans. Remember, Greece would have been part of Rome in the second century. They took holidays and would have used this as a guidebook," Randy explained.

"Much like we're doing?" Tom countered.

Randy gave him a quelling glance. "Something like that," he murmured. When no one else spoke up, he directed his gaze out the coach window and thought of Diana. He looked forward to sharing the tidbit with her whenever they next talked about Pausanias.

Although he would have continued staring at the blue waters of the Aegean, he felt a tap on his knee and turned to discover Marcus leaning in his direction. All the others in the coach were sound asleep. "What is it?" he asked in a hoarse whisper.

"What do you suppose the women are talking about in their carriage?"

Randy blinked. He had secretly hoped he could ride with Diana, and he knew Marcus had planned to be in the same coach as Miss Jane. "Fashion, gossip, and..." He swallowed. "*Us*, no doubt."

Sighing, Marcus sat back in the squabs, tipped his top hat forward, and went to sleep.

Chuckling softly, Randy returned his attention to the sea.

CHAPTER 24
THREE WOMEN IN A CARRIAGE

*M*eanwhile, in the coach directly ahead

Given the amount of space three bell skirts required in a cramped traveling coach, Barbara sat facing the direction of travel while Jane Fitzsimmons and Diana Henley occupied the opposite bench.

Not used to female companionship, Diana had brought along her copy of the first volume of *Description of Greece*, intending to read more about Pausanias' experience at Sounion. She didn't expect the book to remain unopened for so long, but even after two hours of travel, she was still engaged in conversation with Jane and Cousin Barbara.

Her brother Marcus, it seemed, was causing a good deal of consternation for Jane.

"Will you tell me of his true regard?" Jane asked, her brows furrowed. "I beg you share with me what you know about your brother."

Diana exchanged a quick glance with Barbara, the older woman's gloved hand twitching as if she was encouraging her to speak. "Uh, I haven't exactly spent much time in his company these past few years, given he was away at Oxford," she began carefully. "However, I can say with certainty I have never heard him speak of another female as he has spoken of you."

Jane blinked. "What exactly has he said?" There was a hint of breathlessness to her query, as if she feared hearing the truth.

Diana remembered when Marcus had been speaking with Randy up on the roof two nights ago. She recalled what she had overhead. "He is quite smitten with you," she said. "He fancies himself in love, in fact, and is quite vexed that you are apparently betrothed to…" She stopped, realizing she was about to bring David into the conversation. Glancing at Barbara, she sighed.

"My son," Barbara stated, rolling her eyes before she allowed a quiet titter. "Forgive me, Miss Jane, but your betrothal to David was entirely unknown to both Lord Bellingham and myself until only a few nights ago when he admitted he had made a promise to you."

Diana listened intently, curious as to why a young woman of Jane's beauty would accept an offer of marriage during her first Season in London. Surely David was too young to be considering matrimony.

"It wasn't meant to be common knowledge," Jane explained. She leaned forward. "Please accept my apologies. I told no one unless…" Here she allowed a heavy sigh.

"Unless a young man insisted you consider his suit?" Barbara guessed.

Jane nodded. "Or an older man," she added, displaying a wince as she said the words. "Last year was the year of my come-out and my first Season in London. Since my family lives near Bath most of the year, I was entirely unprepared for how I would be received. I didn't know anyone, so I expected to be a wallflower—"

"Oh, my dear," Barbara interrupted with a huff. "You are gorgeous. A viscount's daughter. There was never a chance you would be a wallflower," she said.

Jane dipped her head. "Thank you, my lady. It's very kind of you to say."

"Surely your mother has prepared you for the life of an aristocrat's wife?" Barbara added.

"I believe so," Jane replied, "although..." She turned to Diana. "I never thought I might one day become a... a marchioness. A baroness, perhaps. Mayhap a viscountess. But surely not a marchioness. My mother was from Spain, you see, and although her father was a conte, there are those who believe I cannot be a proper English miss."

Diana gave a start. "But your father is English, is he not?" she asked.

"He is," she acknowledged, lifting a shoulder to indicate it wasn't always enough.

"Well, my son would be lucky to have you as his wife, and he knows it," Barbara insisted.

When Jane didn't respond, Diana did. "But?" she prompted quietly.

The countess' shoulders visibly dropped. "Well, there it is. The truth of the matter," she said sadly. "It's not fair for you to have to wait for David," she said, directing her comment to Jane. "He won't be ready to wed for years, my dear. If you have feelings for someone else—for Mr. Henley or another young man back in England—you are well within your rights to beg off with David."

Jane's eyes rounded. "You would not.. you would not

think me *fast*? Or inconsiderate of your son's regard?" she countered with worry.

Barbara once again tittered. "I would not. Nor would David, I think, given the terms of your arrangement. He is a most amiable young man—"

"Indeed," Jane agreed, her head bobbing up and down.

"—and he falls in love far too easily."

At this bit of news, Jane displayed a look of offense. "Oh?"

Diana could tell from the way Barbara's gaze darted about that the countess realized she had erred with her comment. She placed a gloved hand on Jane's arm. "I'm quite certain she means he easily fell in love with *others* before he met you," she assured her. "But now that my brother has put voice to his desire to court you... for you to be his wife, pray tell, what are your thoughts on becoming the future Viscountess Henley?"

Jane inhaled softly. "Well, Marcus does seem rather attentive," she admitted.

Diana exchanged a quick glance with Barbara when Jane used his Christian name rather than his last name. "Go on," she encouraged.

"I admit I was rather flattered he offered to challenge David to a duel. To gain my affections," Jane continued.

Gasping, Barbara blinked. "When was this?"

Jane appeared to shrink into the squabs. "Whilst we were on our way to the caves. I was quick to inform him he had best not do such a thing. Not because I didn't believe he could win—I think David is probably a crack shot and could take him down with a single bullet—"

"I rather doubt that," Barbara murmured.

"—but I didn't wish for Marcus to become injured because of his regard for me. There are so many other ways he has proven it."

"Oh?" Diana asked, hoping the young lady would elaborate.

"Why, he brought the most wonderful picnic basket the day we toured the caves. *Two* bottles of wine rather than only one, and the very best bread and cheeses," she gushed. "There were even dates, larger and sweeter than I had ever tasted, and figs and olives."

Remembering *she* had been the one to remind her brother about his promise to bring the picnic luncheon, Diana blinked. "Our cook is quite competent," she said in response. "Was there anything else that my brother might have done to impress you?"

A blush colored the young woman's face before she said, "The other night we had dinner at a *taverna* in town. My brother was with us of course, as was David, but it was Marcus who insisted on escorting me. He pointed out all the places where I might have otherwise stumbled on the pavement or tripped on a step."

"As he should have," Diana remarked.

"When he asked me questions, he listened to me."

"Would you not expect him to?" Barbara asked in alarm.

"Well, he didn't interrupt me like Antonio does so frequently. There are times I think my brother believes I am not very clever."

"Almost all men think that about women, my dear," Barbara murmured.

"Well, given the volume of noise in the place—it was quite crowded—it meant Marcus had to lean in closer to hear me."

"He probably liked that," Diana said under her breath.

"Which is when I noticed the scent of him."

Diana blinked, not sure she heard correctly. "His cologne, you mean?"

"A bit of citrus. Amber, surely. But nothing sweet or floral," Jane went on, as if she hadn't heard Diana's query. "For as long as I live, I shall adore that scent."

Exchanging a quick glance with Barbara, Diana swallowed. "I hadn't noticed," she said. Had Marcus begun using colognes? Or had he worn the same one for so many years, she no longer noticed it?

"He wants to live in the capital," Jane continued with excitement. "Learn everything he can about politics and be the very best viscount he can be. Even before he inherits."

Diana stared at Jane for a moment, no longer able to hide her surprise at hearing the young woman's assessment of her older brother. Marcus had never once told her of his desire to live in London, nor of his interest in politics. Up until that moment, she had assumed he would follow in their father's footsteps. Become an archaeologist. Continue the search for the mosaics covering all the floors of what had at one time been the realm of the Greeks and Romans. "Are we still speaking of Marcus Henley?" she asked in awe.

It was Jane's turn to blink before she inhaled softly. "He has not told you any of his plans? Of his intention to apply for a writ of acceleration?" she asked. "He said he should have no trouble given your father's frequent absences from London during Parliament."

Feeling a mix of disappointment and disbelief, Diana shook her head. "Not a bit of it," she admitted, swallowing a sob. "So he must really hold you in very high regard."

Jane displayed a wan grin. "Oh, please, Miss Diana, you must tell me. Am I wrong to want him as my husband?" she asked quietly. "Instead of David?"

Diana inhaled softly. If Marcus and Jane married, she would no longer have him as a pretend protector when her parents were away—or as an impediment to her life as a spinster. As for how he would behave as a husband, she had no idea. "You are not wrong," she said, realizing her brother's interest in Jane must have been far more than an infatuation. "If he should do anything to vex you, though, I can assure you I will scold him most vehemently."

Grinning ear to ear, Jane said, "Oh, would you? He's frightened to death of you, so a scolding from you would mean all the world," she claimed.

Diana gave a start, her attention going to Barbara when she heard her cousin-by-marriage attempting to suppress a chuckle. "I was not aware of his fear of me," she said, finally allowing a grin. "But I assure you, I shall use it to *your* best advantage," she promised.

Jane dipped her head. "I've always wanted a sister."

Swallowing, Diana sobered. "As have I," she whispered. When she turned to Barbara, she saw tears in the older woman's eyes. "Oh, dear. Please don't take offense, my lady," she pleaded. "David is a very amiable young man whom I think shall find the perfect marchioness when he is older."

Barbara shook her head. "Oh, I do not take offense at all," she assured them. "So please do not take offense when I tell you I will be most relieved when David is no longer betrothed. He is simply far too young to marry."

Jane and Diana nodded their agreement.

"I will break off our betrothal with him. Later today, if I'm allowed some privacy with him," Jane promised.

"I will see to it you have that time, my dear," Barbara assured her, her gaze going to the west. "Oh, my. I had no idea we would be traveling so close to the water," she said in awe.

Diana grinned. "The Aegean is especially blue today," she said. "Would you like to hear what Pausanias thought of where we are going?" She lifted her book from the bench and was about to turn to the first page of text when Barbara cleared her throat.

"Actually, I was rather hoping we could talk about you and my nephew," the countess said.

Stunned at the comment, Diana sighed and set aside the book. "You are referring to Lord Forster?" she asked, embarrassed at how her body responded to the mere thought of the young man who would one day be the Earl of Gisborn.

"You know I am," Barbara replied quietly. "And despite the fact that he is only a couple of years older than David, I am of the opinion he is ready to consider candidates to be his eventual countess."

"He does seem older than his years," Jane said brightly. "He carries himself with such confidence, and he seems very responsible, too."

Diana aimed a look of disbelief in the young woman's direction. When had Jane had a chance to spend any time in Randy's presence? When he wasn't annoying her on the Acropolis, he was lying next to her on the roof of the house. "Whatever gave you that impression?" she asked.

Jane angled her head to one side. "I admit I have only had the benefit of his introduction that first day at the Parthenon," she replied. "But he exudes a confidence one can only gain with age and experience. His father has surely put him in charge of something important with respect to the Gisborn earldom." Here she glanced over at Barbara, as if for confirmation of her claim.

"She has the right of it," Barbara agreed. "Although many in London would not agree that an heir should be tasked with physical labor, both Randy and Tom have certainly done more than their fair share of it for the Gisborn farms. Without complaint, I might add."

Diana remembered how easily Randy had lifted her so she could stand atop his shoulders to reach the inscription in the Erechtheion. He had never once complained that her boots were digging into his shoulders, nor had he commented about her weight being a problem as she took care and a good deal of time to trace the figures carved into the marble cella. Even when her descent seemed as if it would be problematic—she hadn't given a thought as to how she would get down once she was up atop his shoulders—his solution had been simple, even if she had felt a good deal of embarrassment at how close he had to hold her body during her dismount.

Trust me, he had said.

What else could she do but trust him?

"Has he made his intentions known?" Barbara queried. "I ask only because he seems more than smitten with you," she added.

Diana glanced over at Jane and noted the young lady's barely suppressed look of anticipation. Apparently it was her turn to be the subject of a discussion regarding a young man's regard. She wasn't about to admit what Randy had said to her, though. Especially the recommendation that she take more than one lover. "Has he said something to *you*, my lady?" she asked.

Barbara seemed to think on the query a moment before she sighed. "I admit I might have overheard him in conversation with my husband."

"Oh?"

A smile suddenly brightened Barbara's face. "It seems you vex him," she said, an elegant brow arching as if to emphasize her words. "Terribly."

Torn between taking offense—he was vexed by *her?*—or feeling triumphant—her methods of rebuffing his interest in her project were apparently having some effect—Diana merely stared at the countess.

"In the very best way, I should think," Barbara added when Diana didn't offer a response.

Diana dipped her head. "I admit we have had some interesting conversations," she said carefully. "Many having to do with my desire to be a spinster."

Here she saw Barbara's happy expression falter.

"Oh? Why ever would you wish such a situation for yourself?"

Diana straightened in the squabs. "I do not wish to become a man's property," she stated. "My father has agreed to give me my dowry so that I might have the funds with which to live. Next year, when I am one-and-twenty."

Barbara seemed to deflate before her eyes. "Oh," she said, sounding ever so sad. "So you won't be having any children?"

"That's correct," Diana replied. "I wish to pursue archaeology as my father has been doing."

"Here in Greece?" Barbara pressed.

The query had Diana pausing a moment before she said, "Well, for now. I do hope to one day explore some of the temples in Egypt. Mayhap look for Roman ruins elsewhere."

"By yourself?" Jane asked, her eyes wide with fright.

"Well, I would require a traveling companion, of course," Diana hedged.

"Servants, too, I should think," Barbara put in. "A laundress, at the very least."

"Possibly," Diana replied, not having thought that far ahead.

"You're terribly brave," Jane said in awe.

Tittering, Diana shook her head. "I do not think I am brave" she replied. "I only wish to unearth the past."

Jane appeared ready to say something, but when she paused too long, Diana asked, "What is it?" She watched as the young woman blushed.

"Will you take a lover?" Jane asked in a whisper.

Diana's eyes rounded. "I... I rather doubt it," she stammered.

"Because, I heard tell of an independent woman in Bath —a bluestocking, I believe she was—who not only took a lover, but had a different one for *every night of the week*," Jane said in a hoarse whisper. "She even called them by the days of the week they were with her. Mr. Monday, Mr. Tuesday... There was talk her favorite was Mr. Saturday because when she attended church, she always displayed rather high color."

Barbara's mouth dropped open as did Diana's, which left them both speechless for a moment before Diana lifted her hand to her mouth and giggled nervously.

Had Randy said something to Jane? Or had Jane overheard their conversation up on the roof? Neither scenario seemed likely. "A bit scandalous, wouldn't you say, my lady?" she asked, directing her words to Barbara.

"Scandalous and rather unlikely," Barbara argued. "I have enough trouble managing *one* man in my life—well, and two boys. I cannot imagine having to manage *seven* of them."

Jane giggled. "Marcus will surely be enough for me, I should think," she said happily.

Diana couldn't help but think of Randy just then. Of their time on the roof. His manner had been teasing and yet not.

He had been entirely too forward. But he had seemed genuinely concerned about her. Worried, even.

The thought of sharing a bed with him had her insides all in a tumble. The most curious sensations darted beneath her skin and left her core throbbing with desire.

Unlike most girls her age, she knew what happened in a marriage bed. Knew what was involved. She had seen the drawings in her father's books. Sexual congress had been happening since the dawn of mankind. Throughout history, every civilization had existed because couples had either chosen or been forced by circumstance to lie together, and women had then given birth to the next generation. Civilizations were never wiped out due to a lack of sexual congress. Quite the contrary in some cases.

History was filled with stories of those who took lovers. Not all of them ended badly. Would it really be so awful if she were to take a lover?

Had Randy encouraged her to take a lover because *he* wanted to fill the role?

Why else would he even bring it up? Unless he only wished to torment her?

She remembered the placement of his hands as he helped her climb onto his shoulders. The feel of his arms as they pressed against her sides when he guided her back down again. The way he had watched her, ready to do what was necessary should she lose her balance and begin to fall.

Trust me.

Diana inhaled sharply when a frisson of pleasure shot through her middle. When she glanced over at Barbara, she discovered the countess watching her with a most curious expression.

"He's not going to ruin you, if that's what you're thinking," she said softly.

Staring at the countess for a moment, Diana finally nodded. "I would not expect him to," she replied.

"I mean to say, not unless you want him to."

Blinking several times, Diana glanced over to discover Jane's eyes filled with amusement.

"And if he does," Barbara went on, her back stiffening so she straightened in the squabs, "he will do the honorable thing and take you to wife."

"Whether I want him to or not?" Diana countered, immediately regretting her words. "Apologies. It's as you said. He's not going to ruin me because... because I won't allow it."

Despite feeling ever so relieved at having declared her intentions—or lack thereof—Diana couldn't shake the niggling feeling she wouldn't have the final word on the matter.

CHAPTER 25
ACCOMMODATIONS CAUSE AN ISSUE

ear Cape Sounion

When the women's carriage halted in front of a simple structure located near a sandy beach, the driver hopped down from his bench and opened the door. "Legrena," he stated, waving in the direction of the water.

"The sand is so white," Jane said in awe, stepping out of the carriage with the help of the driver.

"The water is so blue," Barbara murmured, joining Jane to stare at the scene before them.

"The temple is magnificent," Diana said, her hand lifted to her forehead to shade her eyes as she stared up at the cliff adjacent to the beach.

The other two followed her line of sight and both gasped. "Is that it? The Temple of Poseidon?" Jane asked in surprise.

"Indeed," Diana replied.

"Elena will see to your rooms," the driver said, indicating the older woman who had joined him. She was slightly bent, her back displaying a noticeable dowager's hump. From the gaps apparent when she smiled, she was also missing a number of teeth.

The three women curtsied before they helped themselves to their valises, the groom having lined them up next to the carriage. They followed Elena into the building, waving when the older traveling coach carrying the men stuttered to a halt at the edge of the road directly in front of the lodgings.

Even before the equipage had completely stopped, David already had the door open and was hurrying to offer his arm to Jane.

"Are you well?" he asked, slightly breathless from his quick jog. He took her valise from her and then lifted her hand to his lips.

Jane dipped a quick curtsy and grinned as she placed her arm on his. "I am. It's been a very pleasant trip." She arched a dark brow. "And you, Lord Penton?"

"I spent most of it sleeping," he admitted. "I wondered if I might be allowed a few minutes of your time?"

"Now?" she asked in surprise.

"Well... before we walk up to the temple," he stammered. "I wish to speak with you on a matter of... well, some importance," he said.

Jane inhaled softly. "All right," she agreed. "Perhaps there is someplace inside where we might converse," she hedged.

"Oh, we'll want to eat something, too," he said.

"Very well."

*B*ehind them, Will rushed up to take Barbara's valise from her. Despite the brim of the small hat she wore, he managed to land a kiss on her cheek. "You look especially fetching today," he said, offering his arm.

She tittered before sobering. "You say that as if you hadn't already seen me several times today," she chided.

"I rather wish I could have spent the entirety of it with you," he said.

Barbara glanced up at him, about to thank him for his regard when it dawned on her why he would say such a thing. "Was it terribly uncomfortable for you to be stuffed into that coach with all the boys?"

He chuckled. "Tight quarters, yes, but I certainly didn't expect a history lesson," he said. "Made the trip go by much faster, though."

"Ancient history or... more recent?" she asked.

"A bit of both," he murmured. "All is well, though. Or at least, I think it shall be by the time we return to Athens."

Barbara widened her eyes. "Well, now you have me all curious."

"Fear not. I shall tell you everything I know and all that I suspect," he promised.

"I look forward to hearing about it," she murmured.

*M*eanwhile, Randy had hurried to offer an arm to Diana. "How are you?" he asked, taking her valise from her hold. "I trust your ride was smoother than ours."

She tittered at seeing how dusty their traveling coach had become during the trip from Athens. "It was comfortable enough. The conversation was... diverting, I suppose. A bit unexpected."

They entered the white rectangular building, the shingle above the door painted with the words *Legrena Hotel* in Greek. After the brightness of a day that had grown almost too warm for comfort, the dim interior was blessedly cool. A rug covered most of the marble floor leading to a corridor that split off in opposite directions. To the left, Elena stood behind a marble counter bearing a line of ancient iron keys, and two young women, dressed alike, stood at the end of the counter ready to escort guests to their rooms.

Randy furrowed his brows, his gaze returning to Diana after his quick perusal of the place. "Did my aunt say something—?"

"She was the perfect traveling companion. As was Miss Jane," Diana said, arching a reddish-blonde brow. "I never even had a chance to read Pausanias' account of this place."

"Oh, don't bother," Randy said on a huff. "He got it all wrong on the very first page."

About to ask what he meant, Diana's attention was caught by one of the young women. Dressed in a tight-fitting vest trimmed with gold ornaments and a long, multi-layered skirt —one of red and the other of gold—her hair was covered with a translucent scarf secured beneath her chin. On her feet were tiny slippers, the fronts curled up to a point. She curtsied to them and indicated they should follow her.

Exchanging glances of confusion, they did her bidding and were soon in the first room off the corridor to the left. Furnished sparsely with only a bed, two wooden chairs, and a simple table, it featured a window with a view of the beach and the Aegean Sea. A pitcher and a bowl were perched on a stand next to the window.

The girl handed them a ring from which hung a key. She pointed to the door. "For locking," she said in heavily-accented English. She once again curtsied and quickly took her leave.

Diana blinked. "Uh..." She turned to see Randy

attempting to stifle a chuckle at the same moment Jane and David were being led past their open door by the other young woman. "Oh, dear. I think there's been some misunderstanding," she said in alarm.

"We'll sort it," Randy said, his amusement still apparent. He took two long steps to the open door and glanced out to discover Elena leading Barbara and Will to a room across the entry and down the opposite corridor. "I expect I'll be sharing a room with Tom and—" He stopped speaking when he saw that Tom and Marcus were being led by their escort to the room right next to the one into which Barbara and Will had disappeared. Behind them, Antonio entered the last room.

Joining him at the door, Diana peeked around the corner to the left to see Jane doing the same thing as she was, although Jane was displaying an expression of shock. Diana was about to wave for Jane to join her, but before she could do so, Jane disappeared into the room, the heavy wooden door shutting with a *thud*. "No," she whispered, a hand going to her mouth. She turned to stare at Randy, her eyes rounding with worry.

"He's not going to do anything untoward," Randy said in a quiet voice.

"Does it matter? They're in a room. By themselves," she argued. "And the door is closed."

"As are we," he said at the same moment his coach driver appeared with his small trunk. "*Sas efcharistó*," he said, pulling a coin from his pocket to give to the man.

"Our door is open," she stated.

Randy dipped his head. "I think David just needs a moment with her. I'll move to that room and she can come here when they're finished," he explained.

Diana inhaled softly. "Is he... is he breaking it off with *her*? Their... their betrothal?" she stammered.

The way she asked had Randy furrowing his blond brows. "Was *she* planning to break it off with him?"

Clamping her mouth shut, Diana picked up her valise and moved it to the table. She withdrew a bath linen and moved to the window, removing her straw bonnet as she did so. "It's really not for me to say," she murmured.

About to press for more information, Randy decided he would learn of the couple's situation later. He shoved his hands into his pockets. "What are you doing?"

"Washing my face," Diana replied, pouring some of the water into the bowl. She dipped the linen into the water and drew the wet cloth over her upraised face, sighing as she did so.

Randy watched from where he stood, swallowing at the sight of her. Given the brightness beyond the window, she practically appeared in silhouette. He was reminded of when they had been on the roof watching the shooting stars, her dressed in only a night rail and appearing almost ethereal in the darkness. He could imagine pulling her into his arms and kissing her, pressing his forehead to hers as he used a thumb to caress her cheek and the edge of his palm to push away the riot of fine reddish-blonde curls that framed her face. He was sure he would discover a sprinkling of freckles on her otherwise porcelain complexion.

"I'd like to go up to the temple right now," she said. "While there is plenty of light."

Pulled from his reverie, Randy blinked. "I'll escort you," he offered. He watched as she extracted her leather satchel from her valise. "Did you wish to change clothes?" He waved toward the door. "I can wait for you out in the entry."

"No," she replied. "I wore an old gown for a reason, and I don't wish to take the time," she added, lifting the strap of her leather satchel over her head so it rested on the opposite shoulder. "The sun is already past its zenith."

Suppressing the urge to groan at seeing how the satchel strap accentuated her bosom, Randy said, "I could carry that for you."

"Thank you, but you're going to carry this," she said, pulling a small wooden box from the valise. She handed it to him.

"What is it?" he asked, hefting the rectangular box featuring a brass clasp and and a pair of hinges to determine it wasn't very heavy. He tucked it under an arm.

"My paint box." She extracted another wooden device from her valise and handed it to him. "Here's the easel."

He arched his brows in surprise as he took what appeared to be a number of square wooden sticks with brass bolts at the end of them. "How can this be an easel?" he asked in confusion.

"It's all collapsed now, of course, but when it unfolds, it makes for a serviceable stand," she said, waving a hand in the air dismissively.

"Do you have a canvas?" he asked, tempted to glance into the valise. Had she even brought any clothes?

"I've one in here along with my sketchpad," she said, tapping the satchel as she hurried to the door.

He moved to join her, offering his arm. "Does the fact that you're going to be painting mean you're not going to look for inscriptions?" he asked, managing to sound disappointed as they made their way past the marble desk—he nodded to Elena as they did so—and out the door.

She gave a start. "Of course I am. I plan a thorough walk

all the way around the stylobate," she replied, referring to the base of the temple. "But given there aren't any cellae, I expect I'll only find carvings on the square columns or on the blocks of the stylobate."

"I'm told Lord Byron's name can be found on one of them," he said.

"No doubt," she replied, rolling her eyes.

Randy glanced back at the hotel. "Aren't you... hungry?"

She shook her head, but paused to open her satchel. She reached in and pulled out a linen cloth wrapped around some dates, figs, olives, and a hunk of goat cheese. Offering him the food, she watched as an expression of happiness appeared on his face.

"Oh, bless you, Miss Diana," he said, helping himself to a few of the fruits before they resumed walking up the steep road to the temple.

"You're welcome, Mr. Saturday," she replied, smirking.

Seeing her expression of amusement, Randy realized she was teasing him, but he wasn't about to ask what had her using the odd name. Besides, the uphill trek had them struggling to catch their breath and made conversation difficult.

They were entirely breathless when they reached the top, both stopping to stare at the Temple of Poseidon.

CHAPTER 26
BREAKING OFF A
BETROTHAL

eanwhile, back at the hotel

"Whatever are you doing?" Jane asked in alarm, her eyes wide as she watched David close the door to their hotel room and stand with his back pressed against it.

"Ssh," he responded, holding a finger to his lips. "I need only a moment of your time, and then I will take my leave," he whispered.

"They saw us—"

"They won't say anything," he claimed. "I'll make sure of it," he added. "Would you like to sit down?" He was about to indicate the wooden chair that sat in the corner but realized there was only the one. He instead waved to the bed.

"If it's all the same to you, I would prefer to stand. I've been sitting all day," she replied. "What's this about?" She stripped her gloves from her hands and tossed them and her reticule onto the table.

David dipped his head. "I wish to learn of your true regard for Marcus," he said.

Jane opened her mouth to respond but quickly closed it. "David," she murmured quietly.

"I wish you to know that when I made my promise to you last Season, I meant it."

"I never doubted it," she assured him.

"That you could honestly claim you were betrothed to me as a means to prevent unwanted suitors," he went on.

"I do appreciate what you have done more than you can know," she said, nodding. "You have saved me from having to fend off a number of would-be suitors, most of whom I found rather odious or immature."

"I had every intention to wed you," David went on, as if he hadn't heard a word she said.

Jane's eyes rounded. "Had?" she repeated.

"Have," he said on a sigh. "But Jane, I cannot help but notice how you are with Marcus. How he is with you."

Dipping her head, Jane turned to face the window. "Mr. Henley has been rather attentive," she admitted.

"Jane, he wants to marry you," David stated.

Despite the fact that she didn't want him to see her look of indecision, nor the tears that threatened, Jane whirled around to face him. "He's too young to marry, though, don't you think?" she asked, crossing her arms as if to hug herself.

"Is he?" he countered. "Jane, he may only be three-and-twenty, but he is older in other respects," David said gently. "He already knows what he wants in this life. He is ready to inherit. He has an interest in politics and could easily take his father's seat in Parliament should he be granted a writ of acceleration."

Jane inhaled softly. "Already?"

David nodded. "He is ready for a life in London."

"You... you noticed that, too?" she asked rhetorically.

Chuckling softly, David stepped closer to her. "We all have." He lifted her hand to rub his thumb over the betrothal ring he had given her. "Please know that if you have developed feelings for him... if you feel any affection for him at all—"

"Oh, David," she said softly.

"I will not hold you to our betrothal," he finished. "Remember, my promise was to be your husband should there not be another whom you liked better."

Tears brightened her eyes, and Jane raised her face in an attempt to keep them from falling. "Oh, David. I'm so sorry," she whispered on a sob.

"There's no need to be," he said, reaching into a waistcoat pocket to pull out his handkerchief. He offered it to her at the same moment a tear streaked down her cheek. "You already know I am quick to fall in love," he murmured. "Not that I've ever kissed anyone but you," he quickly added.

She sniffled. "Actually, until earlier today, I didn't know that about you."

David's gaze darted to the side. "Oh. Well, I, um..." He scratched the back of his neck. "I tend to fall in love with nearly every young woman I meet," he admitted lamely. "You, of course, have meant more to me than all the others, though."

Jane sniffled and pulled the ring from her finger. She held it out to him. "So, I suppose this is you telling me I should accept an offer from Marcus should he be so inclined?" she asked curtly.

"Oh, Jane," he said, hesitantly taking the ring from her. "Only if he is what *you* really want."

Once again crossing her arms, Jane sniffled. "If he doesn't make me an offer?"

David held up the ring. "It's yours," he stated. He stepped forward and kissed her on the cheek. "If you do not know it already, let me assure you I have imagined a future with you. A life at Devonville House. Children. Entertainments. Walks in the park," he murmured quietly. "If he does not propose marriage, and if no one else captures your heart, then you can have mine."

Jane inhaled softly. "Oh, David," she whispered, reaching up to place a hand against the side of his face. She pulled his head down to kiss him on the cheek. "Thank you," she whispered.

They both stiffened at the sound of footsteps out in the corridor.

"I need to get out of here," David whispered, tucking the ring into his waistcoat pocket before rushing toward the window.

"You needn't leave," she countered, moving to the chair in the corner. She set it aside and pulled on a rectangular wooden door that was only about three feet tall. Beyond the opening in the foot-thick wall was the adjacent room. "I'll join Diana in her room. Push my valise in after me," she instructed as she grabbed her gloves and reticule from the table.

David watched as she wriggled her way into the next room, her bell skirt making the passage more difficult. At the sound of a knock at the door, he tossed the valise through the opening. "Coming!" he called. He closed the panel and moved the chair back into place.

He opened the heavy wooden door to discover his parents staring at him with wide eyes. "Are we leaving for the temple now?" he asked.

Will stepped into the room and glanced around. "Where is...?"

"Randy? I think Miss Diana asked that he escort her up to the temple some time ago," David replied.

The door to the next room off the corridor opened and Jane stepped out. "Are we leaving for the temple now?" she asked of Barbara.

"Oh, there you are. We were led to believe there might have been some confusion with the room assignments," Barbara said, sounding ever so relieved as she directed a wink at Jane. "We expected to find you in this room. With our son."

"Yes. There must have been some confusion," Jane agreed. "They delivered the wrong trunk to our room."

"That must be Randy's," David said. "I'll move it into this room, and we can be on our way. That is, if anyone knows where I might find some food first?"

His mother tittered as she lifted the basket she held over one arm. "We'll have a picnic next to the temple," she said.

"If I carry it up there, can I get started eating early?" he asked in a pleading voice.

Barbara sighed and handed it over to him. "Don't eat everything," she warned.

"Has anyone seen my brother?" Jane asked.

"Here," Antonio called out from the other end of the corridor. He had changed top coats and was making his way to the entry along with Tom and Marcus.

Jane shook out her skirts, collected her reticule and gloves from her room, and joined them. When Marcus was quick to offer his arm, she took it and gave him a brilliant smile, her gloves still clutched in her other hand. "You must tell me *everything* you gentlemen talked about in your coach today," she ordered.

Marcus exchanged quick glances with the others before he said, "We spoke of history, mostly, but…" he paused. "If you insist…"

Although she pretended interest in his recollection of their earlier discussions, Jane spent most of the climb up to the temple imagining what her life with Marcus Henley would be like in London.

Despite occasionally wiggling her fingers in the hope that he would notice she no longer wore David's ring, Marcus never let on if he did or not.

CHAPTER 27
A TEMPLE DISPLAYS ITS SECRETS

*C*ape Sounion

Surrounded on three sides by the Aegean Sea, the Cape of Sounion would have been a beautiful sight even without the Temple of Poseidon. As the group topped the promontory, a combination of 'oohs' and 'ahs' sounded. The sun, still well above the turquoise waters to the west, cast the twenty-foot tall fluted marble columns in a yellowish white. Pockets of scrub brush, flowers, and the rubble remains of a now-missing temple covered the rest of the site.

"I see my sister has already begun working," Marcus groused, his attention on Diana. She was kneeling before one of the marble blocks making up the base of the temple and writing something on her sketchpad.

"And my brother seems to be at her beck and call," Tom murmured. Randy was in front of the temple assembling what appeared to be an easel.

"Remind me of the mythology of this place," Barbara said to her husband, clutching his arm as they stepped over the uneven ground and around several clumps of gorse and giant fennel. The yellow flowers were interspersed with the purple blooms of phrygana and covered much of the area around the temple.

"Well, this is where Aegeus, the king of Athens, jumped to his death after mistakenly believing his son, Theseus, had died," Will began.

"Was this story in the *Odyssey*?" she asked.

"Indeed. Theseus had gone to Crete to challenge the Minotaur. If his ship returned with black sails, it meant he had been killed, but if he was victorious, the ship was to be outfitted with white sails."

"Well, if Aegeus jumped to his death, then he must have seen black sails," she reasoned.

"He did."

"But I thought Theseus slayed the Minotaur," she argued.

"He did. But he forgot to change the sails from black to white to signal his victory," Will explained.

"How awful." Barbara displayed a grimace at the same moment they joined Diana in her perusal of the stylobate.

"Have you discovered anything unusual, Sister?" Marcus asked.

Diana straightened and took a step back. "Well, it was obviously an important building," she remarked as she regarded the ruin.

"How can you tell?" David asked.

"The stylobate," she replied. "This raised platform," she clarified. "This high base separated it from the other structures that used to be located here." She turned around and waved a hand to indicate the other, mostly flat area they had crossed to reach the temple. "There used to be an Archaic temple in this location before this one was built," she added. "Before the Persians destroyed it." She moved to the southeast corner and bent to study the blocks nearest the ground. "This is so odd," she murmured.

"What do you mean?" Randy asked, joining her. He bent down, his hands pressed to his knees.

"Does this look like the same marble to you?" she asked, pointing to the block at the base of the corner.

Randy gave a start. "Reminds me of limestone," he said, reaching out to scrape a thumbnail over the rough surface. He did the same with the block above and scoffed. "These are different," he remarked. "Do you suppose they—?"

"Built this temple atop the other?" she finished for him.

"If a base was already here, why not?" he reasoned.

"I can hardly wait until Father sees this," she said with a grin.

Standing behind them, Tom surveyed the open area next to the temple. Although no other buildings were located on the headland, there was evidence there might have been given the number of marble pieces embedded in the ground. He kicked the protruding edge of one. "Where did all this marble come from, I wonder? I can't imagine they would transport it all the way from the quarry near Athens."

"It's Agrileza marble," Randy stated. "From the Agrileza mines near here," he added. "There used to be a temple to Athena on this site, made from the same marble," he added. "And a statue of Poseidon would have been inside this one." He pointed to the site's only remaining temple.

Diana gave a start, obviously surprised he knew the history of the Temple of Poseidon. "You'll find this marble is far rougher than that used for the temples on the Acropolis," she said. "That's why it doesn't appear shiny under the sun, like the Parian marble does."

Using a finger, Antonio began counting under his breath,

but before he could say anything, Diana said, "Six columns at the front and back and thirteen along each side—"

"Thirty-eight originally," Tom interrupted, his attention on the travel guide Donald had composed. He glanced up and noted Diana's expression of annoyance. "Oh, apologies. I knew it was in my cousin's notes," he said lamely.

"Seventeen made it to modern times," she continued. "However, about fifteen years ago, two of the Doric columns collapsed. At least one of the two, the fifth from the northeast corner," she lifted a hand to point to where the front columns had at one time been located, "was dismantled on the orders of Commander Paulucci of the Imperial Austrian Navy."

"Dismantled?" Will repeated, his brows furrowed in dismay.

"The columns were originally constructed by stacking the drums one atop another," she explained, pointing to the nearest column to show the seams between the drums. "He took one of the columns to the Venetian Arsenal in 1826," she explained. "Apparently, there were five of the eight original drums as well as the column capital, and they were reassembled in the garden of a palazzo on Fondamenta Briati in Venice." She rolled her eyes. "At least it was a neoclassical palazzo."

"How is it you know about that particular column?" Randy asked as he joined them.

"The blocks bore a number of etchings," she replied. "Graffiti," she added in disgust.

"Venetian?" Tom guessed.

She nodded. "And French sailors," she said. "*Le Zefire Bric Du ROI eighteen-sixteen,* is one that comes to mind."

"Eighteen-sixteen?" Will murmured, his gaze on his mind's eye. "Huh."

"Were *you* here then?" Barbara asked him.

He shook his head. "Not while the French were here, but mayhap shortly after," he replied. He pointed south and drew a line in the air toward the east, indicating a path through the Aegean Sea between the headland and the nearest island. "I remember we passed by here early one morning. I saw this temple at sunrise," he went on.

"You would have seen it with seventeen columns," Diana said in awe.

Will's face took on a look of embarrassment. "I have to admit I did not count them."

"What of the other column that collapsed?" Randy asked, noting that although there were a couple of column bases, there were no separate drums strewn about on the stylobate. Surely someone would have reassembled them if there had been.

"It's in England," Tom stated.

Everyone turned to stare at him. "At the British Museum?" Barbara asked.

"One drum is there," he acknowledged. "I saw it on display before we departed England," he added.

"What of the rest of it?"

"It's under the bust of the sixth Duke of Devonshire. In the garden of Chatsworth House," David stated, his gaze on his mind's eye. "Well, four of the drums are there," he added. "I don't remember there being more than that."

They all turned to stare at David. "You've seen them?"

He shrugged. "I was invited to a garden party there by one of my friends at university," he said. "A huge conservatory was under construction at the time." He motioned with his hands to indicate the unusual shape of the building.

"I haven't been to Derbyshire in years," Randy murmured.

"I hear it's an excellent place to go on one's wedding trip," Jane said, her hand still on Marcus' arm.

"I've heard the same," he said, glancing down to stare at her hand. His attention went to her face when she turned to smile at him.

"When I was your age, my friends used to claim Rome was the best place to go on a wedding trip," Barbara said.

"Which is why I am taking you there after we go to Egypt," Will said.

"You're planning to go to Egypt?" Diana asked. She straightened, her gaze darting to Randy for confirmation.

"When we're done touring Greece," he confirmed.

"Oh," she said on a sigh. She returned her attention to the column base she had been studying near the back of the temple.

From the front of the temple, Antonio shouted, "Jane, you have to come see this!" He scrambled up onto the temple floor to stand before a square column.

Marcus and Jane hurried between the clumps of purple and yellow flowers to join him. When she paused to sort how to negotiate her way onto the base, Marcus said, "Allow me," as he placed his hands at her waist and simply lifted her onto the marble base.

She inhaled sharply but gave him a brilliant smile as she held out a hand to help him up onto the block. Once they were both on the temple's floor, they rushed to where her brother stood with his arms crossed.

"Oh, he *was* here," Jane murmured excitedly. "Miss Diana, you must come and see this." She turned to Marcus. "Did you ever meet him?" she asked.

He shook his head. "I did not have the honor. I do have

one of his books of poems, however. Those that were inspired by his time here in Greece."

Holding up her skirts as she made her way around some brush and up the stairs of the stylobate, Diana stopped short at the sight of the column base that had everyone's attention. Surrounded by other names, the name 'Byron' was carved into the marble in curvy English letters.

"Do you suppose he actually did it?" Randy asked after a moment of staring at the inscription. "The carving, I mean."

"Undoubtedly," Diana said, her attention going to all the other names etched into the flat ancient marble.

"Look at all these other names," Randy whispered, using a finger to trace several that appeared to be of Roman origin. "There's English and French and..." He sighed and moved around to another side of the column to continue his perusal. "Latin and Greek."

"What are those carvings all about?" Barbara asked, pointing up to a frieze located along the top of an interior colonnade.

Diana followed her line of sight to see a long set of carved images. "They are scenes from mythology," she replied. "There's a battle between the Centaurs and Lapiths," she explained as she pointed to one section. "And the Amazonomachy—"

"The battle with the Amazons," Randy interpreted for his aunt.

"And the deeds of Theseus," Diana finished.

"Aren't they all meant as an allegory for the Athenians' victory over the Persians?" Will asked. He had been at the other end of the temple studying the frieze while the others were in search of names they might recognize on the square columns and along the base of the temple.

"Democracy over tyranny," Randy murmured, unaware of how his uncle regarded him with appreciation.

"Is anyone else starving?" David asked. He stood in the middle of the temple holding up the basket of food he had carried for his mother.

A round of chuckles ensued before several joined him, settling on the marble floor or sitting with their backs against the interior columns to enjoy the bread, goat cheese, olives and fruits that their cook in Athens had packed for them early that morning.

"The sun is going down so quickly," Jane remarked, helping herself to one of the figs. "The sky is gorgeous."

"Oh!" Diana said in dismay. She had been studying a series of etchings on the northwestern base of the temple, her back to the setting sun. She hurried to where Randy had set up the easel on the other side of the temple. "Where are my paints?"

"Here," he said, joining her to open the box he had set on a nearby rock. The size of the marble block suggested it had one time been part of a building on the site, but its edges had been worn away by time, wind, and water. "What is your intention?" he asked, before popping an olive into his mouth.

"I'm going to paint the sunset," she said.

Randy moved to stand behind where she had taken a seat on the rough block. The outlines of columns and the base of the temple had already been drawn on the canvas she had mounted on the easel.

He watched as she squirted a number of different colored oil paints onto a small palette. "Do you do this often?" he asked. "Paint, I mean?" He watched in fascination as she quickly mixed a few colors together to create a bright blue that matched the sky.

"When there's time," she replied. "Usually for my father's books."

"For the color plates?"

"Indeed," she replied, not tearing her attention from her subject. She had dipped a large flat brush into a pot of linseed oil and was spreading a band of blue along the top edge of the canvas when Randy noticed the first dot of light appear in the sky.

"Venus," he said.

"What about her?" Diana asked as she mixed some other colors on the palette.

"Not the goddess, the planet," he clarified. He pointed to the only white light in the sky. The bottom edge of the sun seemed to touch the water, and its reflection in the water nearly reached the cape.

She glanced up. "Ah. I shall be sure to include it," she said, before brushing in the next band of color.

Fascinated by the way she quickly mixed colors and applied them in layers, Randy settled onto the rock next to her and watched both the real sunset and the one she created on the canvas.

A series of 'oohs' and 'ahs' erupted when the last of the sun dipped below the edge of the Aegean Sea, leaving behind a sky streaked in oranges, pinks, and purples.

Meanwhile, the columns of the temple appeared as reddish-brown silhouettes—as did all those who watched in wonder.

CHAPTER 28
A CONVERSATION IN
THE DARK

half-hour later

Diana sighed and set aside her palette and brush. "I'll do the temple some other time," she murmured, wiping the brush on a cotton rag from the box before dipping it in the oil again. She wrapped it in the rag and used another to clean off the palette.

Realizing it had been some time since Randy had said anything, she glanced over to discover his gaze was still directed to where the sun had disappeared.

"Magical, isn't it?" she asked, grinning.

He finally turned his attention to her. "Indeed. But I do believe your version is better," he said, waving to the painting.

"Why, thank you," she said, closing up the paint box. "Will you help me with the easel?"

Randy nodded. "Of course. I do hope someone thought to bring a lantern," he said, glancing around to discover that darkness was quickly descending. The others, including Marcus, had already made their way off the temple floor and were heading toward the road to the hotel, his aunt and uncle leading the way.

He grunted his displeasure at seeing Diana's brother escorting Jane whilst David, Tom, and Antonio walked together behind them.

"What is it?" Diana asked as she slid her sketchbook into her satchel.

"Your brother. He seems to have forgotten about you again."

Diana shrugged. "I don't mind. Truly," she said. "Besides, it appears he's finally gained Miss Jane's approval."

"But you knew that already," Randy accused, dismantling the easel into its separate sections.

Stiffening at hearing the censure in his voice, Diana dipped her head. "He was a topic of discussion in our coach today," she admitted. "Although Miss Jane likes Lord Penton very much, I do not believe she would ever feel the sort of affection for him she has developed for my brother."

Randy nodded, tucking the paint box under his arm. "David is too young to marry, but whomever he does take to wife will learn he's a true gentleman," he said, as if defending his cousin's honor. "Despite his tendency to fall in love easily, I expect he will be a loyal husband."

"And you? Will you be a loyal husband when you finally decide to marry?" Diana asked, lifting the flap of the satchel to close it.

Tempted to tease her—was she asking him to marry her? —Randy opted to remain serious. "It's certainly my intention," he replied. He pointed to the canvas. "Can you manage it?" he asked as he watched her pull the strap of her satchel over her head and settle it on her hip.

"I can," she acknowledged, reaching for the painting. She

held the canvas so that the painted side was out, one of the wooden stretcher bars gripped in her fist. Before she dared to take a step forward, though,—the twilight made everything appear in dark shades of gray—she waited until Randy was next to her.

"Hold onto me," he said quietly. "That way, if one of us goes down, we both will," he teased.

"How is it you can joke about such a thing?" she asked. Although she might have been scolding him, her words didn't sound as sharp as they might.

"Well, we can't both be serious all the time," he countered.

She inhaled sharply, and not only because one of her half-booted feet slipped on a slick stone. Randy paused to be sure she wasn't hurt before he resumed his careful steps. "I am not serious *all* the time," she argued.

"I rarely see you display humor," he said when they finally reached the road, the more even surface making it easier to walk.

"That's because there is rarely anything to amuse me," she argued.

"Not even me?" Randy asked, grinning. The faint conversations of the rest of the group reached his ears, and he realized they had fallen far behind the others in their trek back to the hotel.

"How is it *you* are always able to display such a happy countenance?" she asked in dismay. "Your brother and David as well?"

Randy shrugged. "I have no complaints, I suppose. Other than I'm rather hungry at the moment." When she seemed ready to stop to retrieve the linen-wrapped food from her satchel, he added, "We'll be having dinner shortly. I can wait."

"If you're sure." She didn't make it a question.

They walked in silence down the steep slope for a moment before Randy asked, "What does make you happy?"

He heard her soft scoff. "Finding something I've been searching for," she replied. "Discovering something I didn't expect to find."

"Painting?" he offered.

It was her turn to shrug. "I enjoy it," she admitted.

"You appeared rather content whilst you were doing it, although I sensed you felt rushed. As if you wanted more time—"

"I did want more time," she affirmed. "When I'm painting the mosaics for Father's publications, I can take all the time I need. Sometimes the light changes, but the tiles never move about as I'm trying to capture their shape and color."

"Like the setting sun did?" he murmured.

"The sky changed, yes, but so did the color of the columns," she explained.

"So... which color will you choose when you paint them?" he asked. "That yellowish white, or—"

"The color of chocolate with a hint of red bleeding around the edges," she said. "I'll paint them in silhouette, at least, that's what I remember when the top quarter of the sun was above the horizon. Only a few of the details were still visible in the columns. Very little of the fluting, of course, but there were places near the column tops and at the base where it was nearly black."

Randy glanced over to discover she was grinning. Despite the darkness, his eyes had adjusted enough that he could make out her features. When they lightened even more, he gave a start and realized why. The bobbing light of a lantern appeared directly ahead of them.

"*Kalispéra*," their coach driver called out.

"*Kalispéra*," Randy said with relief. Farther ahead and almost to the hotel, he could see his uncle Will was now carrying a lantern in front of him. The driver joined Randy and Diana for the rest of the trip down the hill, and for a moment, he held his lantern so it illuminated Diana's painting.

"Ah, you are an artist?" he asked.

"She is," Randy said, before Diana could answer. "But she has more to do on it before it will be finished."

"The sunset always goes by too fast. I saw it while I helped Elena and the girls," he said. "With the table for dinner."

"Oh?" Randy and Diana exchanged a quick glance. "I didn't see a table in the hotel that looked large enough to accommodate all of us," Randy said.

"That's because it is outside. Elena has your dinner all ready for you," he said in his heavily-accented English. "Drinks, too. You will eat on the beach."

"The beach? Like a picnic?" Diana asked.

The driver shook his head. "At the table, and there are chairs for you to sit," he said. "I cleaned them all so you will not mess your gowns.

Diana grinned. "I appreciate that," she murmured. She glanced over to discover Randy watching her, his lips quirked. "What are you finding so humorous now?"

"Not humorous," he replied. "I'm feeling rather happy at the thought of dinner. Remember, I'm starving."

For the firsts time since he had met her, Diana giggled as they made their way into the hotel.

CHAPTER 29
A RIVALRY IS PUT TO REST

*M*eanwhile, in the hotel

As the members of their party entered the hotel and split off in two directions to dress for dinner, David waited until Jane had disappeared into her room before he followed Marcus down the short corridor in the opposite direction.

About to enter the room he shared with Antonio, Marcus paused when David hurried up to stand before him, essentially blocking his way.

"Might I have a word with you, Mr. Henley?" David asked.

Marcus scoffed. "Look, Penton, if you're sore with me because I escorted…" He stopped speaking when David pulled a ruby ring from his waistcoat pocket and held it up between a thumb and forefinger.

"I wish to make a peace offering," David said.

Confused, Marcus angled his head to glance down the corridor before he returned his attention to the ring. "Isn't that... isn't that Jane's betrothal ring?" he asked in alarm, lowering his voice to a hoarse whisper.

"It *was*," David acknowledged. "And it can be again."

Marcus inhaled, his eyes widening. "I don't understand. Did she throw you over?"

David resisted the urge to grow angry with the viscount's heir. Why couldn't he understand he was trying to help him with his pursuit of Miss Jane? "No, you dolt. I could see she was growing to favor you, so I encouraged her to end our betrothal," he explained. "As a result, we have come to a mutual agreement as to our futures."

Blinking, Marcus looked as if he had been slapped across the face. "What sort of agreement?"

Rolling his eyes, David said, "That's not what's important at the moment. Do you love her?"

Marcus' face reddened, but apparently not with anger, for he asked, "Can we talk about this in private?"

David waved in the direction of his room, and the two filed in. He turned to face Marcus and pointed to the room's only chair. "Do you love her?" he repeated, once the door was shut.

"That's really none of your business," Marcus replied.

When he didn't move to take the proffered chair, David realized they were going to stand for their discussion. "It *is* my business. Jane wishes to marry sooner than later. She wants children," he explained in a low voice. "I am not yet ready to take her to wife, so I have let her know her obligation to me is forfeit, unless she should find herself without a husband when I am ready to take a wife."

Marcus dipped his head. "You know of my regard for her. I have *not* tried to hide it," he said.

"Do you love her?" David repeated.

A growl sounded from Marcus before he finally nodded. "I do. I want her to be my viscountess. The mother of my children."

"Good." David once again held up the ring. "Then propose to her. You can give her this ring to seal your betrothal—"

"Why would I do that?" Marcus asked on a scoff.

David sighed and displayed a look of annoyance. "Because she likes it, and because I'm giving it to you," he said, his exasperation evident. "If you have something better you'd like to offer her—"

"I don't," Marcus admitted, his manner softening. "I don't. I... I thought to ask her father's permission before I saw to the formalities."

David resisted the urge to wince. He had never so much as written to Viscount Reardon regarding Jane's future. He hadn't even met the man. "Damn it, Cousin. She's gorgeous—"

"You don't need to tell me that. I have eyes."

"If she doesn't have a ring on her finger, every man looking for a wife is going to pursue her when she and Antonio make it back to British shores," David stated. "It's why we agreed to a betrothal in the first place. So she wouldn't have to receive callers and put off potential suitors and randy old widowers in search of a second wife."

Marcus gave a start. "What? Are you saying...?" He stopped, his gaze sweeping the floor. "Yours was a *fake* betrothal?" His query was said in a whisper.

David rolled his eyes. "No. Maybe." He grunted. "Yes, but I have every intention of marrying her if she's not married by the time I am ready to wed," he claimed. "And I will *love* her," he added, a finger stabbing the air to emphasize his point.

Marcus visibly swallowed. "You won't have to," he replied. He plucked the ring from David's finger. "I'll propose." He glanced in the direction of the door. "Tonight. After dinner. I'll... I'll write a letter to Lord Reardon to ask his per—"

"Tell him."

For a moment, Marcus seemed uncertain. Then his eyes widened as he seemed to grow emboldened. "To *inform* him of my intention to..." Here he paused and sighed.

"To inform him you intend—"

"To marry Miss Jane," Marcus finished.

"And?" David prompted.

Another look of confusion crossed Marcus' face. "And?" he repeated.

"Marry her, damn it," David stated. "Otherwise, she's going to leave for Spain in less than a fortnight, and who knows how long it will be before you two see one another again? You've already talked about where you would go on a wedding trip. Marry her and take her there on your way back to London."

Marcus began nodding, his head bobbing up and down with every one of David's points. "All right," he replied. "I'll do it."

"Good man," David said. "Now, get the hell out of my room so I can change for dinner, won't you?"

Marcus chuckled softly, but instead of moving to the door, he held out his right hand. "Thank you, Penton," he said.

"Don't make me regret this," David warned.

"I won't," Marcus assured him. He took his leave and closed the door behind him.

David stared at the back of the door for several moments, torn between cursing his loss of Jane and cheering his freedom.

"It's a good thing I fall in love so easily," he murmured, moving to change his clothes for dinner.

CHAPTER 30

A DINNER AND A
DISCUSSION IN THE DARK

few minutes later, behind the hotel
A line of candle lamps illuminated a pair of cloth-covered trestles set up directly behind the hotel, the flames dancing about due to the slight breeze coming off the nearby water. Nine serviettes, pottery plates, and wine glasses were evenly spaced out, each guarded by a set of silver utensils. Scattered about what was left of the trestle's surface were bowls of cut up tomatoes, cucumbers and onions and platters of grilled lamb meat.

"I think we can forego formality on this night," Will said as he escorted Barbara to a place to the right of the head of a trestle. A quick glance at the arrangement showed there was only one place setting at the end of one trestle and four on each side.

Murmurs of appreciation sounded as the others followed them to take their places, Jane and Diana sitting opposite one another while the young men took seats on either side of them.

"I cannot believe this is the first time we've all been

together at the same table," Barbara said, watching as their driver saw to pouring wine.

"Everything smells delicious," Will remarked, placing a skewer of meat on her plate before taking one for himself. He passed the platter to David.

Meanwhile others helped themselves to the various offerings, tearing bread from long loaves and dishing up vegetables doused in olive oil and herbs.

"We've definitely come at the right time of the year for the tomatoes," Randy remarked. He had managed to take the seat next to Diana, glad when she didn't seem annoyed by his closeness.

Across from him, Marcus sat next to Jane, continuing the conversation they had been having when they had entered the hotel from that day's excursion. While Randy would have expected David to sit on the other side of Jane, Tom had that honor while David sat across from his mother and to his father's left. Antonio took the remaining chair on the other side of Diana.

"Do you suppose they would share any of their recipes?" Barbara asked after tasting the meat.

"I'll ask Elena," Diana said, knowing the older woman didn't understand any English.

"We'll have to see if Hannah can grow some of these spices in her garden," Will murmured. "Or mayhap we can take some back with us."

Antonio cleared his throat. "Lord Bellingham, I wondered if it might be possible to reconfigure who rides in which coach for the trip back to Athens tomorrow. Make the numbers at bit more equitable?"

Will glanced up from his plate to discover everyone's attention on him. "Uh, what did you have in mind?"

"Perhaps Miss Diana and my sister could ride with Marcus and me," he proposed.

Randy stiffened. While Marcus and Jane seemed pleased with the arrangement, he expected David would not be. However, his younger cousin seemed indifferent, his attention on his food.

Will's gaze shifted to Barbara.

"If we're in the same coach, I'll be sleeping with my head on your shoulder," she murmured.

"You say that as if you think I will mind," Will countered, his dimple appearing in his lower cheek as he grinned.

"I think I should like to ride with my cousins," Randy announced. "If that's all right with them?"

Antonio shrugged. "It's fine by me."

"And me," Marcus chimed in, his gaze on Jane.

Randy turned to Diana. "You won't mind, I hope?"

She shook her head. "I expect I'll be reading most of the time."

"Pausanias?" he asked.

"Indeed. I find his descriptions of the artwork on the Acropolis quite thorough."

"Better than his descriptions of the buildings," David said. "Almost as if he couldn't see the forest for the trees."

Randy heard Diana softly gasp, and he dipped his head down. "What is it?" he asked in a whisper.

She lifted a shoulder and tittered softly. "My mother used to say that my father saw only the forest while she saw the trees."

He watched how the flickering candlelight played across her features, how her expression of humor changed to lift her cheeks and the corners of her lips. His chest seemed to contract in response, and his breathing hitched. "Because of her poor eyesight?" he guessed.

"Indeed. But there have been times in the past when I've understood exactly what she meant. Father can look at a dig site and tell you where all the walls will be found while completely overlooking the perfectly preserved pot resting in the middle of it."

Randy chuckled. "I do try to notice the obvious," he murmured, keeping his voice low enough so that only she would hear.

"Perhaps I should be glad you have failed when it comes to me," she countered, keeping her voice equally low.

Lifting an open hand to his chest, Randy feigned offense. "You wound me," he accused.

Diana tittered and returned her attention to her meal.

"What shall be our next adventure in Athens?" David asked.

"The agora," Tom replied. "And the Temple of Hephaestus."

Murmurs of agreement sounded from around the trestle as Elena brought out small glasses of ouzo on a tray. Toasts were made and the spirits drunk before members of the party made their way back indoors.

"*M*iss Jane, might you remain out here a moment longer?" Marcus asked when she seemed ready to leave the table.

Jane settled herself back in the chair. "Certainly. What is it?" she asked, her gaze darting about to discover everyone else had gone inside.

Marcus glanced around, sure Elena and her staff would be

returning to clear the table at any moment. "Would you walk with me? Closer to the water?"

Inhaling softly, Jane allowed him to help her from the chair and then placed her hand on his proffered arm. They slowly made their way to where the ground met the sandy beach, their shadows barely visible from the little light cast by the candle lamps on the trestles.

"Penton told me you and he are no longer betrothed," Marcus said, turning to face her.

Jane dipped her head. "He was a dear to have offered a betrothal when I was most in need," she said. "But he knows me well enough to recognize I am ready for marriage when he is not."

Marcus reached for her hand and raised it to his lips. He kissed the back of it. "Then might I discover if the feelings you once had for him could instead be for me?" he asked. "If you were to learn that I feel affection for you?"

Her eyes rounding, Jane scoffed as a grin lightened her face. "Do you?" she asked in awe.

He nodded.

"Then I believe they already are, Marcus."

Appearing unstable on his feet, Marcus inhaled and let the air out in a whoosh. "Oh, Jane," he whispered. "Will you do me the honor of becoming my wife?" He felt around in his waistcoat pocket for the ruby ring David had given him. "I believe this belongs to you."

Jane didn't have a chance to give him an answer before he slipped the ring on the hand he still held.

"Marcus," she whispered.

"Penton... he gave me his blessing," he said, touching his forehead to hers.

"Then, yes, I will be your wife."

"Oh!" he responded on an exhalation of breath.

"On one condition."

He stilled himself and swallowed. "Put voice to it, and I shall do my best," he said.

"Don't make me wait," she replied. "I wish to wed as soon as possible."

"As do I," he countered.

"You'll take me on the wedding trip you talked about?"

He nodded. "Roma first," he confirmed. "And then to Derbyshire after we're back in England." He drew his brows together. "I was going to send a letter to your father to let him know of my regard for you," he stammered. "To ask his permission, but instead I shall simply inform him I am taking you to wife."

She laughed, the musical sound nearly lost in the noise from the waves lapping onto the beach. "Oh, my. He'll despise and respect you all at the same time," she claimed.

Dipping his head, he once again took her hand to his lips. "May I kiss you?" He dropped a kiss on the back of her knuckles before she pulled her hand away and wrapped it around the back of his neck.

Their lips met after a moment of hesitancy, barely touching and for only a moment before the two straightened and stared at one another. "Perhaps we should wait until after I've had a chance to tell your brother before announcing it to everyone," he suggested. "I shouldn't want him to plant a facer on me."

Jane tittered. "Antonio wouldn't do such a thing, but I can keep a secret for as long as we must," she agreed.

She glanced toward the small hotel and then back at him. "Might we kiss once more?" she asked in a whisper.

It was Marcus' turn to chuckle, and he lifted a hand to the

side of her face to place his lips to hers. When she turned her head slightly and parted her lips, he deepened the kiss and moaned softly.

They might have continued kissing long into the night but for the sound of a shutting door.

"I'll escort you back," Marcus said, offering his arm.

Grinning, Jane accompanied him to the hotel, but once they were inside, they went in separate directions to their rooms.

Neither noticed Randy as he exited his room and left the hotel.

CHAPTER 31
A NIGHT ON THE BEACH

*L*ater that night

The remains of their dinner had long been removed from the trestle and most of their party had disappeared into their rooms when Diana made her way to the beach. She was barefoot and carried a bed linen in one arm. Up ahead, closer to the water's edge, she could barely see the shape of a standing man.

From the bit of silhouette she could make out in the darkness, she knew it had to be Randy. There was something about the way he stood, the angle of his body at ease, that gave him away.

Confidence, she remembered Jane saying. At some point in his future, that air of confidence would serve him well as an aristocrat.

Diana had departed the room she now shared with Jane when the young lady claimed she was ready for bed. Already dressed in a white nightrail and braiding her long, black hair, Jane displayed an enigmatic expression suggesting she and

Marcus had come to some sort of agreement. When Diana had asked, Jane sighed and said, "I cannot say anything. I promised him I would not."

Well, if Marcus was still up and about, Diana was determined to learn what she could from him.

From the sound of male voices coming from outside his room, though, she realized four of them were engaged in a game of cards.

So much for a late night discussion with her brother.

Bored and not the least bit tired, she decided to watch the stars from the beach. With any luck, the meteor shower usually seen at the end of August would be putting on its celestial show for anyone still awake and out of doors.

Diana unfolded the bed linen and spread it out on the sand before carefully stretching out on the expanse of fabric. For a moment, she wondered if Randy wouldn't notice it in the dark and accidentally walk over it—or her—as he made his way back to the hotel. She had barely settled into place on one half of the linen when he was suddenly there.

He didn't say anything as he lowered himself onto the linen and lay back next to her, his hands clasped behind his head. He was the first to break the silence, however. "I wondered when you would come out," he whispered.

Swallowing a sound of surprise at hearing his words, Diana sighed. "Jane's abed and the boys are playing cards," she replied. "You were expecting me?"

Murmuring his positive response, he seemed about to say something when a bright light arced across the sky. "That was especially impressive," he remarked.

"Indeed."

"I've been thinking..."

"Oh, dear," she whispered, although she made sure to smile when she did so.

He turned his head and scoffed in surprise. "You're in good spirits," he accused, pulling his hands from behind his head to slide them down the side of his body.

"I am. I enjoyed spending time at the temple today," she said. "I didn't have to do any digging to discover what I was looking for."

"Which was?" he prompted.

She inhaled slowly. "A garrison general's dedication. About the temple," she murmured. "Poseidon's temple wasn't the only one for which he was responsible, though. He was apparently very concerned about the health of his troops, so he also built one to Asclepius on the same site." She motioned up toward the cliff.

"You're speaking of the dedication by Theomnestos?" he guessed.

Gasping, she stared at him. "You saw it, too?"

"Theomnestos, son of Theomnestos of Xypete, having been erected by the people general in charge of the seaside place—"

"Coastal countryside," she corrected him.

"—in the archonship of Menekrates,... then some date—I haven't yet done the calculation to determine exactly when it was—dedicated *this*," he finished.

"I think it's from two-eighteen BC," she murmured.

He glanced over at her. "Did you write it all down?"

Diana nodded. "In my sketchbook." Until that moment, she hadn't realized how close Randy was, how his hand brushed hers. She glanced over to discover his face displaying a grimace. "What are you thinking?"

"About you. About spinsterhood," he replied.

The shock she felt at that moment nearly turned to anger. They had been having a perfectly reasonable and interesting conversation about an ancient Greek general, and yet Randy was thinking about…

Me.

She swallowed as a streak of light lit up the black before it dissipated as quickly as it appeared. Inhaling softly, Diana let out the breath in a huff. "If you intend to lecture me with reasons I should not—"

"As a spinster, you wouldn't be held to the same standards as any other young woman," he stated, sounding rather insistent. "You can do what you like. You can take a lover, and when you grow bored with him, you can simply move on to another."

Diana closed her eyes and took a deep breath in an effort to tamp down the temptation she felt to respond with a verbal lashing. "Do you mean like what men do with their mistresses?" she finally asked.

"You know about that?" he countered, surprise in his voice.

Despite the dark, she gave him a quelling glance. "As we have ascertained, I have read a great number of books in my nineteen-and-a-half years, and, so, yes, I know about men and their mistresses," she said. She didn't try to hide the disgust she felt at discussing the topic. "Throughout all of history, men—especially powerful men—have employed mistresses," she claimed.

"Plenty of women have taken lovers," he countered, his words barely heard over the sound of the small waves washing up on the beach. He nearly missed a shooting star directly above them, its tail shorter than those that had streaked across the western sky. "You're going to require a lover. At least one," he stated.

Once again sounding her disbelief with a scoff, Diana remained flat on her back and stared at the sky. The new moon was barely visible, so the cloudy band of stars making up the Milky Way, splitting the sky in half, was evident in the inky blackness above. "Require?" she repeated.

"Yes."

She glanced over at him. "Why?"

He rolled onto his stomach, bringing him so close their bodies nearly touched. "Because there will be nights—mornings, perhaps—when your body will demand it be touched. Held. Stroked. Kissed," he said softly. "Made love to."

She recoiled at hearing the insistence in his voice. "You know this... how?"

He moved a hand closer to her face, one finger bent so he could stroke a knuckle along her cheek. "You're human. History has shown over and over we require someone with whom to share our lives, or at least a few hours of our day."

"How is it you can be so certain?"

"Because it is how I awoke this morning. How I will feel before I go to sleep tonight," he replied without pause.

She lifted a hand to grasp the one stroking her cheek. "You should stop that," she whispered.

"Why?"

Her breaths increasing in number, she stared at him. "I may require *you* be the one... to... to fill that position," she whispered. "It would serve you right."

He turned her hand in his and pulled it to his lips. She gasped when his lips took purchase on her bare skin, kissing the back of her hand and turning it around to press his lips into her palm. "You say that as if you think I would deny you."

Her eyes rounded when she realized her dare hadn't worked to deter him. "You're not going to?" Although she thought to pull her hand from his hold, she didn't think he would easily let go. She also knew his words about touching were true. She had't realized how much she craved it until her hand was engulfed in his.

"I would be honored to be your lover." He lowered his voice so his words could barely be heard. "You would have to… guide me, of course. Tell me what to do. How you like it."

The gasp she made wasn't due to a meteor. "Guide you?" she repeated, at the same moment a shooting star did arc across the western sky. Was it some sort of sign she needed to end this entirely inappropriate conversation?

"Well, it's not as if I…" He stopped speaking, embarrassment apparently halting his tongue.

"As if… what?" she pressed.

"Have experience. With a spinster," he stammered. "Or any other woman, for that matter."

Diana stared at him before she drew her brows together. "How old are you?"

"Three-and-twenty."

"You went to university."

"Three years," he acknowledged.

She lifted herself onto an elbow and stared down at him. "And you're trying to make me believe you have not lain with a woman?"

He shrugged. "I may have heeded my father's warnings a bit too much," he said.

"What sorts of warnings?"

He dipped his head between his shoulders. "Bastard children. Venereal disease. Broken hearts."

"Yet you offer yourself as a lover knowing I could end up with child," she accused, settling onto her back.

"I would employ a French letter," he quickly countered.

Her breathing hitched before she realized how very serious their conversation had become. How she never could have imagined discussing such intimate details with any man. "I will not reach my majority for another year and a half," she whispered, almost glad she had an excuse to put him off.

Almost.

"So?"

Damnation. "I can't really be a spinster until then," she reasoned. "By that time, you'll be—"

"I can wait," he stated. "Be at your beck and call, although..."

"Although?" she prompted.

"Would one man be enough for you?" he asked in a quiet voice. "I would be quite jealous if you showed favor to any others."

Diana swallowed at hearing the confession. He would feel jealousy? That implied... well, surely he wasn't professing anything more than lust at the moment, although even that was more than she had ever thought to incite in a man.

She thought back to the story Jane had told in the coach earlier that day and allowed amusement to sound in her voice. "Well I can't imagine trying to manage *seven*," she said on a soft chuckle.

"Seven?" Randy countered, sounding shocked, his expression conveying a host of conflicting emotions.

"One for every night of the week," she replied, grinning at how ridiculous it sounded. "Miss Jane told us about a bluestocking in Bath with seven lovers. She even calls them by their day of the week…" She stopped, clamping her mouth shut when she remembered she had called him 'Mr. Saturday' when they were making their way up to the temple.

For a moment there was silence, and then Randy rolled onto his back. "Was her favorite 'Mr. Saturday' by any chance?" he asked, clasping his hands together atop his waist as another shooting star crossed the sky.

Glad her reddening cheeks didn't show in the dark, Diana said, "I believe so."

He chuckled softly in the dark before turning his head in her direction. He leaned over and kissed her cheek. "You minx," he accused. "If I don't leave you this instant, I'm going to thoroughly ruin you," he warned. "Not that anyone would see, it's so damned dark out here."

The oddest sensation passed through her body just then. Pleasant and exciting. Warm and welcome. Tingly and altogether foreign to her.

Desire.

"Then you had best go," she whispered, glad for the reminder they couldn't be seen by anyone and for the hypnotic sound of the waves as they lapped onto the beach. She had a thought she would simply close her eyes and fall asleep, although it would be some time before her body would stop whatever it was doing to leave her so discombobulated.

"I'm not leaving you outside by yourself," he murmured.

She inhaled deeply and let the breath out in a *whoosh*. "Oh, all right. I'll go to bed."

Randy was already up and reaching out to help her to stand before the words were out of her mouth. "If you wake early and would like, I'll walk with you up to the temple. We can watch the sunrise."

"Yes, I'd like that," she agreed, not intending to sound as breathless as she did. She bent to lift the bed linen from the sand and shook it out before quickly folding it into a square.

They made their way into the building and down the corridor to their respective rooms, neither saying another word.

CHAPTER 32
A RETURN TRIP FLIES BY

The following day

After a leisurely breakfast around the same trestles they had dined at during the dinner the night before, Will announced it was time they finish packing to head back to Athens. "We'll want to be home before dark," he reminded them when murmurs of disappointment sounded from around the table.

Will remembered the arrangements they had discussed over dinner the night before. "It seems you and Tom are riding with Barbara and me," he said, directing his comment to David.

"It's fine, Father," David assured him.

"More room for me. I'm going to sleep the whole trip," Tom claimed.

Barbara tittered, although she seemed troubled by her son's reaction to the arrangement. "I can be ready to leave in ten minutes," she said.

"Hah!" Will responded. "You've all been challenged," he said with a chuckle.

Nearly twenty minutes had passed before the coaches were loaded and their occupants settled in for the trip back to Athens.

In the coach which included Randy, Jane was sandwiched between Marcus and Antonio while he shared a bench with Diana, Volume 1 of Pausanias' *Description of Greece* separating them. He waited until they had been traveling for a few minutes before he broke the awkward silence. "Is there some announcement you're withholding from us?" he asked, directing his query to Marcus.

For the entire time during breakfast, Marcus and Jane had exchanged looks that could only be described as flirtatious. If he hadn't known of David's betrothal with the young lady, Randy would have simply concluded Marcus had succeeded in securing some sort of promise from Jane.

"Jane has agreed to be my wife," Marcus blurted.

Diana, who had settled her head into the corner of the squabs to stare out the coach window, straightened and stared at her brother. "What?"

"I... I proposed last night after dinner—"

"And I accepted," Jane said happily, pulling off her glove and lifting her left hand to wiggle her fingers.

Randy furrowed his brows in confusion. "Wh... what of David?" he asked. "I thought—"

"He broke it off," Jane said. "*We* broke it off. Last night. Before dinner. He... he wished to wait to wed, and I do not." She sighed contentedly. "Oh, Diana, thank you so much for your words of encouragement yesterday," she added. "It made all the difference, and I'm so sorry I didn't tell you last night. I know you must have wondered at my odd behavior."

Diana's eyes rounded in wonder, but she quickly recovered when she got a closer look at the ring. "Well, you're forgiven, of course, but isn't that the same ring you were wearing yesterday in the coach?"

"It is indeed," Jane replied in delight.

"Penton gave it to me," Marcus stated. "He was such a sport last night. Said it belonged to her, and that I should use it as a betrothal ring. I'll give her another when we wed, of course," he added.

Randy turned his attention to Antonio, surprised to see his eyes were closed, his breathing suggesting he was fast asleep.

"Oh, he knows. I told him last night," Marcus said, aiming a thumb in Antonio's direction.

"And he agreed?" Randy pressed.

Jane nodded. "His only concern is that Marcus doesn't have our father's blessing," she said. "But he will after he writes to him."

"That could take weeks. Months," Diana murmured.

"Jane accepted my proposal on the condition that we marry quickly," Marcus explained, his face briefly displaying a wince. "I am in agreement, of course. I plan to take her to Rome and Derbyshire for our wedding trip before we go to London. That's where we'll live."

Diana blinked several times at hearing her brother's itinerary. "You've made all those plans since last night?" she asked in alarm. "You haven't even spoken with Father," she added in disbelief.

"I will. When he finally arrives in Athens. Which... should be any day," he added. "He knows I want to go back to London. I've not made it a secret," he argued. "He says I can live in the townhouse." He took another breath and let it out. "I will require some help to see to finding someone who can perform the wedding ceremony." His gaze settled on Randy.

"Why are you looking at *me?*"

Marcus chuckled. "I thought you might have an idea. Some suggestions."

"Well, we're not going to find an Anglican priest here in Greece," Randy countered. "But if you agree to a civil service, there might be someone who can do the honors. The mayor. A state official, perhaps. The king," he said, grinning at mentioning the last option.

"The king?" Jane repeated, excitement in her voice.

"I, uh… I have never met King Otto," Marcus stammered.

"Queen Amalia is said to spend time in her gardens, and apparently she isn't much older than me," Diana remarked. "I do know where you can find the mayor, though," she added.

"The mayor would do," Marcus replied. He glanced over at Jane for confirmation, and she allowed a brilliant smile.

"The mayor will do," she affirmed.

*M*eanwhile, in the other coach

"Thank you for arranging this trip, Uncle," Tom said as he settled onto the bench facing away from the direction of travel.

"You're welcome," Will replied, grinning, He sobered when he noticed his son staring out the coach window, an expression of sadness on his face. "It appears this wasn't a good trip for everyone, though." When David didn't respond, he glanced over at Barbara.

"David, you've been awfully quiet… since before dinner last night," she commented.

Her son gave a start. "The temple was… fine. I quite liked the sunset," he said.

Tom elbowed his cousin. "Why aren't you in the other coach?"

David sighed. "Jane and I broke off our betrothal last night."

"What?" Barbara and Will replied in unison.

"He loves her. And she… I think she likes him very much. I told Marcus. I think he proposed after dinner last night. Jane has obviously accepted his suit. I don't think I've ever seen her as happy as she was during breakfast."

Will leaned forward. "What about you, though?"

David lifted a shoulder. "I didn't expect it to hurt this much," he admitted.

"Oh, David," Barbara whispered.

"I thought I would feel relief. Especially after what happened in the caves," he went on. "I never meant for my cousin to despise me so much because we were in love with the same girl."

"So… you *were* in love with her?" his father asked in confusion.

David nodded. "Well, at least I think I was. Am. Although, I knew we would probably never wed," he admitted. "I think I aways knew she would be of a mind to marry long before I would be ready, so I cannot say this was a surprise."

"It wasn't a real betrothal, though, right?" Tom asked. Despite his comment that he would be sleeping for the entire trip back to Athens, Tom seemed particularly interested in the conversation.

"It was conditional, yes," David agreed. "It still is. I told her if something should happen and she's in need of a husband when I am ready to wed, then she can have my heart."

"Oh, how romantic," Barbara murmured.

Will glanced over at her before he wrapped an arm around her shoulders and pulled her closer. "You may wish to guard your heart, son. You have a tendency to fall in love far too easily," he warned.

David nodded, chuckling softly. "I know." He took a deep breath and let it out in a *whoosh*.

After what he thought was only a quick nap, he awoke to discover the coach had halted in front of Engels Mansion.

He had to wake up everyone else.

CHAPTER 33
CAUGHT IN THE ACT

The following afternoon at Vouros Mansion

After a day spent at the Erechtheion searching for inscriptions on what was left of the marble cella, Randy had helped Diana pack her tools into her satchel. He watched as she rolled up the rubbing she had completed at great risk to herself, the memory of what she had done forcing him to suppress a chuckle as he slid the roll into her tubular carrying case and slung the strap over his shoulder.

"Thank you for walking me home," Diana said, removing the case from Randy's shoulder. Before she could do anything with it, the butler took it from her and helped to divest Randy of the leather satchel.

"I appreciate you allowing me to do so," he replied, watching in confusion as the servant disappeared from the vestibule.

His gaze took in the mansion's decor. Although he had been here for dinner only a few nights before, he had been escorted to the dining room almost immediately upon his arrival and hadn't seen most of the house. He had already been shown the curved marble staircase from the main hall, but the ceiling hid its ultimate destination. He had climbed those stairs, though, all the way to the roof.

Twice.

The reminder of his time with Diana in the dark, under a curtain of stars, had his cock twitching. The first time she had been dressed as if she were a proper English lady, even if she had been flat on her back. The second time, she had been wearing a nightrail, the thin fabric doing nothing to hide the mounds of her breasts or the tops of her thighs. Despite the dark, he was sure her nipples tented the muslin.

Their night together on the beach had nearly been his undoing. Desire for her—desire to discover what would please her, to become her one and only lover—had consumed his thoughts ever since.

Seeing her now, garbed in breeches and a man's shirt, a cloud of soft curls surrounding her dirt-smudged face, only increased his desire for her.

How was that possible?

"You're staring as if you've never seen the inside of this house before," she accused. "You were here for dinner," she reminded him before lowering her voice to add, "And the night before last."

He gave a start. "It looks rather different in the daylight is all," he said, his gaze sweeping the interior. He was tempted to say something about only having eyes for her, but he didn't think she would welcome the sentiment. Instead, he waved to indicate the ground floor parlor. "I don't remember seeing this room," he said. "You certainly have the better house," he added as he passed beneath an arch and into the parlor. "Italianate, is it not?"

Diana crossed her arms and joined him. "Or what passes

for it here in Athens," she replied. "One of the servants and I finally finished unpacking the crates the day before yesterday," she added. "I didn't wish for my parents to arrive to find the house still in disarray from the move."

Randy picked up a small vase, realizing almost immediately it was an ancient Greek rhyton. The drinking vessel, shaped like a horn, featured the face of a cat at its base. He carefully returned it to the table. "So you set up all this by yourself? After you spent most of the day on the Acropolis?"

"I did," she replied, as if it were no trouble. "Though, I expect some of it will be rearranged once Mother arrives."

"You don't think she'll like it?" he asked in alarm.

Diana lifted a shoulder. "She does have issues with her eyesight," she said. "Even when she's wearing her spectacles, she might discover a piece of furniture has suddenly jumped out to collide with her shin."

"She's that blind?"

Diana seemed to think on her response a moment. "When she doesn't wear her spectacles, she may as well be. Father told me she nearly fell off a cliff near Girgenti," she said. "Trying to take in the view from the Temple of Hera."

Randy's eyes rounded. "What happened?"

"Father saved her. Apparently scolded her something awful for not wearing her hideous spectacles at the time. Made her cry so hard, he felt terribly guilty. At least, according to Father."

Frowning, Randy was quick to defend the viscount. "He was probably frightened out of his wits," he said with more force than he intended. His family had visited the temple whilst on their tour of Sicily. Although an ancient city wall lined most of the Valley of Temples, the area around the

Temple of Hera was open, its few remaining columns perched on a cliff visible from the sea.

Diana blinked at hearing his reaction. "I suppose," she replied. "He took her to Palermo and found an oculist who could make her a decent pair of spectacles. They've been back there several times over the years so he could make her new ones when her eyes worsened."

Randy nodded. "I am glad to hear it."

When he seemed about to say something else, she pressed him to continue. "What else were you about to say?"

He inhaled and let the breath out. "Mother told me once that Cousin Marianne was forced to marry Viscount Henley. That they were discovered—"

"Kissing. Next to a fountain featuring Cupid," Diana finished for him. "And he wasn't *forced* to marry her. He *wanted* to marry her," she added defensively. "Even if she was blind."

Randy furrowed his brows. "Are you saying he made sure they were caught?"

Diana gave a start, as if she hadn't considered that possibility. "He hasn't said so, but he did have a gleam in his eye when he relayed the story to me."

Allowing a smirk, Randy chuckled softly. For a moment, he imagined how Diana would react should she be caught kissing him. He rather doubted she would be amenable to marriage—forced or otherwise. Despite their conversations in the dark, he was fairly sure she still intended to be a spinster. As for if she would ever consider taking a lover—*him* for a lover—he still didn't know. "I look forward to finally meeting them."

"Well, I expect you'll have your chance in the next day or

so," she replied. "We received word they were departing Rome on a sailing vessel."

"Going through the Strait of Messina?" he asked, remembering when the captain of their ship, *The Fairweather,* had instead taken the southern route around Sicily rather than through the strait when they were on their way to Catania.

"Oh, I don't know," she said. "I don't believe they planned to stop anywhere on the way, but they could, I suppose. There are certainly a number of ships that go in and out of Piraeus," she added, referring to the nearest port to Athens.

"Do you plan to stay... for a long time?" he asked. "In Athens, I mean." He moved closer to where she stood.

She nodded. "Given my father's new patron and his desire to discover the evidence of a temple he thinks must have been on the Acropolis," she explained. "I expect we'll be here for several years."

Randy continued to study the artifacts set up around the room before he moved to join her in the middle. Finally facing her, he seemed unsure of what to say. "I... I doubt we'll be here for more than a month or so before we move on," he murmured. He lifted a hand to the side of her face. "Maybe we'll go to, uh, Delphi," he stammered. "Or one or two of the islands." He tilted her head up with two fingers placed along her jaw.

She swallowed. "I hear Crete is quite nice."

"Mayhap we'll stop there on the way to Egypt," he whispered.

"That's a good plan."

"But I suppose it all depends."

"Oh? On what?" she asked, sounding breathless.

He didn't respond, his attention moving from her eyes to her lips.

"Why... why are you looking at me like that?" Diana asked, shivering when Randy slid his thumb along the edge of her bottom lip.

"I'm trying to memorize every bit of you," he whispered.

"Why would you want to do that?" She inhaled when his thumb moved up and slid across one cheekbone, dislodging a layer of dirt from where she had wiped her face with the back of her glove earlier that afternoon.

Although he had been tempted to wipe it away with his handkerchief when it happened, he knew it would help with her attempt to appear as a boy when they were walking through the city.

"I like to imagine your face while I'm falling asleep."

She swallowed. "I...I don't think that's such a good idea."

He was pulled from his reverie at hearing her words. "Why ever not?"

Her brows drew together. "Because I'm fairly sure my face is covered with a layer of dirt. My hair is filthy and in need of a comb. My..."

Her words ceased when his lips suddenly covered hers, her intake of breath deepening what might have been a simple touching of lips.

*D*iana froze in place, as much from surprise as from how Randy's lips had captured hers in what was becoming one of the most pleasant sensations she had ever experienced in her entire life.

A kiss. A kiss so enchanting and consuming, so deep and demanding, she was no longer aware of anything but the two of them. She felt relief when one of his arms wrapped around her back. She needed it for support, for she was sure her knees were about to buckle. When his fingers splayed over the back of her shirt, she was sure he could feel the cravat she had wrapped twice around her chest in lieu of a corset.

Perhaps he would know how to undo it through her shirt, for she wanted to be rid of the damned binding. When she lifted her arms to his shoulders in an effort to hold onto him, she knew he could feel where the ends of the cravat were tucked under her arms, the wrap no longer tight enough to be secure.

For a moment, she wanted it to slip down her torso. Wanted there to be less fabric between her breasts and his chest. She wanted her tightened nipples to rub into the planes of his body and provide the surcease she didn't know she needed.

When he angled his head in a different direction, his lips never leaving hers, his other hand moved to grip her waist. His thumb brushed the side of a breast, and she felt the touch through the fabric of her shirt and the cravat. Inhaling sharply, she briefly broke off the kiss.

"Take me as one of your lovers," Randy murmured, his lips moving to nibble on one of her earlobes.

She made a sound of disbelief. How could he speak coherently at a time like this? "I rather doubt I would take more than one," she whispered, her breaths coming in short pants. The idea of more than one man seeing her—knowing her—was almost as frightful as giving in to the idea of accepting a lone lover for the rest of her life.

"Then take only me." His lips moved back to hers, his tongue invading her mouth to slide along her teeth and tangle with her tongue.

Unable to reply, Diana could only do her part in helping to deepen the kiss. To press her body closer to his until she felt his arousal against her middle. To softly moan when his tongue retreated from hers. His lips didn't move from hers, though, but simply captured her lower lip to nibble it before once again claiming her mouth.

At some point, she moved a hand to the side of his face, her fingertips reaching beyond the whorls of his ear to thread through his hair. She was sure she felt his body shiver when her fingernails scraped his scalp.

As if in retaliation, he slid a hand along her side, his thumb sliding between their bodies to circle the nubbin of a hardened nipple.

Inhaling, which only seemed to deepen the kiss, Diana lifted her other hand to his ear, her thumb tracing the top whorl before she tugged his lobe between two fingers. The sense of satisfaction she felt when he once again shivered nearly had her smiling against his lips, but it was his audible groan that nearly had her laughing.

When he finally ended the kiss, he left his forehead pressed to hers. "I will be yours and yours alone," he vowed out loud.

"Well, I should hope so."

Randy blinked, sure Diana's lips hadn't moved. He also realized the words were spoken in a much deeper voice than she possessed.

Alarm gripped him. He lifted his head and turned to discover a middle-aged man and woman staring at them in disbelief. The woman wore spectacles and an expression of bemusement while the gentleman's dark brows were furrowed in what could only be interpreted as anger.

Or perhaps it was confusion.

Although he really should have given up his hold on Diana—he remembered something about needing to behave—Randy instead pulled her closer, one arm moving in front of her as he stepped forward to act as a shield.

His move proved fruitless, for Diana pulled her hand from his as she moved to stand next to him.

"Hello, Mother. Father," she said, sounding even more breathless than she had when she had been speaking to him. She rushed forward to pull her mother into an embrace before turning to kiss her startled father on his cheek. "Welcome to Athens."

"What a welcome it is," Marianne, Viscountess Henley, said, her gaze still on Randy. When she finally turned to look at Diana, she scoffed. "Oh, darling, your poor face is covered in dirt, and I do believe an introduction is required," she added, lifting a blonde brow as her attention returned to Randy.

Stunned by the woman's resemblance to his mother—her facial features were so similar he would have mistaken her for his mother in a crowd—Randy was dumbstruck.

Except for the spectacles.

Surrounded by gold wire, the thick lenses caused Marianne's eyes to appear smaller than they really were.

"Lady Henley. Lord Henley," Randy said as he bowed, sure his face was bright red with his embarrassment. "I am Randolph Forster, heir to the Gisborn earldom." He stepped forward and lifted Marianne's hand to his lips. "It's very good to finally meet you, Cousin."

"Oh, well, I suppose I am your cousin," she said, grinning. "And this is my husband, Jasper Henley," she said before Diana could do the honors. "It's very good to finally meet you, Cousin Randolph."

When Randy straightened from his bow, he discovered Jasper's expression had changed to one of confusion. "You... you are Cousin Hannah's son?"

"Her oldest son, indeed." He took Diana's hand in his. "Miss Diana's second cousin," he added. "I apologize for the situation in which you found us. My fault entirely."

"Oh, I rather doubt that," Marianne said, her face displaying a grin of delight.

Diana gave her a quelling glance. "Mother."

"I take full responsibility, my lord," Randy stated, his words directed to her father.

Jasper's attention went to his daughter. "You *do* understand what this means?" he asked in a quiet voice.

Randy watched as Diana visibly swallowed. Before she could respond, he said, "Lord Henley, might I have your permission to marry your daughter? So that she will one day be my countess?" Although he had never intended to use his future title as a means to induce a betrothal, he realized it couldn't hurt in this instance.

What else could he say to help his cause? They had been caught in the very same act that had forced Diana's parents to marry.

He didn't have to see Diana's reaction to know how she felt about the matter. The way she attempted to pull her hand from his grip told him she didn't agree with what he was trying to do. He reluctantly let go of her hand, dipping his head in an effort to hide his disappointment.

Jasper cleared his throat. "Before I give you permission to do anything, I think it best I have some time to, uh, discuss it," he stammered. "With my daughter." When Marianne's elbow intersected his ribs, he quickly added, "And my wife, of course."

Randy stiffened. "Of course, my lord. I'll, uh, take my leave and, if it's agreeable, return on the morrow?" He was well aware Diana was staring at him, although he didn't dare tear his attention from the viscount to discover if she was angry with him or not.

He knew she was. Either that, or she was panicking. He had a thought that he, too, should be feeling panic, but instead, he was experiencing something altogether different— a sense of impending loss.

"Are you staying here in Athens?" Marianne asked, stepping forward to place a hand on his arm.

"Yes, my lady. We have taken a residency at Engels Mansion in Adrianou Street," he explained, noting how she aimed them in the direction of the front door. He fell into step next to her.

"We?" she prompted.

"I've come with my uncle Will—your cousin Will," he said, determined to emphasize their relationship. "My aunt Barbara, and their son David, Viscount Penton—he's Uncle Will's heir—and my brother, Thomas," he added.

"But not Cousin Donald?" she asked, concern evident on her face. She lifted her free hand to tap a finger against her cheek as a grin lit her face. "Oh, I suppose you have left him behind in Catania with his new bride," she guessed.

Randy's eyes widened with his surprise at hearing her comment. "We did," he replied. "Lady Montblanc is increasing with child. Donald thought it best they remain there rather than travel with us," he explained. "She's due to give birth in a month or two." His brows suddenly furrowed. "You... *you* know about Cousin Donald? That he married the Marchioness Montblanc?"

Marianne nodded as she beamed in delight. "Despite the

distance, I receive a letter from Aunt Cherise every month," she said, referring to the Marchioness of Devonville.

Cherise was Donald and David's grandmother. And Thomas and Randy's, as well.

"I actually first learned of it from reading a Sicilian news-sheet, though," she added, her voice kept low as if she were sharing a secret. "I used to buy them every week in Girgenti," she added happily as they entered the vestibule.

"Grandmother Cherise must be thrilled to know Donald married a marchioness," Randy said, knowing full well she was. Cherise wrote to Aunt Barbara every month as well.

"Oh, I think she was more thrilled to learn that his *son* is a marquess," Marianne countered happily.

Despite her thick spectacles, Randy noticed how she winked. "No doubt," he said, grinning.

"Well, I'm so glad to hear so many of our family are here in Athens," she said. "I should like to finally meet my cousin Will. And Lady Bellingham, of course," she said. She turned to glance back at her husband. "We'll have you all to dinner once we're settled, but in the meantime, do join us for breakfast in the morning. Say ten o'clock?"

Heartened to hear the invitation—perhaps she would be his ally when it came to convincing Lord Henley—and Diana —to accept his offer—Randy nodded. "I shall be here, my lady," he assured her, his gaze darting to the front door. He gave a start and angled his head to one side and then the other, his attention on the ancient painted panel. Blinking, he stepped back and then leaned his head forward before he scoffed softly and returned his attention to Diana's mother.

Despite her thick lenses, he could see how her gaze darted to the front door before she returned her attention to him. "Do call me Marianne," she insisted, turning to face him when the butler opened the front door. "Have you a coach... or another means of transportation?" she asked, looking toward the street to see there weren't any vehicles other than the one in which they had arrived from the port in Piraeus.

"I'll walk. It's not far," he assured her. He once again lifted her hand to his lips. "I do feel affection for your daughter," he said in a quiet voice. "If that has any bearing at all on the matter."

Marianne angled her head to one side and sighed. "Well, that much was obvious," she replied with a grin. "Good day, Lord Forster."

"Randy. You can call me Randy," he said before he bowed again. "I'll come back at ten o'clock in the morning," he added. "And if you could, maybe mention the door to her? She'll understand."

Marianne blinked. "I'll be sure to do that. Oh, do give my regards to your family," she said before she allowed the butler to shut the door.

Inhaling deeply, Randy made his way down the pavers to the street, his thoughts on what his uncle would say when he learned what had transpired.

Behaved, he had not. The temptation to kiss Diana had been so great, he wasn't sure if he could have stopped himself if she had attempted to push him away. The pillows of her lips had been so soft against his mouth. They had tasted of dates and wine—a combination that reminded him of the joy she had exhibited at discovering the name inscribed in the marble of the Erechtheion.

How would she react if he ever had the honor of making love to her? He remembered her soft inhalations of breath when his fingers grazed the side of one of her breasts. The way her eyes darkened when his thumb brushed over her hardened nipple.

If he hadn't been behaving the last night they had spent on the roof, he would have continued what he had started. Pushed her sleeve down her arm and taken her bare breast in his mouth. Suckled her nipple with the fervor of a man starved for sustenance. Lifted her nightrail so his fingers could skim up her thighs to her pussy.

Would he have been able to pleasure her by simply rubbing her quim with his hand? Perhaps she would have allowed him to insert a finger inside her most private place. He was sure she had been aroused, even if they had only been speaking of her taking lovers, for he remembered the light scent of musk teasing his nostrils in the darkness.

He wondered if she had been as wet as his cock was hard. Wondered at how it would feel if she were to spread her legs and allow the tip of his manhood to enter her.

It would not have been enough, though.

His cock would have demanded surcease. It would have forced him to thrust the entire length of his rod into her. Bury his cock as deep as it would go. To claim her. To brand her as his own.

I don't wish to be anyone's property.

The reminder of Diana's words acted as if a bucket of cold water had been dumped on his head. She was determined to be a spinster in order to avoid becoming someone's property. From a legal perspective, marriage meant she would be her husband's property. It's why he had proposed the idea of her taking a lover instead, hoping she might choose him.

He hadn't given a thought to where they might live or

what he might do if she wanted to continue her search for secrets from the past—especially outside of England.

Would she ever willingly give up her avocation?

No. At least, he rather doubted it.

Which meant he would have to accommodate her avocation, at least until he inherited the Gisborn earldom. After that, he wasn't sure what he could offer her. He didn't think she was the least bit interested in becoming a countess —her reaction to his mention of it to her father had proved that point.

What could he offer her?

He was determined to do the right thing, and not only because he wanted to experience the sorts of kisses he had shared with her moments ago. Not only because he enjoyed lying next to her. Not only because he yearned to find her still there the following morning. Not only because he wanted to experience again the sort of sensations he had felt when she scraped his scalp with her fingernails.

He wanted to impart those same pleasures for her. Wanted to kiss and to hold her in the dark. Wanted to protect her. Wanted to make love to her until she begged him to stop. Wanted her to wake up happy next to him.

Yes, he wanted to be her one and only lover. But now he was discovering he wanted more.

He hoped Lord Henley would insist she marry him—it's what he wanted. He could only hope Diana would agree once she learned what he planned.

What he hoped she would agree could work for now and after he inherited.

Surely what he had seen etched in the front door would help in that regard.

"Marriage it is," he murmured, his steps quickening as he made his way back to Engels Mansion.

CHAPTER 34
A FATHER-DAUGHTER TALK

*M**eanwhile* Jasper Henley glanced behind him as Marianne escorted Randolph Forster to the front door.

Although her words were quiet, he had overheard a few of them. From her manner with the heir to an earldom, he knew his wife was happy about what they had witnessed.

Diana kissing a young man.

Willingly, it appeared.

A hand in his hair and the entire front of her body pressed into his.

Only a month ago, he had assured her she could choose the life of a spinster. She could have her dowry when she reached one-and-twenty. Live the life of an independent woman wherever in the world she wished to be.

He had hoped she might join him on his excavations on the Acropolis. That she might continue to live with Marianne and him as they adapted to life in a new country. That she would remain under his protection.

Having arrived in Piraeus only two hours earlier, the very

last thing he would expect to discover was Diana with a young man.

He quickly glanced around the ground floor parlor to realize the crates that contained the stuff of their life in Sicily were nowhere to be found. The furnishings, rugs, and decor were all unpacked and in place. Portraits and paintings were already hung on the plaster walls—familiar and yet not, given their new home.

In the middle of it all stood Diana, her face displaying an expression that seemed to vary from that of panic to despair to resignation. What he didn't expect to see were tears.

"It's rather remarkable what you've managed to accomplish in the short amount of time you've been here," he said, waving to indicate the parlor.

Diana sniffled. "Thank you. I didn't wish for Mother to find it a mess."

"Your brothers were probably of no help," he guessed.

She shook her head. "They, um..., they have been exploring. Michael has been working on the Acropolis, and Marcus has been... courting," she stammered.

Jasper gave a start. "Courting? Huh. Must be something in the water?" he gently teased.

Dipping her head, Diana covered her face with her hands and sobbed.

Taking the five steps that separated them, Jasper wrapped his arms around her shoulders and pulled her into an embrace. "Oh, there now. No need to cry," he whispered hoarsely. "I'm not going to make you do anything you don't wish to do," he assured her.

She straightened her head in an attempt to look over his shoulder. "I know, Father. It's silly of me to think you would make me marry him," she said, watching her mother as Randy took his leave. Marianne was standing at the front door, and despite the butler having closed it, she still faced the carved wooden panel.

"You're not going to make me marry him, are you?" she pressed.

Jasper shook his head. "No, but I do think you'll want to…" Aware his daughter's attention was no longer on him, Jasper let go of her. He turned to see his wife's back, her light redingote wrinkled from their ride in the coach. "Sweeting?" he called out. "What is it?"

He watched as Marianne raised a gloved hand, one of her fingers tracing a pattern in the back of the door. "This door is amazing," Marianne replied, briefly glancing over her shoulder. "You must come interpret the words for me."

Diana and Jasper exchanged quick looks of confusion before they moved to join her.

Although there was a transom window above the door, the entry was too dark to make out any detail directly. Lifting the lantern she used whilst working from where it rested on a nearby table, Diana turned up the flame and held it close to the door.

"It appears to be an inscription of some sort," Jasper murmured, taking the lantern from Diana and lifting it even higher.

"It's Greek. Old Attic, I think," Diana whispered.

"You haven't noticed it before?" Marianne asked in surprise.

Diana started to answer in the negative and instead shook her head. "Mr. Kyknos always opens the door before I get this close," she said.

"Leave it to your blind mother to discover the most

interesting things," Jasper murmured, his face mere inches from the painted panel.

"Jasper," Marianne scolded. "I am wearing my new spectacles," she said proudly, reaching up with a gloved hand to push them up her nose. "But I only looked at it more closely because I noticed Randolph's fascination with it."

Diana gave a start. Surely he wouldn't have been able to read all of it. The faint carving was barely visible through the paint.

"I don't think this is wood," Jasper said, opening the door to examine the edge of it. "This is, though," he added, his gaze sweeping the exterior. He fisted his hand and knocked on it, listening intently to the sound it made.

"It's an inlay," Marianne said, beaming at her discovery. "I think it's marble." She removed one of her gloves and scraped a fingernail along the edge where the inlay met the wood. Flakes of thin, brown brittle paint—the same paint as what covered the wooden interior of the door—fell away to reveal white stone. "Whoever would paint marble?" she asked in complaint.

"The Greeks," Diana and her father replied in unison. The two grinned at each other before returning their attention to the carving.

"Do you know what would make this easier to see?" Jasper asked, one finger tracing the shape of a letter.

"We scrape away the paint on the surface. Whatever remains is the inscription," Diana answered.

"Exactly."

"Might you have a razor we could use? I don't have one in my satchel," she said, her attention still on the carving.

Jasper glanced around. "Did someone bring in our trunks?" he asked of the butler.

Kyknos dipped his head. "I was about to, my lord." He motioned to the door. "But I did not wish to disturb her ladyship and Lord Forster and whatever it is you are doing."

"Oh, do go about your duties," Marianne said, pulling her husband and daughter from the door. "We really should take a tour of the house and get settled before we go about excavating anything."

Diana sighed with disappointment. "Of course, Mother. I'll show you to your rooms," she said. "And take you to the roof. From there, you can see almost all of Athens."

Marianne hurried into the front parlor, obviously happy to see their possessions in place. "Have you left anything for me to do?" she asked, turning to see for the first time that her daughter had been crying.

"I wasn't sure where you wanted things exactly, but I didn't want you to have to contend with the crates," she replied before a sob interrupted her breath.

"Where are your brothers, dear?"

Diana gave a start. "Uh, Marcus is... he's with the Fitzsimmonses," she replied. "I believe they were going to the National Gardens this afternoon."

"The Fitzsimmonses," Marianne repeated quietly. "As in Lord Reardon's children?" she asked.

"Well, they're no longer children," Diana hedged.

"So Marcus is courting Miss Jane?" her father guessed.

Surprised her father would jump to that conclusion, Diana was about to ask how he knew when he said, "We came upon Viscount Reardon and his wife in Rome," he explained. "They mentioned that they had already toured Northern Greece and were heading back to England. They said they allowed Antonio and Miss Jane to come to Athens. Apparently he wished to experience a bit of a Grand Tour for himself and agreed to allow Miss Jane to join him for a time."

"They were only planning to be here for a fortnight," Diana said. "They're expected in Spain soon."

He chuckled softly. "When we arrived here, I thought perhaps Antonio was the young man who was kissing you."

Diana's face flushed red. "Although he is a very handsome young man, I barely know him, Father," she replied. "I feel as if I know Miss Jane much better, though. I thought for a time Marcus was only interested in her because..." Here she paused and rolled her eyes. "She's gorgeous, and well-educated, and she would make the perfect viscountess."

Marianne blinked. "If not for those reasons, then is there another?"

Her shoulders dropping, Diana shook her head. "She is truly a very amiable young woman," she said on a sigh. "Despite having agreed to a betrothal to a future marquess who is equally amiable, it seems she would prefer to be married to my brother and have lots of babies with him," she added, sounding flummoxed at the thought Jane would choose Marcus over David.

"So... you have spent time with her?" Jasper asked, obviously concerned his heir was already courting.

"Nearly two entire days of traveling to and from Cape Sounion in the same carriage," she replied.

"You've already been to see the temple there?" he asked, his disappointment evident.

"Randy invited me to join his family, and Marcus and the Fitzsimmonses had already made plans to go, so we all went the same day." She inhaled softly. "Oh, I would go again. Whenever you'd like. The sunset was... truly beautiful. I tried to paint it, but I don't think I captured the colors quite right.

And there was a new moon, and Venus was perched halfway up the sky, a brilliant white diamond against a rather rich cerulean blue," she said in a rush.

Jasper exchanged quick glances with Marianne. "And the Temple of Poseidon?" he prompted.

Diana blinked. "Oh. Well, the temple was... quite spectacular. It's missing half its columns and the cella, of course, but it's in far better repair than I would have expected given its location," she gushed. "The inscriptions around its base are rather varied. Lots of graffiti. Lord Bryon even carved his name in one of the square columns."

Furrowing a brow at hearing his daughter's description, Jasper said, "It all sounds rather romantic."

"Oh, it was," she assured him. "I think it's where Miss Jane decided she rather liked Marcus. She, uh, begged off her betrothal with Viscount Penton—it was all very amiable—and accepted Marcus' offer of marriage the same night. And although he really should ask permission from her father, at least according to Antonio, he has every intention of marrying her within the week. He was going to speak with the mayor about a civil ceremony today."

Jasper scoffed softly, but it was Marianne who asked the most important question.

"And you?" her mother prompted. "Is the Temple of Poseidon where you and Cousin Randy fell in love?"

Diana's eyes rounded before she dipped her head. She was saved from having to answer when the butler appeared under the archway. "Your trunks have been taken to your rooms, my lord, my lady," he announced.

Jasper nodded to the servant. "Let's have a look about the house," he suggested, offering his arm to Marianne. "Although I was going to pay a call on Mr. Pittakis this afternoon, I think I shall do so on the morrow," he said, referring to the archaeologist in charge. He turned to Diana. "And I can see you are anxious to start scraping paint from the front door," he murmured.

She allowed a watery grin. "Is it that obvious?" she asked rhetorically.

He chuckled softly. "Come, daughter. I know that even if I tell you to wait until the morning, you'll have the paint removed before you take to your bed."

Diana nodded. "You have the right of it."

A half-hour later, razor in hand, she began at the top of the marble inlay and began scraping away brown paint from the marble. Occasionally, the housekeeper would appear with a broom and dustpan to clear the entry floor of the paint chips, her initial sounds of protest changing to approval as the marble was revealed.

She only had a few inches exposed when she heard her brothers approaching from the other side. Sighing, she set aside the razor and opened the door before Michael and Marcus had reached it.

"Hello, Sister," Michael said with surprise. His brows furrowed. "What are all those brown flecks all over your shirt?"

"Old paint," she replied, stepping aside to allow them into the house.

"Is something wrong with Mr. Kyknos?" Marcus asked. "I don't ever recall him not opening the door for us."

"No. He's unpacking Father's trunk," she replied. "Mother and Father arrived only an hour ago." She grinned, knowing the news would have them hurrying up the stairs.

Left alone again, she continued her scraping while she considered all that had happened on this day.

CHAPTER 35

A DISCOVERY LEADS TO A REVELATION

*M*eanwhile, at Engels Mansion

Deep in thought, Randy was about to follow the pavers leading to the front door of Engels Mansion when someone called out to him.

"Pardon, but are you him?"

Blinking, Randy turned to see a young man carrying a leather satchel, a white missive clutched in one hand. He stopped and moved to join him. "What have you there?" he asked in Greek.

"Correspondence for Bellingham. From England." The postal courier appeared frightened for a moment. "Will you pay?"

Randy glanced at the writing, grinning when he recognized his mother's penmanship. "Yes, yes, how much for the postage?" he asked, digging into a waistcoat pocket for some coins.

"Two-hundred-fifty lepta," the boy replied, as if he feared Randy's response. His eyes rounded when Randy pulled out a handful of drachma and offered him three. Obviously relieved at seeing the coins, the courier handed over the letter.

"*Sas efcharistó*," Randy said, not bothering to wait for any change. "I will take it to him," he added, practically running to the house.

Having fished fifty lepta from his pocket, the carrier stood in confusion for a moment and finally shrugged before continuing his deliveries.

"*Y*ou're back earlier than I expected," Barbara said when Randy joined her in the parlor. She was pouring tea from a pot made from pottery, the hand-painted design far different from any of the porcelain teapots that could be found in the butler's pantry at Ellsworth Park.

Reminded of why he was home before dinner would usually be served—he had hoped to spend more time in Diana's company—Randy sobered somewhat as he handed the missive to his aunt. "It's from my mother," he said.

Barbara gasped, an expression of delight crossing her face. "Where did you get it?" she asked in awe. She offered him the cup of tea she had just poured, but he shook his head.

"There was a courier out front. I paid the postage," he said. "Left him with the extra in the hope he'll see to expediting future deliveries," he explained. He watched as Barbara carefully undid the folded missive, the paper in surprisingly good shape considering it would have arrived in Athens via a ship and then overland transport. Mail sent only over land was considerably cheaper.

When Barbara had the sheet completely unfolded, she

studied the writing for a few minutes, one hand going to her chest as she inhaled softly.

"What is it? Is something wrong?" Randy asked in alarm.

"Hardly. It seems your mother has dug up what might be an old coin," she replied, tittering softly. "She wonders if it might still have some value."

"Digging? Where?"

"In the garden. Next to the orangery," she replied, holding out the sheet to Randy. "She's talked about having a row of tulips along the front of the brick, and I think she's finally received the bulbs she ordered," she added as she waved to the middle of the letter. The coin was depicted in a crude drawing in the middle of the sheet. "It appears she traced the outside of it," she added, "so this must be its exact size and shape."

Giving the illustration a passing glance, Randy said, "It's Roman," his manner rather sullen. "Father found a few when he plowed close to the river." The Gisborn lands, directly north of the River Isis, were extensive, the farms providing livings for a number of residents in Bampton and enriching the Gisborn earldom's coffers. The reminder of what he was to eventually inherit brought with it the thought that Diana wouldn't be by his side.

Barbara glanced up and regarded her nephew with furrowed brows. "Randy, what's wrong?"

He blinked several times. "I... I think I'm in love." He practically fell into the chair adjacent to hers, his hands scrubbing his face as he planted his elbows onto his knees.

Scoffing softly, Barbara set aside the letter and angled her head to one side. "Why does it take men so long to realize the obvious?"

"Aunt Barbara," he countered, his face screwing into a grimace.

"Miss Diana?" she guessed.

He nodded.

"You two did seem rather attached whilst we were at the cape," she said softly. "But from what she told us in the coach, I gathered she wasn't interested in matrimony."

"She's not," he affirmed, swallowing hard when a lump in his throat suddenly formed. He dipped his head and struggled to breathe.

"Oh, dear," Barbara whispered. "Have you spoken with her? Told her of your regard?"

He straightened in his chair. "In a manner of speaking," he said. "I... I kissed her."

"You did *what?*"

Randy blinked, sure his aunt's lips hadn't moved. The query was also said in a much deeper voice than hers, which had him turning to discover his uncle standing on the threshold of the parlor.

"I kissed her," he repeated. "I escorted her home from the Acropolis, and we were in the front parlor, and... I don't know, I couldn't help myself," he admitted. "She started kissing me back, and I told her I would be hers always, and then we were... caught."

"*Caught?*" Barbara repeated, her eyes wide.

Will took one look at Randy's face and apparently sorted what had happened. "The Henleys arrived in town about an hour or so ago," he stated. "I saw Cousin Marianne in an open carriage. Thought she was my sister at first. The resemblance is remarkable."

"It sounds as if history might be repeating itself?" Barbara asked gently, her gaze darting between her husband and her nephew.

Randy shook his head. "Except Lord Henley won't require

me to marry her. He's already told her she can have her dowry and live as a spinster," he bit out. "Besides, she would hate me if she was forced to wed me."

"So... you *want* to marry her?" Will asked, settling into the chair facing Randy's. Barbara saw to making him a cup of tea and held it out to him over the low table that separated them.

"I do," Randy affirmed. "Lady Henley invited me to breakfast in the morning, where I expect Diana will make it clear she's not interested in marrying me."

"Marianne invited you to breakfast?" Barbara asked in surprise. "Well, that's encouraging."

"I think she's on my side," Randy said, allowing his first moment of humor to show since leaving Vouros Mansion. He remembered what he had seen on the front door and hoped Cousin Marianne understood what he meant with his gesture.

He hoped it wasn't a trick of the eye. Hoped it wasn't because the grain in the wood had somehow formed what he was sure was a dedication in Old Attic.

If Diana was made aware of it, he was sure she could find a way to expose the entire inscription. Make out all the words. Find the one that he had seen.

All the time she had spent in the temples on the Acropolis, and what she sought was probably etched on the inside of her front door!

"Well, if she's like any other mother, I rather imagine she wants to see her daughter wed," Barbara said, pulling him from his reverie. "Wants her to have a protector, especially given her avocation," she added.

"I've been trying to sort how we could make it work," Randy murmured. "I know she wants to go to Egypt. We could go there for our wedding trip," he explained. "She wants to continue to do her archaeology, though. She's good at it. She's terribly clever. Remembers everything she's ever read or heard or seen. But..."

"You're going to be an earl someday," Will reminded him in a quiet voice. He took a sip of tea and gave his wife an appreciative nod.

"I know. I know. But there must be something I can offer her. Some way we can make a marriage work," he reasoned.

Barbara lifted the letter from the low table and held it up. "Perhaps there is," she murmured softly.

"What's that?" Will asked.

She passed the creased sheet to him. "From your sister. Seems she's discovered what Randy says is a—"

"A Roman coin," Will said in awe, studying the drawing in the middle of his sister's perfect penmanship. He chuckled softly. "Henry found a few of these near the River Isis about ten years back, when we were checking the irrigation gates," he added.

"You're sure it's Roman?" Barbara asked in awe, her gaze darting to Randy. He had his head down, obviously still smarting from what had happened with Diana.

"I'm fairly sure. We could have Lord Henley..." Will stopped and scrubbed a hand over his face, a slow grin forcing a dimple to appear at the base of one cheek. "We should have *Miss Diana* confirm it, don't you think?" he asked in a teasing voice. "Mayhap, encourage her to take a trip to Oxfordshire and verify it in person? Allow her to... oh, I don't know. Dig up so more?"

Randy suddenly straightened, his eyes wide. "Uncle, you're a genius," he said, rising from his chair to rush toward the door.

Will stood as well, but he held out his hands. "Steady,

Lord Forster," he stated, his simple words sounding as a warning.

Halting, Randy huffed and turned.

"Her parents have only just arrived in town. She's probably not accepting callers, especially this close to dinner," Will warned. When he saw Randy's crestfallen expression, he added, "I know exactly how you're feeling right now," his gaze darting to Barbara.

"You'll see her at breakfast in the morning," Barbara said softly. "Surely you can wait until then."

Randy finally nodded, although he had already begun forming another plan.

A plan to see Diana later that night.

CHAPTER 36
AN INSCRIPTION REVEALED

a few hours later, Vouros Mansion

Marcus angled his head first to one side and then the other as he studied the marble inlay of the front door of Vouros Mansion. "How did you even think to do this?" he asked of his sister, who was at that moment sitting on the marble tile floor, cross-legged, scraping paint off the bottom half of the marble. Brown flakes of paint covered her breeches and littered the floor around her.

"Randy noticed something when Mother was escorting him out earlier," Diana replied.

Blinking, Marcus stepped away from the door and glanced down at her. "Escorting him out?" he repeated. "Forster was here?"

Diana sighed and set aside the wooden-handled scraper she had been using to clear away the paint. When the butler understood what she was doing, he had offered the tool normally used for masonry work. The flat metal allowed her to clear away larger sections of paint than she had been able to with her father's razor. "He insisted on walking me home and was here when Mother and Father arrived," she explained.

"Did something happen?" he asked, turning to lean against the adjacent wall, one booted foot crossed over the other.

Diana glanced up from her work, not sure how to respond. After their attention had been captured by the inscription in the front door, nothing more had been said about her discovery with the Gisborn heir. "Nothing of note," she said with a shrug.

Even during dinner, the conversation had been all about their parents' time in Rome and subsequent sailing to Piraeus. During the dessert course, Marcus announced he planned to marry Miss Jane and wondered if their father would agree to assist with acquiring a writ of acceleration so he could take his place in Parliament.

Although their father seemed hesitant at first, he soon agreed to Marcus' plan—especially when their mother displayed such glee at learning her son would soon be marrying.

"Best wishes, by the way," Diana said. "Miss Jane is a lovely girl. She'll make a perfect viscountess."

Before the small glasses of liquor had been served, their mother, obviously weary from the day's travels, had retired, and their father soon joined her. Michael was next, claiming he needed to be up early for work on the Acropolis.

Marcus and Diana remained at the table until the liquor was drunk and she excused herself to change back into a pair of breeches to resume scraping the front door.

"Thank you. It means a lot coming from you," Marcus said.

Diana furrowed a reddish-blonde brow. "What do you mean?" she asked. "Coming from me?"

He shrugged, uncrossed his arms, and pushed himself away from the wall. "You're planning a life as a spinster," he reminded her. "There will be no wedding in your future."

"That doesn't mean I would deny others the right to marry," she argued. "Besides, I'll be gaining a sister," she said, allowing a grin.

Apparently surprised she wasn't trying to disabuse him of the idea of marrying Jane Fitzsimmons, Marcus turned and headed for the stairs. "Don't stay up too late, Sister. Mother said we have a guest coming for breakfast," he said. "Good night."

"Good night," Diana replied, her attention going back to the marble while the reminder of Randy had her reliving their kiss in her mind's eye.

Before this afternoon, she never expected to discover the joy found in a kiss. The all-consuming sensations of pleasure and desire the touching and suckling of lips could incite beneath one's skin. The sense of security she had felt at being held in another's arms.

The odd way her heart seemed to contract when the kiss had ended.

Actually, that hadn't happened until he had spoken words that sounded like a vow.

I will be yours and yours alone.

The knock coming from the other side of the door had her jerking in surprise. She reached up and pulled down the handle, opening the door only a few inches. A pair of Hobys were in her direct line of sight. When her gaze slowly went up, she wondered if her thoughts of Randolph Forster had somehow conjured him into existence, for her second cousin stood there, ramrod straight, his breaths coming in short pants as if he had been running.

For a moment, she didn't say anything, and for the same amount of time, he didn't seem to realize she was on the other side of the door, watching him from below.

"Hello," she said, scrambling to her feet as she opened the door wider.

She saw him blink in confusion before he said, "Hello." He visibly swallowed. "Might I be allowed—?"

"Come in," she whispered quickly, reaching out to capture his wrist with one hand. "And see what you've made me do," she added, her voice sounding accusatory.

His confusion still apparent, Randy slipped inside, his attention immediately going to the brown paint chips that were scattered all over the marble tile floor. Two lanterns were lit, as was the overhead light hanging from the ceiling. Beyond the entry, a candle lamp burned in the parlor, apparently the only other source of light on the ground floor.

Then his gaze went to the back of the door. Nearly all the marble had been exposed, its brown paint almost entirely scraped away. Left behind were lines of paint embedded in the Old Attic inscription.

"For the good fortune of the Council and the People of Athens—"

"*Athenians*," Diana corrected him. "We greet—"

"*Welcome*," he countered, "the Roman known as—"

"Pausanias," Diana said, grinning in delight.

"But he was Greek," Randy argued, although he displayed a grin matching hers.

"Yes, but Greece was under Roman rule at the time," she reminded him.

"Oh, of course," he replied, one finger tracing the next

line of Ancient Greek words. "A son of Lydia." He paused and sobered. "A mention of a mother but not a father?" he questioned.

"He was born *in* Lydia," she replied. When she noticed his blank expression, she added, "It was once an Iron Age kingdom in western Anatolia. Sardis was its capital," she explained.

"You really *do* remember everything," he said in awe.

She nodded before turning her attention back to the inscription. "Who has arrived..." She shook her head. "Come to...?" she guessed.

"*Reached* our city for the purpose of recording our..." He sighed in frustration when he struggled to interpret the last word of the inscription. "History?" he guessed.

"Heritage," Diana said in a whisper.

"Heritage," he confirmed. He chuckled softly. "Where do you suppose this was originally located?" he asked, waving to the marble. At some point, the thin slab had been inlaid into a wood panel that was now the front door, a carved wooden frame around it keeping it in place.

"The agora, perhaps," she replied. "At some point, someone must have realized it was in danger of breakage and thought to preserve it this way."

"And then someone much later must have decided they didn't want it to show and painted it over."

"They may not have been able to read it," Diana said on a sigh. "The inscription isn't particularly deep."

Randy crossed his arms and stared at the marble for a moment before he said, "I like it much better like this."

"As do I," she said. She inhaled softly and let the breath out in a *whoosh*. "You're here rather late. Did you expect to find me up on the roof?"

"Would you have been there if not for this?" he asked, pointing to the door.

She shook her head. "I think the nights of falling stars have come to an end, at least until the next meteor shower," she murmured.

"Pity," he said. "I rather enjoyed our nights together. In fact, I am here because... because, well, I don't want them to end."

"Randy," she whispered.

"I love you, Diana." He ignored her look of shock and added, "I meant what I said about being yours. For life. I want us to be wed. I want you to be my countess."

She swallowed, unaware he had taken one of her hands in his. Before she could put voice to a response, he took her other hand and kissed the back of it.

"We can go to Egypt on our wedding trip and then to Rome and then to... Oxfordshire," he said, obviously trying hard not to make the last destination sound as disappointing as it would be to her.

"Oxfordshire?" she repeated.

"Where you can continue your avocation."

She scoffed softly. "How?" she asked in disbelief.

Randy extracted his mother's letter from his waistcoat pocket and unfolded it. He held it out to her and said, "It seems the Gisborn lands contain a number of these," he said, pointing to the drawing of the coin.

"A Roman aureus," she said in awe.

"My uncle said my father found several about a decade ago. They were near the River Isis."

Her eyes widened as she studied the drawing. "If there are coins, then surely there must be ruins there," she reasoned. "Mayhap a Roman settlement?"

"My thought as well," he said. He dipped his head as he raised her hands to his lips, kissing the knuckles of both before he straightened. "Will you marry me, Diana?"

She visibly swallowed. "You would truly allow your countess to dig in the dirt?"

His gaze darted to the side. "Yes," he replied. "If it makes her happy, of course." At her look of disbelief, he added, "Mother does it all the time. She likes to tend to the garden."

Diana seemed satisfied with his response, but then she asked, "Would you allow your countess to travel?"

He pretended to think for a moment before allowing a shrug. "As long as I'm welcome to join her."

"Would you allow your countess to wear breeches?"

He nodded. "Oh, most certainly."

She displayed a smirk. "You've given me much to consider," she said, crossing her arms.

"Do you require more? In order to make your decision in my favor?" he asked.

"Are you trying to bribe me?" she accused.

"Maybe," he replied. "Is it helping?" His attempt at keeping a straight face failed, and he chuckled softly. "I don't expect an answer right away," he admitted. "Even if you haven't decided by the time I come for breakfast in the morning, I'll try very hard to be patient."

She nodded and sighed.

"Oh, and congratulations on your discovery," he said, waving to the marble inlay.

"It was actually yours," she countered.

"But you had to do all the work to uncover it," he said, motioning to the paint flecks that littered the floor. He lowered the handle on the front door, pulling the door open a few inches. "Sleep well, my love," he whispered. He lifted her hand to his lips, holding it a moment longer than necessary before he bowed and disappeared out the door, carefully pulling it closed behind him.

He made it almost all the way to the waiting town coach before the front door opened again. He turned and was nearly bowled over when Diana ended up in his arms.

"You forgot to kiss me," she accused, her hands gripping his arms as she stood on tiptoes.

Randy grinned and heaved a sigh of relief. "I promise I shan't make that mistake again," he replied, wrapping an arm around her waist as he captured her lips with his own. Although it wasn't nearly as long as the kiss they had shared earlier that afternoon, the shorter kiss seemed to satisfy Diana. She lowered herself until she was standing on both feet.

"I'll give you my answer in the morning," she whispered.

He gave a start, thinking she already had with her demand for a kiss. "Then I'll be sure to bring your betrothal ring with me," he countered.

"You really are trying to bribe me."

He placed a hand at the back of her head and dropped a kiss on her forehead. "Apparently, it's working," he whispered. "Now, off to bed, or I'm going to take you to Engels Mansion with me and have my way with you," he threatened.

Giving him a slight curtsy, she turned and headed back toward the house. Before she opened the door, she turned and asked, "Are you staring at my derriere?"

His back against the coach door, Randy crossed his arms and grinned. "I am."

When she huffed and went into the house, he sighed and called up to the driver. "Back to Engels Mansion."

"Yes, my lord."

• • •

eanwhile, in a bedchamber on the second floor

"Whatever are you doing over there?" Jasper Henley asked. He sat up in bed and leaned over to turn up the flame on the nightstand's candle lamp.

Marianne, wearing a night rail, her newest spectacles, and a huge grin, let go of the edge of the velvet drape she had been holding and stepped away from the window. "I was sure I heard voices is all," she said. "Thought I would try out my new spectacles to see if they worked in the dark."

He watched as she climbed back into bed. "And do they?" he asked.

"Not a bit," she whispered happily, removing the eyewear to place them on the nightstand.

Grunting, Jasper turned down the candle lamp flame before he gathered her against his body. "Now you've given me all sorts of ideas," he complained.

"Of all the things you can do to a blind woman in bed?" she asked hopefully.

His gasp was loud as she tittered in delight.

CHAPTER 37

A BREAKFAST BETROTHAL
SEALS THE DEAL

The following morning

Although he had considered walking to Vouros Mansion for that morning's breakfast with the Henleys, Randy reconsidered and spoke with the butler about having the carriage made ready.

"Are you leaving for your breakfast with the Henleys?" Barbara asked. She was in the Engels Mansion breakfast parlor writing a letter whilst enjoying a cup of tea, the rest of the family not yet up and about.

"I am," he replied.

Barbara dropped the quill she held and directed a critical gaze at his apparel from top to bottom. "Well, you look especially handsome this morning," she said, admiring his snow white cravat, top coat, yellow embroidered waistcoat, buff pantaloons, and freshly polished Hobys. "And a bit frightened, if I might say."

Randy winced. "I'm so nervous. What if she says no? What if her father says no?" he asked in dismay. "What if Marcus says no?"

Tittering, Barbara folded up the letter she had been writing and handed it to him. "Take this to Marianne for me, won't you? I'm inviting them all to dinner this evening."

He gingerly took the missive from her. "You think that will help my cause?" he asked.

"Oh, Randy, Marianne is no doubt on your side. It won't matter what Jasper or Diana or even Marcus might say on the matter. Marianne will have the final word," she assured him.

Randy's brows furrowed. "I don't want Diana forced to marry me," he murmured. "She'll hate me."

"She won't hate you, darling. Trust me when I tell you she's a very clever girl. She's already come to value your opinion, and she trusts you."

About to ask her how she knew, he remembered Diana had ridden in the same coach as Barbara when they traveled to Cape Sounion. Knowing his aunt, she would have been able to learn all she wished to know without Diana realizing she was being interrogated.

"I hope you're right," he said. When he saw the butler waiting for him at the door, he leaned over and kissed Barbara on her cheek. "Wish me luck."

"Luck," she said, pulling another sheet of stationery in front of her. "I'm writing to your mother next, and I expect to finish it with your news, whatever it may be."

About to ask that she not, Randy realized it would do no good. He was sure Barbara had promised his mother she would tell her everything whilst they were on this trip, no matter if it was good or bad.

"Oh, and one more thing," she said, holding out her hand.

"What's this?" he asked, moving closer to see what she held in the palm of her hand. "A ring?" he said in surprise.

"Well, you don't have one, do you?"

"Uh..."

"Take it," she ordered.

"But... isn't it yours?" he asked, carefully plucking the ring between his thumb and forefinger to examine the gemstone. The simple gold band featured a single sapphire with a tiny diamond on either side.

"Part of a parure your uncle gave me years ago. I've never actually worn the ring—I've worn all the other pieces, of course—it came with a necklace, bracelet, hair comb, and a brooch—but I could never come to wear rings other than the wedding rings your Uncle Will gave me," she explained.

Randy scrubbed a hand over his face. "You're sure?" he asked in a whisper.

"Yes, I'm sure. Now, go get your girl," she ordered.

Nodding, Randy tucked the ring into his waistcoat pocket and rushed out of the breakfast parlor.

A *half-hour later, at Vouros Mansion*

When Kyknos opened the door to Randy's knock, he waved off his offering of a calling card and stepped aside. "Lady Henley is expecting you," he said.

Randy's gaze darted to the floor, and he wasn't surprised to see the marble had been swept clean of all the paint chips shaved from the marble inlay. A quick glance at it showed the marble had been polished, the inscription now much easier to read.

"There you are," Marianne said. Dressed in a bright apple green day gown, its bell skirt adorned with embroidered flower buds, her pale blonde hair rolled into a bun atop her head, he could have been his mother. He hadn't noticed the resemblance so much the day before, but with everything that had happened prior to her sending him out the door, he wasn't surprised.

"Am I late?" he asked, taking her hand to his lips.

"Not at all. The boys haven't yet come down."

"Michael is here?" he asked, expecting the youngest to have already left for the Acropolis.

"Yes. He and Jasper will go up together when we're done with breakfast," she explained.

"And Miss Diana?" he asked, his nervousness returning.

"She was in her room painting this morning. Said something about wanting to finish something she had already started."

Randy inhaled softly, fairly sure he knew exactly which painting she was finishing.

"First door on the left, second floor," Marianne said. "But not yet."

Blinking, Randy was about to ask what she meant when a knock at the door had Kyknos hurrying to open it. Randy chuckled softly when he saw Antonio and Jane enter the vestibule.

"Oh, good. They received my note," Marianne said, her brilliant smile appearing.

"Have you already been introduced, or would you like me to do the honors?" Randy offered in a whisper.

"Oh, please do. This will be the first time I'm to meet my new daughter-to-be," she said with excitement. "Oh, my, she is quite gorgeous," she added in a whisper. "And quite striking in yellow."

Randy once again chuckled. "So I've been told, but I prefer Diana," he said in a hoarse whisper. He heard her slight inhalation of breath and took the opportunity to perform the introductions.

The two newcomers had barely finished their greetings when Antonio asked, "Marcus invite you?"

Randy shook his head at the same moment footsteps sounded on the marble stairs.

Marcus appeared, one hand tapping his chest. "Ah, please accept my apologies, my sweet," he said, capturing Jane's hand to kiss the back of it. "I intended to be the one to introduce you to my mother."

"Apology accepted," she replied, her face displaying more color than usual.

"You look especially lovely this morning," he said. "Like a yellow rose," he murmured.

Jane tittered, dipping her head as she thanked him.

"Please, come take a seat in the parlor," Marianne said. "Mr. Kyknos will see to some coffee or tea," she said, gasping when Jasper and Michael quickly stood from where they had already been seated in the parlor. "Oh, darlings, here you are," she said. "However long have you been down here? I must be blind to have missed you."

The two chuckled. They had been enjoying cups of coffee during their guests' arrivals, but they now saw to greeting the newcomers, bowing and kissing the back of Jane's hand.

While everyone else made their way to the parlor, Randy hung back near the bottom of the stairs, and when he was sure no one was watching, he bolted up the steps.

Pausing when he reached the second story, he discovered the first door was open. The faint odor of paint reached his nostrils even before he peaked around the edge of the door frame. He grinned when he saw Diana standing before her easel, her back to the bedchamber's only window.

"Good morning," she said, her gaze never leaving the canvas to which she was applying paint with a small brush.

"Good morning, indeed," he replied. He made his way to stand next to her, and when it appeared she had lifted the brush from the canvas, he kissed the side of her head. He stepped back to admire first the gown she was wearing—a peach sprigged muslin with lace trim—before adding, "You look especially fetching in peach."

She tittered. "I suppose you were expecting to find me wearing breeches this morning?"

"Actually, yes, I was," he admitted.

"Later, perhaps," she said. "I'm told we're having guests for breakfast this morning."

Randy turned his attention to the painting. "Oh. You've managed to match the color of the columns exactly as they appeared that night," he marveled. He watched as she dabbed a bit more paint into one of the column tops, the slightly darker brown providing the detail of the Doric column capital. "You're quite good at this," he whispered.

"Thank you." She stepped back and angled her head to one side. "I think it's finished." She placed her brush into a glass jar, the dark liquid giving off the scent of linseed oil.

He continued to study the painting, noting the simple details she had added since he had last seen it. Not only had she filled in the columns with the rusty brown as they had appeared during the sunset, their edges slighter redder, but she had also added highlights to the flowers and other vegetation in the foreground, as well as darker details to enhance the tops of the fluted columns and at the base of the blocks making up the floor. "I shall remember this always," he whispered.

"The Temple of Poseidon?"

He nodded. "This was where I fell in love with you.

When I fell in love with you," he quickly added, waving to indicate the moment she had captured in the painting, the silhouettes of the temple's columns against a sunset of blazing colors under a crescent moon. There was even a dot of bright white above the moon, exactly where Venus had appeared.

He turned his head to find her staring at him, her eyes wide. Before he could say anything else, she stood on tiptoes and kissed him, her hands clutching his shoulders. He immediately wrapped his arms around her waist and deepened the kiss, finally pulling away to leave his forehead resting against hers. "Does this mean you'll marry me?" he asked. He left one hand behind her waist while he dug into his waistcoat pocket for the ring his aunt had given him.

"I... I suppose?" she replied. When he straightened slightly and held up the ring between them, he watched as she focused on it. Watched when she blinked and finally displayed a watery grin. "Oh, Randy."

He didn't wait for her to say anything else. He captured her wrist from his shoulder and slid the ring onto her fourth finger. "It matches your eyes," he whispered. "When they're in the dark, like they were that night."

She swallowed. "It's beautiful," she whispered.

"Does it fit all right?"

She nodded. "It does."

She wrapped her hands around his shoulders and embraced him for a moment. He grinned as he tightened his hold on her. "You've made me a very happy man."

"You're already so happy, I can't imagine making you more so," she countered.

He laughed and once again kissed her forehead.

Her eyes suddenly widened. "Oh, we should go

downstairs. We're expecting guests at any moment," she said in alarm.

He chuckled. "Actually, they're already here."

"What?" She stepped out of his hold. "Why didn't you…?" Realization dawned and she sighed. Mother sent you up here, didn't she?"

Randy angled his head first to one side and then the other. "Well, she only told me which room was yours," he said. He offered his arm. "Shall we?"

She placed her hand on his and they made their way down the stairs to the entry.

"I noticed the marble inlay has been polished," Randy remarked as they paused before the front door. "It's much easier to read the inscription now," he added.

"The housekeeper must have done it," she said, studying the carving. "It does look much better than how I left it last night."

"Well, it couldn't be helped. You were interrupted," he said.

She grinned and turned to discover that everyone in the parlor was watching them. "Good morning," she called out. "Uh, I apologize for my tardiness," she added as she and Randy joined them, the men standing upon her arrival.

"It's all my fault," Randy said, leading her to one of the few remaining chairs in the room. "I was admiring her work of art." He moved to stand before Jasper to bow and shake his hand before he took the adjacent chair to Diana's.

"Your painting?" Jane guessed. She was ensconced in an upholstered chair next to Marcus, her yellow gown adding more color to the floral array. "Is it finished?"

"It is," Diana said. "Only a moment ago. Right before I accepted Randy's marriage proposal." The words tumbled out so quickly, she lifted her left hand to cover her mouth. The announcement along with the appearance of a betrothal ring had the others gasping in surprise.

"Oh, best wishes, Diana," Marianne said as she sighed contentedly. "We have two betrothals to celebrate this morning!"

"Thank you, Mother." Her gaze went to her father, but his attention was on Randy, his expression one of worry.

Randy noticed his future father-in-law's regard and cleared his throat. "Not only has Miss Diana agreed to be my eventual countess, she will also be the Gisborn earldom's archaeologist," he announced.

"What's this?" Jasper asked in surprise.

"A number of Roman coins have been found on our property," Randy explained. "Evidence of what we believe to have been a Roman settlement along the River Isis in Oxfordshire."

Jasper chuckled softly. "And you're going to allow her to dig it up?" he asked.

"I am," Randy replied. "I'll offer assistance should she ask for it—"

"I'm going to make him do all the heavy shoveling," Diana said, a teasing grin lifting her lips.

"But I've learned she likes to make her own discoveries," Randy finished, aiming a grin in her direction.

"Well, then about the question you had for me yesterday, I suppose my answer is yes," Jasper said. "Best wishes to you both."

"Thank you, my lord," Randy replied.

"Thank you, Father."

"So, Forster, where are you planning to take your bride for a wedding trip?" Marcus asked. "We're off to Roma after we say our vows before the mayor next week," he added. "Then it's to Derbyshire."

Randy arched a brow. "Well, not to one-up you, Cousin, but we may be joining you when it comes to seeing the mayor next week, and then, after we complete our time here in Greece, Diana and I are off to Egypt for an expedition up the Nile and then to Roma before heading back to England."

The others in the parlor boggled at hearing the itinerary. "Egypt?" Jasper repeated.

Diana nodded. "I can hardly wait to walk through the Temple of Luxor," she said. "And see the pyramids and the Colossi of Memnon."

Blinking, Randy scoffed softly. "You mean, you've never been to Egypt?" he asked in confusion, remembering her tale of Romans on holiday in Egypt sounding as if she had actually witnessed it for herself.

She shook her head. "I've only ever read about it," she admitted.

Randy chuckled softly. "You really do remember everything you've ever read," he commented.

"Or seen or heard," her father said, as if in warning.

She gave Randy the most brilliant smile he had ever seen on her. "I really do."

Although he might have felt a moment of unease, Randy merely smiled back at her. "When next we play cards, you're on my team," he said.

CHAPTER 38
MORNINGS MAKE THE DAY

A week later

Unlike most mornings, when she would awaken suddenly and practically jump from her bed, Diana awoke slowly on this day, wiggling her toes and stretching her fingers before finally opening her eyes. She stretched her entire body, her arms burrowing beneath the pillows until they collided with the upholstered headboard.

There was a moment of unease, an unsettling feeling that something was not quite right, that had her heart rate increasing. A sudden awareness of a warm body next to hers.

There were memories of pleasures she had never before experienced and that awkward moment when she had finally succumbed to her new husband's gentle urgings and allowed him her body.

He had been absolutely right in claiming she needed a lover.

How he could have been so patient, so sure he could hold off satisfying his own needs before seeing to hers—despite her insistence that he should simply get it over with—she wasn't about to sort so early in the morning.

Then, after he had finally had his turn at experiencing pleasure, during a much slower and more careful coupling than she had expected, she had watched in wonder as his body seemed to seize, every muscle in his torso and the cords of his neck and the planes of his face straining as if his orgasm was almost painful. A moment after, and it was as if every muscle in his body gave way all at the same time.

If he thought for one minute she was going to allow him to simply roll off of her and fall asleep somewhere off to the side of her, he learned rather quickly she wasn't going to let go of him. Not even if she was terribly warm. Not even when he claimed to be too heavy for her soft body.

She had clung to him, her body quaking with tremors she had never before experienced. She needed his weight atop hers to keep her from floating away, for she was quite sure she was weightless.

So until she had finally succumbed to sleep, he had stayed atop her, his head tucked into the space between her shoulder and neck, his breathing becoming less labored, and his pulse slowing until it matched hers.

They might have remained that way all night, but at some point, he was on his back and she was atop him, their legs tangled and his heavy manhood pressed into her hip.

Later, she found herself on her side, his knees behind hers and her body tucked into the front of his. Although she would have expected to feel trapped by the heavy arm around her waist, she thought it rather comforting.

That his hand cupped over one of her breasts as they slept made it seem more intimate, even if she found it humorous that another part of him seemed intent on finding a resting place between her thighs.

One thing was certain. She was going to enjoy spending winters in the same bed as Randolph Forster.

As for summers, she hadn't yet decided.

A hitch in his breathing had her lifting herself onto an elbow, and she scoffed softly.

His eyes still closed, Randy asked, "What is it, my love?" in a voice that sounded as if it was coming from far away.

"You're smiling," she accused in disbelief. "In your sleep."

The grin on his face widened until his white teeth gleamed in the early morning light. "Of course I'm smiling. I'm waking up to my very first day as a married man," he murmured happily. "A huntress has caught me in her trap, and I'm rather happy as her prey." He finally opened his eyes, his lashes nearly invisible as he stared at her. "Your prey," he added before he moved to kiss her on the forehead. "Good morning."

Diana gave a start. "And here I thought it was the other way around."

Randy's eyes widened. "You thought *me* a hunter?" he asked, his face screwing into a grimace. "I only chased you 'til you caught me," he teased.

Grinning at hearing his claim, Diana leaned over and kissed him on the lips. When she pulled away, she lifted a hand to the side of his face and studied his features in the morning light.

Reminded of the last mosaic her father had uncovered near Girgenti—the Roman hunter she had found more handsome than any of the others he had discovered during his excavations—Diana was struck by how much her new husband resembled him.

She had completed the painting of that mosaic the day after its discovery, and she was sure her father had already submitted his latest manuscript to his publisher along with that painting and all the others she had done for him.

Until it was in print, she might never see it again. Although she would have expected such a thought to lessen her unusual good mood on this morning, it didn't.

A better model—a live model—was right next to her at that very moment, his eyes darkening with desire.

"A hunter, yes," she affirmed. "You're going to be one in my next painting."

Randy chuckled softly and relaxed back into his pillow. "Well, until then, can I be your prey?"

It was Diana's turn to chuckle. "You can be my favorite lover," she countered. "Mr. Saturday."

He didn't hesitate to prove himself.

EPILOGUE

Two years later, near the River Isis, Oxfordshire

Under a cloudy summer sky, Diana pitched a shovel full of rich soil onto a pile she had started earlier that morning. Even before she watched it cascade down the slope of dirt, she knew it contained something metallic. She had heard the telltale sound of metal-on-metal when she plunged the shovel into her growing hole.

Dropping to kneel next to the pile of dirt, she reached out and plucked the coin from where it was sliding down.

"Another one?" Randy asked from where he was lounging against a grass-covered mound, a white-garbed bundle resting on his chest. He held an open letter in one hand, the masculine scrawl barely legible.

Diana glanced up, a grin lightening her face. "Another aureus," she said proudly. She tossed it to him, and he dropped the letter to catch it in one hand.

He chuckled, which sent the bundle on his chest to bobbing up and down. Securing it with his free arm, he turned his attention to the gold Roman coin, examining it with a critical eye. "This is exactly like the others," he said, adding it to the stack of gold he had started next to his shoulder.

"Have you been able to interpret my brother's poor penmanship?" she asked, referring to the letter he held.

"Barely. He and Jane are enjoying their life in London. Seems we have a new niece. They named her Marianne." He paused to note how Diana lifted an approving brow before he continued reading. "Her older brother Michael is apparently not pleased to have a contender for his mother's attentions, however," he added.

Diana inhaled softly. "Mother will be so glad to hear it," she said. "But two babies already?" she said with worry.

"Jane did say she wanted to have lots of babes," he reminded her.

She lifted another shovelful of dirt and cast it onto the growing pile. This time, two coins, shinier than the gold coins she had already unearthed, reflected the sun's light. "Silver?" she said in confusion.

"Silver?" he repeated. "A denarius?"

He watched as she studied the impressions on both sides of the silver discs. "They both are," she murmured.

"You're going to be the richest woman in all of England," he said. He glanced down at his son. "Did you hear that? You're mother is going to be rich. And I think she still has her dowry, unless she has been secretly spending it in Bampton. Although I cannot think there is that much for her to buy there."

Although Jasper Henley had offered to give Randy her dowry the same day they were married by the mayor of Athens, Randy had insisted he give it to Diana. "She is my wife. Not my property," he had said back then.

Diana laughed. "You're being ridiculous," she admonished him. "I put it into a savings bank in Oxford," she reminded him. She rose to lean against the handle of the shovel, her buff breeches stained at the knees and her forehead displaying a streak of dirt from where she had rubbed the back of a glove across it. "And these belong in a museum," she countered, waving to the gold and silver coins.

He furrowed his brows and inhaled deeply, which nearly sent his four-mouth-old son rolling off his chest. He quickly captured the babe and held it above his body. "Should we build your mother a museum?" he asked, his face screwing into a frown when he realized the babe was still asleep. "The Gisborn Museum of Roman Gold Coins—"

"I expect to find more than just coins here," she argued.

"The Gisborn Museum of Ancient Roman Artifacts," he amended. "Father might allow us to build one somewhere 'round here," he said. "George could help if we built it after the harvest," he added, referring to his youngest brother. "The Cavendish boys would probably help as well."

He brought the babe back down to his chest and continued to think out loud. "We built mother's orangery in a month," he claimed, "We could certainly build a museum in two or three months." Angling his head to one side, he scoffed when he saw his son was still sound asleep. "How are you sleeping through all this excitement?"

Attempting to suppress a giggle, Diana lifted a gloved hand to hide her mouth. "Careful, that's your heir, and he's about to land on his head," she warned.

"I've got him," he assured her. He moved the babe to rest in the crook of his arm. "He's rather heavy," he remarked.

"I'm aware," she said, continuing to widen the hole by removing another shovelful of dirt. This time, a number of coins appeared, and she gasped. "Uh..." She stepped back from the edge of the hole.

Randy sat up. "What is it?" He placed the babe on the grass next to him before he scrambled to his feet to join her. He stared down into the wide depression she had created, his eyes rounding in shock.

A cache of gold coins could be seen at the bottom of the hole, appearing as if they had been inside of a container that had long ago disintegrated.

"I think I may have broken the sack they were in," she said in awe. She glanced back at the pile of dirt, as if searching for remnants of fabric or leather.

"Have you ever found this many at one time before?" he asked in awe.

She shook her head. "I've never found any coins before today," she replied.

He straightened and regarded her with surprise. "Well, then congratulations are in order, my love." He leaned over and kissed her. "Should you wish to celebrate, Mr. Saturday will be at your beck and call this evening."

Scoffing, she sighed and noticed their son was awake. "You say that as if he isn't always," she teased. She lifted one of the coins from the hole and slid it into her pocket. When she noticed his raised brow, she said, "I'm going to show your father what I've discovered on his land."

"The Gisborn lands are entailed, so they're not really his," Randy reminded her. For the first time that day, he sobered and considered the repercussions of her find. "Which means, the idea of a museum is probably best."

"You did hire me to be the Gisborn archaeologist," she reminded him.

He grinned, not about to argue with anything she

remembered. "We'll build a museum," he stated. He picked up the boy from the ground when he noticed she seemed ready to head back to the house. "Are you already abandoning your dig site?"

"I'll return in an hour or so," she replied. "But your son is about to realize it's his feeding time and he no doubt needs his nappy changed. Besides, you know how your mother worries if she hasn't had him in her company for more than a couple of hours."

Chuckling softly, Randy said, "She is a rather attentive grandmother. I hope you don't find her…. overbearing."

"Your mother is a dear. She rarely allows the nurse to take him," she commented. "And your father… well, I never would have expected to discover an earl on the floor of the nursery playing with a babe," she claimed as she displayed a brilliant smile.

"He wanted to be sure the toy he invented for him would entertain him," Randy said, referring to a contraption that featured a winding key and wheels. The small cart had their son screeching in delight when it darted out the door and into the corridor, sending a housemaid scurrying for cover.

They walked in the direction of Gisborn Hall in silence for some time before Randy announced he was hungry.

"That's because someone forgot to bring the picnic basket."

Randy displayed an expression of contrition. "That damned Mr. Saturday… he forgets as much as his wife remembers," he murmured.

"And I'll never let him forget it," she said as she giggled in delight.

AUTHOR NOTES

Frankish Tower

The last rulers of the Duchy of Athens, the Acciaioli family are believed to have constructed the Frankish Tower when they took over the duchy in 1388. Others think it may have been built even earlier—by the first dynasty of Frankish dukes of Athens, the 13th-century de la Roche family, who also had a residence on the site.

Situated on the western corner of the Acropolis, the eighty-five foot high, square fortress was built using the materials from earlier structures on the Acropolis. The stone block walls were nearly six feet thick. A wooden staircase provided access to the top of the crenelated tower. From there, the entire plain of Attica and the surrounding mountains would have been visible. Beacon fires could be set atop a small square turret that jutted from the north wall, the light visible from Acrocorinth in the Peloponnese.

When the duchy fell to the Ottoman Empire in 1458, the Turks used it as a salt store and a prison.

After the Greek War of Independence, archaeologists

called for the tower's demolition as they believed the blocks used in its construction might include inscriptions. Although many agreed, some argued it should remain. Despite it being a home for hundreds of owls and a long-time part of the Athenian horizon, German archaeologist Heinrich Schliemann finally gained permission to take it down when he agreed to pay for its demolition in 1875.

National Garden

Completed in 1840, this green space in the middle of Athens was commissioned by Queen Amalia and completed when she was but twenty-two years old.

Plaka District

The oldest historical neighborhood in Athens, Plaka is clustered around the northern and eastern slopes of the Acropolis and is built on top of the original ancient city.

Hotel Aiolos

Designed by the architect Kleanthis and built from 1835 to 1837, this 25-room hotel was located in the intersection of Aiolou 3 and Adrianou 64. The building is still there.

Kyriakos S. Pittakis

A largely self-taught Greek archaeologist, Pittakis served as Ephor General of Antiquities (the head of the Greek Archaeologist Service) to carry out the conversation and restoration of several monuments on the Acropolis, including the Erechtheion, the Parthenon, the Temple of Athena Nike, and the Propylaea. He was a founding member of the Archaeological Society of Athens, which undertook the excavation, conservation, and publication of archaeological finds. He was prolific both as an excavator and as an archaeological writer, publishing more than 4000 inscriptions.

From 1837 to 1840, Pittakis, Swiss sculptor Heinrich Max Imhof, Prussian Eduard Schaubert and the Saxon architect Eduard Laurent carried out restoration work in the Archaeological Society's name on the Acropolis, where Pittakis insisted on removing any post-classical remains.

On a side note, Pittakis befriended Lord Byron during the aristocrat's time in Greece, and his wife's sister, Aikaterini, is believed to be the inspiration for the 1811 poem "Maid of Athens".

The Mayor of Athens

Angelos Gerontas was the mayor of Athens during the time of this story, and yes, he could perform civil marriages.

ABOUT THE AUTHOR

A self-described nerd and lover of science, Linda Rae spent many years as a published technical writer specializing in 3D graphics workstations, software and 3D animation (her movie credits include SHREK and SHREK 2). Mythology, immortality, and ancient Greece have been lifelong interests.

A fan of action-adventure movies, she can frequently be found at the local cinema. Although she no longer has any tropical fish, she does follow the San Jose Sharks. She makes her home in Cody, Wyoming.

For more information:
www.lindaraesande.com
Sign up for Linda Rae's newsletter:
Regency Romance with a Twist
For articles on research and travels, read Linda's Rae blog:
Regency Romance with a Twist